FROM BAD TO WURST

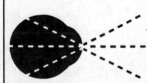

This Large Print Book carries the
Seal of Approval of N.A.V.H.

A PASSPORT TO PERIL MYSTERY

FROM BAD TO WURST

WITHDRAWN

MADDY HUNTER

WHEELER PUBLISHING
A part of Gale, Cengage Learning

GALE
CENGAGE Learning·

Farmington Hills, Mich • San Francisco • New York • Waterville, Maine
Meriden, Conn • Mason, Ohio • Chicago

GALE
CENGAGE Learning®

Wheeler Publishing Large Print Cozy Mystery.
The text of this Large Print edition is unabridged.
Other aspects of the book may vary from the original edition.
Set in 16 pt. Plantin.

LIBRARY OF CONGRESS CATALOGING-IN-PUBLICATION DATA

Names: Hunter, Maddy, author.
Title: From bad to wurst : a passport to peril mystery / by Maddy Hunter.
Other titles: From bad to worst
Description: Large print edition. | Waterville, Maine : Wheeler Publishing, 2016. | © 2015 | Series: Wheeler Publishing large print cozy mystery
Identifiers: LCCN 2015047433| ISBN 9781410487926 (softcover) | ISBN 141048792X (softcover)
Subjects: LCSH: Andrew, Emily (Fictitious character)—Fiction. | Tour guides (Persons) —Fiction. | Large type books. | GSAFD: Mystery fiction
Classification: LCC PS3608.U5944 F76 2016 | DDC 813/.6—dc23
LC record available at http://lccn.loc.gov/2015047433

Published in 2016 by arrangement with Midnight Ink, an imprint of Llewellyn Publications Woodbury, MN 55125-2989 USA

Printed in the United States of America
1 2 3 4 5 6 7 20 19 18 17 16

To our wonderful friends
Marge and Jim Converse
and Barb and Ron Schuler
who bussed the 2,200 whirlwind miles
through Germany with us

ACKNOWLEDGMENTS

My heartfelt thanks to Sarah Weers, Sean Patrick Little, and Josephine Mori for exercising their collaborative genius to arrive at the truly clever title for this book. I'd be lost without you guys! Thanks a million.

ONE

"You're going to meet a tall, dark, hand-some stranger."

Bernice Zwerg snorted with derision. "Is he rich?" Bernice's voice is a real attention-getter because it grates against your ear-drums like 40-grit sandpaper scratching the surface off a chalkboard. "If he's not rich, you can tell him to go meet someone else." She cast a disdainful look at the mob of people swarming around us. "And if he's wearing a pair of these dopey-looking leather shorts and suspenders, send him Lucille Rasmussen's way. Her taste in men blows."

We were killing time in Munich's bustling city center, in the main plaza known as the Marienplatz, a name derived from the gilded statue of the Virgin Mary that stands atop a marble column in the center of the square. Before us the new town hall sat in all its pinnacled glory like a Gothic cathe-

9

dral, its soaring bell tower capped by what looked like the top three tiers of a giant wedding cake. In precisely two minutes the bells in the tower were due to ring out the hour, after which the mechanical figures in the tower's glockenspiel would execute the same moves they'd executed for the past hundred years to the chimes of a German-engineered carillon.

"So you got nothing for me other than the tall, handsome stranger bit, huh?" Bernice snatched her hand away from the red-headed woman who'd offered to read Bernice's future by simply holding her hand. "If you can't come up with something more original than that, honey, you better change your shtick."

The redhead, whose guest ID badge bore the name Zola Czarnecki, emitted a peal of laughter that jiggled all the excess flesh on her freckled face. "You're the first skeptic of the trip — and probably not the last — but my skin is pretty thick these days, so you can doubt me all you want." She jabbed a finger into Bernice's shoulder. "You'll change your tune when your handsome stranger shows up. I predict you'll become my biggest fan. Mark my words."

Bernice swatted a strand of over-permed hair away from her face. "Don't hold your breath."

As the bells in the tower began ringing out the hour, I shot a cursory glance left and right in an attempt to keep tabs on the guests who were traveling with us on our tour of Bavaria, Germany's most picturesque state.

I'm Emily Andrew-Miceli, co-owner of Destinations Travel in Windsor City, Iowa — an agency opened by my husband, Etienne, and operated by the two of us. Our specialty is international tours geared toward adventurous retirees, and we've been fortunate to have found a core group of loyal Iowa seniors to fill seats even when the economy is in free fall.

This trip, we're overflowing with guests thanks to a marketing idea Etienne thought up. Since we'll be traveling in Bavaria during Oktoberfest, he made arrangements to have four of our local brass bands strut their stuff in several of Munich's famous beer halls. We'd been peppered with so many inquiries, we had to turn people away. For the first time in our travel experience, we're hosting seniors who are, quite literally, even more accomplished at tooting their own horns than Bernice, which is why we're calling our tour the Sounds of Music.

"Do you have one of those 1-900 numbers?" asked a female guest who was dressed in a traditional Oktoberfest costume of long skirt, apron, fitted bodice, and provocatively low-cut blouse. If not for her high-end shoulder bag with the designer's initials stamped all over it, she could have been mistaken for a time traveler from another century. Her name was Astrid Peterson, and though she was eyeing sixty through the rearview mirror, she was still a knockout with her winter-white hair and ultra-fit figure. "You know, like a person dials 1-900-PSYCHIC and they have their fortune told over the phone for a big fat fee?"

"Psychics have 900 numbers?" asked Dick Teig, a native Iowan whose potbelly was rivaled only by the size of his unusually large head. "I'll be jiggered. I thought that 900 exchange was reserved for phone sex."

Helen Teig pinned her husband with a look that caused her penciled-on eyebrows to collide above her nose. "And you know that *how*?"

"I'm not a psychic," corrected Zola, raising her voice to be heard above the tolling bells. "I'm a clairvoyant."

"What's the difference?" asked Astrid.

"*Psychic* sounds cheesy. It makes people think of credit card scams and those 900 numbers. *Clairvoyant* affirms my status as a professional."

"So you're a *professional* psychic," clarified Margi Swanson, our resident Windsor City Clinic nurse whose war on germs had single-handedly caused the price of hand sanitizer stock to go through the roof.

Zola humored her with a smile. "I'm a certified public accountant. The clairvoyance is just a sideline, but it comes in handy at work — not to mention church fairs and cocktail parties."

Applause and whistles rang out from the festival crowd as the tolling bells morphed into the unexpectedly tinny chimes of a carillon. "Can anyone name that tune?" I asked as the notes clunked out over the square.

"There's a tune?" questioned Helen Teig.

"Oh, look!" enthused Margi, pointing at two Punch and Judy-like stages high on the tower where figures reminiscent of marionettes suddenly came to life. Trumpeters, jesters, guildsmen, and bannermen paraded in both clockwise and counterclockwise directions like decoys in a circular shooting gallery. Dancers in white hose and breeches spun and twirled. Knights on powerful steeds charged straight at each other with lances raised. "Aww. How adorable is that?" Margi cooed.

Holding up her smartphone at arm's length, she rounded her lips into an expression of pleasant surprise and snapped a photo of herself.

"Okay, my curiosity is getting the better of me," said Astrid, "so if you want to tell my fortune, I'll give it a whirl. You do it for free, right?"

"You bet. No one in the family has charged for a reading since my grandmother got in trouble with the IRS for failing to report her income. Gramma was pretty flamboyant with her flowing scarves and crystal ball, so she made a killing. But she ended up having to use most of it to pay off all the government penalties and fines."

Astrid giggled with enthusiasm. "So what do I do?"

Zola made a gimme gesture. "Give me your dominant hand."

Astrid angled the handle of her rolling instrument case toward me. "Would you hang onto my accordion case, Emily? And whatever you do, don't let go. It's my baby."

"Sure." I clasped the handle and regarded the molded shell. It was the same color as an airplane — platinum silver — and looked obscenely expensive with all its state-of-the-art hinges and locks. The other band members were schlepping their instruments, too

14

— in trumpet cases, trombone cases, clarinet cases, banjo cases, and enormous tuba cases — but none of them were quite as spectacular as Astrid Peterson's.

Zola Czarnecki sandwiched Astrid's hand between her own, bowed her head, closed her eyes, and concentrated.

"I actually have butterflies in my stomach," whispered Astrid.

"No talking, please," said Zola.

Bernice rolled her eyes. "How 'bout we cut to the chase?" She squinted into Astrid's face and in a raspy vibrato declared, "You're going to meet a tall, dark, handsome stranger."

"Shh," Zola scolded, her concentration unbroken.

High on the bell tower, the jousting match ended as the blue knight unseated the red knight, sending him toppling backward over his horse's rump. A cheer went up from the crowd, but I wasn't sure whether they were celebrating the blue knight's victory or the fact that the discordant carillon chimes were finally ending. Laughter. Clapping. And then, as if they'd been jolted by a sudden seismic shift, they were on the move, heading off in every compass direction.

"Destinations Travel guests," our tour director called out as he raised his striped

15

umbrella high into the air. "Gather 'round, please."

We'd hired friend and longtime tour director Wally Peppers to manage the troops on this outing. Middle-aged and chipmunk-cheeked, he wasn't embarrassed to admit that when it came to the ladies, his batting average hovered around zero. But he was a consummate professional who knew Europe better than most people knew their backyards, so we felt fortunate to have him aboard.

"The walk to the Hofbräuhaus is a bit tricky," he announced in a loud voice. "I don't want to lose anyone in this mob, so I encourage all of you to stay together. I'll lead the way, and Emily and Etienne will bring up the rear in case any of you get waylaid."

The bands were scheduled to make their debut appearances at Munich's famous beer hall later this afternoon, so we were making the trek on foot — which, Wally assured us, was the quickest way to travel short distances in Munich during Oktoberfest. The plan was to arrive with plenty of time to spare so guests could take a seat, order some authentic German cuisine, wash it all down with a pitcher of Germany's best beer, and soak up the festive atmosphere before hitting the stage.

Margi Swanson waved her hand over her head. "What if we accidentally take a wrong turn?"

"If you stay with the group, there's no way that'll happen," Wally affirmed.

To my left, Astrid Peterson bobbed her head and smiled nervously as she waited for her fortune to be divulged, her gaze riveted on Zola, who was steeped in a trancelike state despite the surrounding chaos.

"How do you want us to line up?" asked Alice Tjarks in a voice that had kept listeners tuned in to KORN radio's hog market reports for decades. "By age?"

"No fair doing oldest first," complained Bernice. "That automatically puts Osmond in the front of the line."

Osmond Chelsvig was nearing the century mark, so the "oldest first" system was always rigged in his favor.

"How 'bout height?" tossed out Dick Stolee, whose salon-styled toupee rocketed him to two inches over the six-foot mark. In a stiff wind it rocketed him to three. "Tallest first."

"Show of hands," Osmond piped up in his ongoing role as pollster-in-chief. "How many people think we should line up by height?"

17

"Objection!" shouted George Farkas, waving his Pioneer Seed Corn hat above his head. "Tallest first always forces Marion to the back of the line."

George and my nana, Marion Sippel, have been an item for years now. At four foot eight inches tall, Nana was the shortest one in the group. She used to be four foot ten, but on her way to eighty-something she lost another couple of inches, which sticks her in the same height percentile as the seven dwarves. What she lacks in stature, however, she more than makes up for in street smarts, common sense, and TV knowledge. Her formal education might have ended in the eighth grade, but she's the smartest person I know, not to mention the wealthiest. Her financial savvy has allowed her to translate a modest win in the lottery into millions.

"As a consideration to the vertically challenged," George continued, "I motion that we do shortest first."

"I know!" All eyes riveted on my mom, who was hovering at Nana's side like an unwanted shadow, her little moon face bursting with excitement. "Alphabetical order!"

This was a pretty typical suggestion coming from Mom, whose affinity for order had started with the Dewey decimal system and

18

escalated into an obsessive compulsion to alphabetize everything from canned soup to clothing labels. Mom was so busy re-arranging stuff for everyone that she had yet to realize that Nana and George were an item, and that suited Nana just fine. Mom viewed Nana's independent lifestyle as a problem that needed fixing, so their clashing opinions always managed to spark fireworks.

"You don't need to line up in any order," Wally instructed. "If you should happen to lose sight of the group, which is highly unlikely, either consult the map I handed out earlier or access the GPS on your smart-phones. Are you all carrying your phones?"

In one fluid motion the group seized their phones and whipped them into the air as if they were flashing police badges — all except my dad, Bob Andrew, who had his eye glued to his camcorder, capturing the sights and sounds of the exiting crowd, which would no doubt include a slew of unwanted pavement and shoe shots. Dad could dismantle a John Deere tractor engine and piece it back together again, but operat-ing the standby, record, and power off func-tions on his camcorder continued to befud-dle him.

"It'll be about a ten-minute walk," Wally

continued. "Fifteen if the crowd doesn't thin. Everybody ready?"

Tapping her foot with a hint of impatience, Astrid Peterson stared at Zola as if to impart her own psychic message: *Hurry up!*

My phone chimed with a sudden text alert. I dug it out of my shoulder bag and scanned the screen — a one-word plea from Nana in caps: *HELP!*

I shot a glance in her direction to find her eyes screaming with desperation as Mom fussed over her with the fervor of a lioness tending to her cub. "You don't have to worry about losing me in the crowd," Mom assured her. "I've come prepared."

With a quick sleight of hand, Mom slapped a band around Nana's wrist.

"What the devil?" Nana raised her arm to display a long strap tethering her wrist to Mom's.

"I found it at Pills Etcetera," Mom burbled with excitement.

"Which section?" Nana clawed at the wristband. "The pet aisle?"

Mom shooed her hand away. "It's a toddler tether."

"It's a leash," squawked Nana.

"Stop poking at it, Mother. It needs to last all the way through Bavaria." Mom cocked her head, regarding it with an emotion akin to adoration. "It was either this or a body harness, so I decided a wristband would be less conspicuous. Besides, the harnesses were labeled one size fits all, and I'm pretty sure you'd need a husky. What do you think?"

Nana gave a hard suck on her uppers, chins quivering, bosom heaving, eyes narrowed to slits. "I think if I'm still wearin' this dang contraption by the time I count to three, there's gonna be consequences — *dire* consequences. One . . ."

Oh, God! My worst nightmare realized. A showdown between my mother and my grandmother. Eh!

". . . two . . ."

Wally stabbed his umbrella high into the air and aimed it at a boulevard guarded by a church and a soaring bell tower whose main architectural features were a witch's hat roof and four corner turrets. Then off he went in that direction, the rest of the group falling in step behind him, bumping hips, elbows, and instrument cases.

". . . *three.*"

Ignoring Nana's threat, Mom gave the strap a gentle tug. "Come on, Mother. We don't want to fall behind. Oh, look, Bob's filming us. Smile for the camera." Mom waved at Dad like a schoolgirl. Nana rolled

21

her lip into a sneer that curled all the way to her nose.

I fired a look left and right. Where was Etienne? Maybe he could run interference between Nana and —

"Uhh, Zola?" Astrid's voice grew anxious. "I hate to break your concentration, but . . . everyone's leaving."

The muscles in Zola's face remained still, her expression blank.

"I'll be able to predict my own future if we don't get going," teased Astrid. "Lost in Munich."

Zola's brows dipped slightly, giving her face an unsettled look. With her breath suddenly catching in her throat, she snapped her eyes open and stared at Astrid. "I'm sorry." She looked unnerved as she released Astrid's hand. "What did you say?"

Astrid gestured to the departing troops. "Wally's leaving. We've gotta go." With a nod of thanks to me, she gripped the handle of her accordion case and searched Zola's freckled face with breathless anticipation. "So? What'd you see?"

Zola hesitated, eyes dimming and lips twitching with what appeared to be indecision.

Astrid looked suddenly frightened. "You don't want to tell me. Did you see something bad?"

"No, no." Zola waved off the accusation and soothed her nerves with a conciliatory smile. "I didn't have enough time, is all. Let's try again later, when I'm not under any time constraints and there's less background noise. I should know better than to try this in the middle of a mob scene in a city plaza."

Astrid gasped out her relief. "So you didn't see anything horrible?"

"I saw nothing horrible," swore Zola. She raised three fingers in a pledge. "Scout's honor."

"Is there a problem, ladies?" Etienne came up behind me and circled his arm around my shoulder, his voice calm, resonant, seductive. "The group is heading toward the church. Shall we join them?"

Astrid let out a peep of dismay. "Uff-da! We've gotta catch up before we lose sight of them completely."

"I've got this," assured Zola. "I predict they're going to walk under that arch in the bell tower."

"No kidding?" The two women shuffled off, Astrid's accordion case rattling over the concrete pavers. "Did you just get a vision?"

"Better than a vision. I studied the map."

"Just the man I was looking for," I chimed

as I grasped Etienne's hand. "Have you ever mediated a hostage crisis?"

Before he'd married me, moved to Iowa, and opened our travel agency, Etienne had been a police inspector in Switzerland, so there was an outside chance that my handsome black-haired, lean-muscled, six-foot-tall husband might be a crackerjack hostage negotiator.

He narrowed his impossibly blue eyes. "Why do you ask?"

"Because I need you to negotiate the release of a hostage. Mom strapped a leash around Nana's wrist to keep track of her in the crowd, so you have to convince Mom to lighten up."

"You want *me* to negotiate a truce between your mother and your grandmother?"

"You have law enforcement skills. You'd probably rock at it."

"Thank you for the invitation, bella, but as my Italian grandmother was fond of saying, I'd rather chew carpet tacks."

"Aww, c'mon. Nana's absolutely miserable, and it's not going to improve any until someone in authority physically separates them or destroys the stupid leash."

"And you're volunteering me?"

"Who better? They both adore you. Please?" I flashed my most irresistible smile.

He smiled back, exposing the dimples that split his face from cheekbone to jaw. "There is no way I would *ever* step between your mother and grandmother."

I blinked in amazement. "Is that a no?"

"That's a no." He tweaked my nose. "Don't feel too badly for your grandmother. No one gets the better of her for long. In a test of wills between her and your mother, my money is on your grandmother. Come on." He squeezed my hand and pulled me along beside him. "We're supposed to be guarding the rear, not preparing to play Family Feud."

I hurried to keep pace with his long stride, still stunned that he'd refused me. Wow, had I lost my touch already? But we hadn't been married that long! When I smiled like that, he was supposed to laugh uproariously and give in.

Okay, maybe not uproariously. He was part Swiss, after all. The Swiss were wound a little too tight to understand the concept of uproariously.

We caught sight of the tail end of the group and fell in line behind them. As we threaded our way through the friendly crowd, we passed by a long section of the plaza that was set up for outdoor dining beneath a canopy of blue umbrellas. Men in leather shorts and alpine hats milled around the perimeter of the café, while women who were dressed like Astrid Peterson in fitted bodices and long aproned skirts flaunted some truly impressive cleavage. Little girls twirled in their long skirts and hovered by their elders. Little boys chased each other in circles and terrorized the pigeons.

Beyond the bell tower, the area opened onto a wide boulevard that was flanked on either side by multi-storied buildings that were as long and boxy as Monopoly game hotels. There were no wrought-iron balconies or window boxes breaking up their stark façades. No flower pots hanging from decorative street lights. No planters festooning the walkways with greenery. The buildings were solid and no-nonsense and hulked over the sidewalk like linemen bunched together in an impenetrable wall of defensive muscle.

On a more upbeat note, what the area lacked in ambiance and charm, it quite made up for in cleanliness. The pavement sported not one wad of gum, strand of hair, or grain of dirt. It was so pristine, it looked as if it might be hosed off twice daily with soap and hot water.

We followed Wally's umbrella for a full block, past a lederhosen outlet, a Häagen-

Dazs store, and a McDonald's that offered al fresco dining curbside so you could enjoy your Big Mac with a hearty side of diesel fumes. Rounding a corner, we turned onto a narrow side street where a mysterious torrent of water was gushing downhill along the curb to a storm sewer on the boulevard. Tall buildings jammed the sidewalks on either side, giving the place a claustrophobic feel, but there was less foot traffic to fight here, so it looked like a good find.

Short cut!

Ahead of us, Astrid hot-footed it up the street while Zola paused on the sidewalk, staring up at a sculpture that was attached to the corner building like a figurehead to a prow. "You have any idea what this thing is supposed to be?" she asked as we approached.

It looked like something that might be found in a contemporary women's clothing catalog — a hooded cloak without a model inside. But even though the face and body were missing, two hands that resembled antlers were poking out of the sleeves. "It looks like one of Tolkien's Black Riders," I concluded. "Kind of spooky, actually."

"That's what I thought, too," agreed Zola, anchoring herself to the spot as she studied it with more intensity than seemed warranted.

I glanced down the lane to find the group disappearing from sight as they rounded a bend in the road. "Everyone's getting ahead of us, Zola. Are you about done here?"

Making no effort to move, she shot a look down the street.

Etienne swept his hand toward our intended route. "After you, Ms. Czarnecki."

She shook her head. "I'm sorry. I can't go down there." Alarm in her voice. Apprehension in her eyes.

"But . . . that's the way to the beer hall." I didn't think it would hurt to point out the obvious.

She hugged her arms to herself as if to ward off a chill and shook her head more emphatically. "I can't. It doesn't feel right. Is there another route I can take?"

I leveled a meaningful look at Etienne. "Have I mentioned that Zola is a practicing clairvoyant?"

Without skipping a beat, Etienne consulted his phone. "You could take a left at the next block. It's a longer walk, but you'll arrive at the same cross street. From there it's a left onto Ledererstrasse and a right onto Orlandostrasse."

Her features knotted in confusion. "A left

28

onto what?"

"How about letting Etienne escort you on the alternate route," I suggested, "and we'll plan to meet up at the Hofbräuhaus."

Etienne nodded agreement. "If you'd prefer to hike to the next street, Ms. Czarnecki, I'll be happy to accompany you."

"Yes," she said enthusiastically. "That's very kind of you. I'd prefer to do that. Thank you."

"I'll catch up with the rest of the group," I said, bobbing my head down the lane. "If we arrive at the beer hall before you, I'll let Wally know where you are."

"Plan A is now activated." Etienne planted a quick kiss on my cheek. "See you there."

He'd been playing video games with my nephews recently, so he was picking up some seriously non-adult jargon.

Zola hesitated, her unease palpable as she put a bead on the place where the street curved out of sight. "Be careful, Emily."

"You bet."

"I mean it." She drilled me with a look that caused all the down on my arms to stand on end. "I wish you wouldn't go down there."

"I'll be fine." But as I sprinted down the narrow walkway, I questioned the benefits of having a clairvoyant on the tour. We'd had one spot left on our guest roster after the musicians had signed up, so Zola, traveling by herself, had claimed it. But how many streets would she be unwilling to walk down because they didn't feel right? How many museums would she advise guests against entering because she sensed the collection wasn't up to snuff? How many historic sites would she refuse to visit because the karma felt "off"? She might be a novelty at church fairs and cocktail parties, but on an international tour her psychic abilities could augur financial disaster.

As I rounded the curve in the road, I caught sight of the group up ahead, Dad with his camcorder rolling as everyone toodled along in single-file, hugging building fronts as closely as possible to avoid a team of city workers who were performing emergency repairs on a broken water main. The men, dressed in official phosphorescent yellow vests and hard hats, had cordoned off a section of the street with traffic cones. Jackhammers lay on the pavement. A backhoe loader idled at the curb, close to the hole it had excavated in the middle of the street. Three men huddled at the edge of the hole, heads together as they assessed the situation, while the heavy machinery operator sat at the controls, observing the fountain of water that was bursting onto the asphalt with the force of a geyser.

Despite the distraction, the group kept moving forward, all except Astrid, whose position at the back of the pack allowed her to pause at the curb to take a picture of what crumbling infrastructure in other countries looked like. I dug my camera out too, not because of the infrastructure thing but because of the backhoe loader. It was a John Deere. My youngest nephew would adore a picture of it.

With a hand signal from his supervisors, the backhoe operator roared into action again, dropping his bucket into the flooded hole. Astrid snapped her shot and continued on her way, rolling her accordion case —

KABOOOOOOOOOOM!!!

The case flew into the air in a hailstorm of tar pellets and sludge, hanging motionless for a fleeting moment before slamming back to earth. My head snapped back as the shock wave struck my face. I felt the sharp sting of flying debris needling into my flesh and a searing heat assaulting my eyes. I saw the ground suddenly disappear beneath a cloud of dirt and dust, and then . . . I saw nothing at all.

Two

"Unexploded ordnance?"

My attending physician, Dr. Helmut Fischer, a head trauma specialist with a shaved head and rimless glasses, stood at the foot of my gurney, hands buried in the pockets of his lab coat. "Unfortunately, Mrs. Miceli, we're still finding unexploded munitions throughout the country decades after the Allied forces dropped them. You should be thankful that this particular bomb was a relatively small one. Three years ago 45,000 residents were evacuated from Koblenz while the disposal squad defused a 1.8-metric ton bomb that could have wiped out the entire city center." He shook his head and shrugged. "Detonations are not uncommon."

The treatment room where I was being tended was glass-fronted, brightly lit, and equipped with all manner of high-tech monitors and machines that beeped, hummed, and whirred. I'd been given a CT scan as a precautionary measure, and though I'd been knocked out in the blast, the results indicated no bleeding, swelling, or other type of cerebral trauma. Dr. Fischer was right to imply that I was one lucky tour escort.

"Other than the cuts on your face from the debris splatter, you've weathered the event with minimal injury," he continued. "Vital signs are normal. No visual impairment. Auditory report is excellent, which is a bit surprising. Proximity to even minor blasts can cause perforations and ruptures in the ear canal, but you were apparently far enough away to escape injury, although should you experience a sudden ringing in your ears in the days to come, don't be alarmed. It could be a delayed reaction, but this type of tinnitus often resolves itself in a few days or weeks. Any questions before I release you?"

"Was anyone else hurt?" I hadn't regained consciousness until I was in the ambulance, so I'd seen none of the devastation. "Is everyone in my tour group all right?"

Dr. Fischer exchanged a glance with Etienne, who stood at the side of my gurney, squeezing my hand. "Your husband has asked to share that information with you,

Mrs. Miceli. Do you have any other medical-related questions?"

"You don't think she needs complete bed rest?" asked Etienne, his voice strained with worry. "It could be a little tricky to pull off, but —"

"I believe that would be an overreaction, Mr. Miceli."

"What if she starts complaining about headaches or dizziness or fatigue?"

"If she experiences any of those symptoms and they become acute, I would encourage you to seek medical attention, but our tests indicate that your wife isn't likely to suffer anything more severe than a few minor muscle aches, which can be treated with over-the-counter pain relievers."

"You don't think we need to cancel the rest of our tour?"

"Not on your wife's account." Dr. Fischer smiled indulgently. "I hope she won't be dancing a polka in the Schottenhamel festival tent this evening, but by tomorrow or the next day she should feel well enough to resume her normal activities. I'll see about signing those release papers now." He shook both our hands and departed. I boosted myself to a sitting position and swung my legs over the side of the gurney, coming eye to eye with Etienne.

I inhaled a deep breath, bolstering my courage to ask the question I dreaded to ask. "Is everyone all right?"

He shook his head, his voice soft. "Ms. Peterson, the lady with the enormous rolling instrument case . . . she didn't survive the blast."

"Astrid?" I stared at him, numbed. "Omigod." In my mind's eye I saw her accordion case being catapulted skyward again, a speck of gleaming silver lost in a gale of swirling asphalt. "She . . . she stopped to take a picture, and then . . . I mean, I stopped to take a picture, too. I thought David would get a kick out of seeing the John Deere backhoe. But I was farther away, so . . ." A knot vibrated in my throat. "I . . . I can't believe it."

Etienne folded me in his arms, cradling my head against his chest. "I've spoken to her family back in Iowa. Not the kind of news anyone ever wants to deliver. But I've given them our personal cell numbers and have assured them that we'll render whatever assistance we can with flight arrangements for Astrid's remains."

"What about Nana?" I choked out, blinking away an onslaught of tears that welled up from the throbbing knot in my throat. "And Mom and Dad. Are they okay?"

35

"Everyone received a clean bill of health from the paramedics at the scene. Wally tells me that the musicians had been so anxious to reach the Hofbräuhaus that they'd set a pretty fast pace for the group, which literally saved their lives. When the bomb detonated, they were outside the danger zone. They're all back at the hotel, anxiously awaiting your return."

"And the workmen?"

"Cuts, bruises, and broken bones, but nothing life threatening."

I sniffled with relief. "That . . . that's wonderful." At which point I proceeded to dissolve into a blubbering heap of sobs and tears. I guess when you come to the realization that you've just escaped death by mere inches, the emotional blowback eventually hits you between the face and eyes.

"My poor bella." Etienne kissed the crown of my head. "Shh. Shh." He held me more tightly against him. "We can't shield our guests from unforeseen mishaps, Emily. We both know that. Accidents are inevitable. No one could have predicted what happened on that street today, but we should celebrate the small miracle that more people weren't hurt."

I grew suddenly still.

No. That wasn't true.

One person *had* sensed what would happen down that street. And I hadn't believed her.

The taxi dropped us at the front door of our hotel, which was conveniently located midway between the city center at Marienplatz and the Oktoberfest grounds at Theresienwiese. I'd regained my self-composure before leaving the hospital, so I wasn't blubbering any longer, but I suspected another crying jag might be in order once I saw myself in a mirror. I was sure I hadn't packed near enough concealer.

Etienne escorted me through the revolving door, where I was immediately swarmed by a dozen Iowans who looked pretty relieved to see me.

"My baby!" cried Mom, throwing her arms around me in a death grip. "I'll never let you out of my sight again!"

That could only mean one thing. She'd bought more than one toddler tether at Pills Etcetera. *Oh, God.*

"Group hug," said Tilly Hovick as she used her walking stick to direct everyone into a Farmer in the Dell–type circle. Looping arms around waists, they formed a human daisy chain around me.

"We thought you were a goner for sure,"

confessed Dick Teig from somewhere in front of me.

"It was the most terrifying moment of my life," sobbed Mom.

"I wish you coulda seen George and your dad," Nana chimed proudly. "When they looked back and seen you layin' on the sidewalk, they leaped right into action."

"It wasn't just me and your dad," said George. "Osmond found your pulse. And Margi made a clean spot on your face."

"I used the very latest in the fall collection of unscented mini sanitizers," gushed Margi. "It's called Air."

"Wally tried to herd us farther down the street in case there was another explosion," Alice reported. "The musicians followed his orders, but the fellas wouldn't leave your side."

"Margi done triage for them workers in the street," continued Nana, "and she done a real good job. She even sent them off to the hospital with complimentary bottles of sanitizer."

"We used Dick's sock as a tourniquet for the backhoe driver," announced Grace Stolee.

"Happy to make a contribution to the cause," boomed Dick. "It had a hole in the toe anyway."

"Them musicians sure hightailed it to safer ground real quick," added Nana. "That's on account of them expensive instruments they're carryin'. They didn't wanna wait around for no more blasts to blow the things sky high."

"I would have helped with the rescue efforts," Mom apologized. "Really, Emily, I would have, but I was so overcome with fright when I saw you that I . . . I collapsed right there on the sidewalk."

"I woulda helped, too," deadpanned Nana, "but I couldn't go nowhere with your mother on top of me."

"Enough togetherness already," groused Bernice. "Lemme out of here. I can't breathe."

"Even Bernice did her part," acknowledged Helen as they broke ranks, adding in an undertone, "unbelievable as that might sound."

A bomb exploding and hell freezing over on the same day? Wow. Talk about momentous.

"What role did you play in the rescue effort, Ms. Zwerg?" Etienne inquired.

"Photographic historian." She elevated her chin at a haughty angle. "I got pictures of the whole disaster. Someone had to. Bob was so obsessed about holding Emily's hand

39

that he set his camcorder aside." Her mouth slid into a sultry smile. "Did you know I used to be a magazine model?"

Dad held my hand while I was unconscious? Aww.

I spotted him on the periphery, calm and quiet amid all the chatter, peeking out from behind Dick Teig's head, a shy smile on his lips. Catching his eye, I mouthed, "Thanks, Dad."

He gave a quick nod and flashed a happy face before Dick moved his head, hiding him from view.

Dad was a man of few words. We weren't sure what all the words were, but among his favorites were yup, sure, and uh-huh.

Dad was nothing if not positive.

Bernice paused in front of me, studying my face. "Have you seen yourself in a mirror yet?"

"I haven't quite mustered the courage."

She nodded sagely. "Smart." Then, under her breath, "That was actually a compliment. Don't let it go to your head."

"Aren't you a sight for sore eyes!" Wally's voice echoed throughout the lobby as he hurried toward me. Banding his arms around me, he smothered me in a huge bear hug. "Don't ever do that again. We all aged about ten years watching them load you into

40

that ambulance today."

"I didn't," countered Bernice. "Unlike the disturbing number of milquetoast lefties on this trip, I'm not a bleeding heart."

Margi sniffed. "That's because you don't have one."

"Do so."

"Do not."

"Well, I sure added ten years to my life," hooted Osmond. "Practically speaking, I should be dead."

"Seriously, Em." Wally held me away from him and searched my face. "Are you all right?"

I shrugged. "So far, so good. A little weepy, a little wobbly, but I'm hanging in there."

He glanced at Etienne. "Any recommendations from the hospital?"

"Her scans came back negative, so she can resume normal activities as soon as she feels up to it, although the doctor discouraged her from dancing the polka at the festival tent tonight. I'm thinking a light schedule for the next couple of days might be in order."

"She should do *nothing* for the next few days," Mom insisted as she hovered close by. "You boys have your hands full with the tour, so I'll take over responsibility for Emily." She waved off any objections. "No need to thank me. It's no bother at all. I'll stick to her like bark to a tree. Won't that be fun, Em?"

Oh, no.

"Really, Mom, I'm not going to ruin your vacation by saddling you with guard duty. I'm perfectly fine. The doctor said so."

Nana shuffled up to us in her size 5 sneakers, her eyes twinkling with mischief behind her wire rims. "You better listen to your mother, Emily. If she's got a notion to keep an eye on you, let her, on account of worry can cause strokes, and we don't want your mother to suffer no stroke."

"That's right," said Mom, adding a little fist pump for emphasis. "I —" Pausing in sudden reflection, she cocked her head and arched a brow at Nana. "A stroke? Seriously?"

Nana shrugged. "You're creepin' up there in age, Margaret, so who knows?"

Omigod. Nana was using fear tactics to sic Mom on me.

"I think it'd do your maternal instincts a whole world of good to watch over Emily for a few days," Nana encouraged. "You don't need to be dividin' your attention between me and her, so I'm givin' you my blessin' to ditch me so's you can focus on her. She's the one what needs you right now."

Mom beamed with gratitude. "That's so unselfish of you, Mother."

"You bet. It'd be downright criminal for me to hog all the attention. I'm fine. Emily's not. Just lookit how peaked she looks."

Mom peered into my face, her head bobbing in agreement. "Your grandmother's right, Emily. Under all your scabs, you *do* look peaked."

"That's because they scrubbed all my makeup off at the hospital! I always look like this without foundation and blush."

"It's all settled then." Mom launched herself at me again, all arms and hugs and smothering kisses. "You have nothing to worry about from now on, Emily. Your mother's going to take good care of you."

I fired an evil look at Nana, prompting her to slink away like the faithful dog who'd made an ill-advised feast of the new sofa cushions, the family bird, and everyone's homework. I was her favorite granddaughter — her *only* granddaughter. How could she do this to me?

"Can I have your attention, folks?" Wally's voice silenced the chatter. "Now that we've had a chance to see for ourselves that Emily is okay, we need to address another issue.

43

Our musicians are grieving the loss of one of their colleagues, so I'd like to have a group meeting to discuss what happens next. They might not feel up to keeping their performance schedule without Ms. Peterson, so we may have to consider changing our itinerary. Let's get it all on the table, though. They're waiting for us in the Prince Ludwig room." He motioned to a corridor that angled around the front desk to the right. "I won't keep you long, but I'd appreciate your extending a few words of sympathy to the other guests. Ms. Peterson was apparently an all-round nice person, well liked by everyone, so they're taking her death really hard."

They followed behind Wally without jockeying for position or cutting each other off, which made me question why they couldn't do that *all* the time. Mom locked her hand around my arm, excitement oozing from her every pore as she burdened herself with my well-being. "Can you manage baby steps, sweetheart, or should I request a wheelchair?"

"If you'll allow me, Margaret." Etienne laid claim to my other arm. "I'll be happy to relieve you of duty for the rest of the day."

"Nosiree," said Mom, tightening her grip. "When I make a commitment, I follow through."

"I insist." He smiled, favoring her with a dose of Old World charm that affected the average woman like catnip affects cats.

"Nonsense. We're good. Aren't we, Em?"

Mom had apparently developed an immunity to Old World charm.

"I suspect Wally could make good use of your people skills in the Prince Ludwig room, Margaret." Etienne gave my arm a gentle tug in his direction.

Mom tugged me back toward her. "You're much more diplomatic than I am — you go. I'll stay with Emily."

"You have a better touch with grief-stricken people, Margaret." Right, toward Etienne.

"No, I don't." Left, toward Mom.

Feeling like the proverbial wishbone from the Thanksgiving Day turkey, I decided to end the tug of war before someone yelled, "Close your eyes and make a wish."

Or was I confusing wishbones with birthday candles?

Uh-oh. Maybe my brain was more addled than the CT scan had indicated.

"Enough already!" I said, wrenching my arms free. "Geesh." I glanced from one to the other. "Trust me. I'm not unappreciative, but there's gotta be a better way. Can

45

we compromise? Like, say, Etienne runs ahead to join the guests in the Prince Ludwig room, and Mom and I follow behind at a more leisurely pace?"

Mom cleared her throat and snorted delicately. "Isn't that what I just suggested?"

"Are you sure this is what you want to do?" Etienne asked me, sounding perplexed.

"Yup. That'll work. But before you head off, you need to refresh my memory about something. Do you remember how long the doctor said we should wait before we . . . you know" — I lowered my voice to a whisper — "resume normal marital relations?"

Stuck between an inhale and an exhale, Etienne broke out in a fit of wheezing that had him thumping his fist against his sternum to clear his air passages. Mom froze on the spot, speechless and red-faced, her eyes popping out of their sockets as if they'd been inflated with helium. "Alrighty then," she tittered nervously, because if there was anything that could force Mom to run from a room, it was the thought of having to listen to another human being talk about that most forbidden of all subjects: S-E-X.

"The two of you must think I'm so selfish," she blurted, aiming herself in the direction of the Prince Ludwig room. "Now that

I think about it, Wally's people skills really are far inferior to mine, so I'll just scoot down there to help out. Those poor grief-stricken souls deserve a huge outpouring of sympathy and support, and no one can dole it out better than I can."

Abdicating any further claim on my arm, she launched herself toward the meeting room as fast as her feet would fly. Etienne hazarded a smile. "She does make a habit of fleeing when the conversation turns to seemingly indelicate subjects, doesn't she?"

"Thank God. How would we ever deal with her if she wasn't so predictable?"

He studied my face for a long moment before trailing his finger down my cheek. "Tell me honestly, do you feel up to facing the masses or would you rather go back to the room?"

"I'll go back to the room after the meeting. We can't abandon Wally. No matter how good he is at what he does, he might need reinforcements. My legs are still a little rubbery, but I'll be okay if I can sit down."

Cupping his hand around my elbow, he guided me around the front desk and down the long corridor toward the Prince Ludwig room. "Since when has your grandmother resolved her issues with your mother by throwing you under the bus?"

"You noticed the tire marks, did you?"

He laughed. "For an octogenarian, your grandmother seems to enjoy living quite dangerously."

Maybe *too* dangerously. She never should have sicced Mom on me; that was a no-no. So she and I were going to have words, and my nonprofessional prediction was that she wasn't going to like them.

THREE

The heartache in the Prince Ludwig room was palpable.

Guests were clustered in small groups around the perimeter, speaking in hushed tones, tissues in hand, dabbing their eyes. Quiet weeping. Loud nose blowing. Earnest hand squeezing. I scanned the area in search of Zola, desperate to speak to her privately, but I caught sight of her red hair at the opposite end of the room, about as far away from me as she could possibly be.

I was encouraged to see that my guys were making the rounds with Astrid's friends, offering sympathy and remaining respectfully low-key. Even Bernice was displaying a level of decorum that was remarkable for Bernice. Not only did she seem disinclined to badger any of the bereaved guests into taking pictures of her, she was actually offering tissues to guests who needed them. Truth be told, I wasn't sure if this was a random act of kindness or an optical illusion.

Mom was practicing her people skills by giving everyone in the room a big squishy hug. She could have limited it to band members only, but to her way of thinking, overkill was a much less grievous sin than discrimination.

The only guest who wasn't engaged in conversation or offering unsolicited hugs was Dad, who occupied a chair in the last row of seats at the back of the room, happily detached from everyone while he studied the floor.

Wally hurried over to us, clipboard in hand. "I received a text from Astrid's brother. He's wondering if we could pack up Astrid's belongings and carry them back to the States with us. I told him it wouldn't be a problem."

"I'll take care of it," said Etienne.

"What about her accordion?" I looked from one man to the other. "Did it survive the blast in one piece?"

Wally's expression went blank. "I didn't see an accordion — not that I had time to look. Was her instrument case the big rolling silver thing that looked like it was on the cutting edge of spaceship technology?"

I nodded. "It's the last thing I remember seeing before I blacked out."

He jotted a note on his clipboard. "I'll track it down. I should think her family would want that back, too, if there's anything left of it. So where's the best place to start an inquiry about a missing instrument case? Local authorities?"

Etienne quickly leaped into former police inspector mode. "Why don't you let me handle the missing accordion? I might be able to navigate the police system a little easier than you."

Wally nodded. "No complaints from me there."

"In fact, while you're calling your meeting to order, I think I'll make a few inquiries at the front desk to get the ball rolling." He gestured toward the orderly rows of folding chairs before us. "Can I offer you a seat, Mrs. Miceli?"

Talk of Astrid's accordion case caused a sluggish synapse to fire in my brain. "Where's my shoulder bag?" I clutched my shoulder in search of the strap, startled that it had taken me this long to realize it was missing.

"Your dad recovered it after you collapsed," said Wally. "He gave it to your gramma for safekeeping."

"OhthankGod." I blew out a long relieved breath. "My whole *life* is in that bag. Did you realize it was missing?" I asked Etienne.

"I never gave your bag a passing thought, bella. I'm afraid worry overtook my awareness of fashion accessories."

Aww. I swallowed around the lump in my throat, forcing myself not to burst into tears again.

Crisis averted, Etienne ushered me to the aisle seat in the front row, then headed out to the reception desk. Wally took up a position in the front of the room. "I apologize for the interruption, but would all of you be kind enough to find a seat?"

Sniffling. Shuffling. Chair scraping. Mom claimed the chair beside me, beating Margi out by a nose, but Nana had obviously decided to keep a low profile because she'd grabbed a chair at the far end of my row, a location so distant, if we were in Iowa, we'd refer to it as the "back forty."

Wally squared his shoulders, eyes somber, voice subdued. "Speaking on behalf of Emily, Etienne, and Destinations Travel, I'd like to express my deepest sympathy to all our musicians on the loss of your colleague. I know Ms. Peterson was an esteemed member of your group. I've heard you compare her musical ability to the accordion virtuoso on the old *Lawrence Welk Show.*"

"Myron Floren," said a woman with a nasally voice.

"She was better than Myron Floren," insisted a male guest. "Her fingers were so nimble, she could practically tie them in knots."

"It helped that she was double jointed," snuffled a man behind me.

"And not only that," agreed another man, "her motor skills were so highly developed, she could work the bellows, play the keyboard, and hit the bass buttons with a blindfold tied around her eyes. Our audiences loved that routine. They always rewarded her with a standing ovation."

"And a tip jar full of five-dollar bills," added the woman who talked through her nose.

"I don't know how our band can survive without her," lamented a man whose voice trembled with emotion. "On so many levels, Astrid was one in a million."

More sniffling and nose blowing. I angled my chair around slightly so I could see the entire room.

Wally regarded us, a questioning expression on his face. "Would the remaining members of her band like to join me up front to share a few of their favorite Astrid memories with those of us who never got to know her?"

Whispers. Throat clearing. Chair creaking.

"That's mighty nice of you to ask," said the man whose voice still shook with emotion. I glanced toward the center of the room as a big, burly guy with a white Santa Claus beard and apple cheeks stood up. "We'd like that."

He gestured to several others as he snaked his way across the row of folding chairs. Up popped three more people, two men and a woman, who followed him to the front of the room. They huddled together in an awkward clump, looking out at the rest of us with red noses and bloodshot eyes.

"Would you mind re-introducing yourselves to the group?" asked Wally. "I know everyone attended the meet and greet, but no one ever remembers names, so repetition helps."

Breaking out of their huddle, they rearranged themselves in a line that I suspected would mimic the way they appeared on stage. The burly guy with the shaky voice lifted his hand in greeting. "Otis Erickson. I'm on tuba."

"Hetty Munk," said the woman beside him. "Clarinet." She was dressed in the same traditional long skirt and fitted bodice that Astrid had been wearing, but there was less of her to fill out the blouse. Her brown hair was shoulder length and stick-straight, with bangs that practically fell into her eyes and a neck whose sagging flesh was falling victim to gravity.

"I'm Wendell Newton." The man next to her bobbed a head that was so shiny, it reflected a glare from the overhead lights. His face was Happy Face round. His upper lip lay hidden beneath a fastidiously trimmed salt-and-pepper mustache whose waxed ends curled onto his cheeks. He reminded me of the guy on the orange Chance cards in Monopoly, only without the tuxedo and top hat. "I play trumpet."

"Gilbert Graves," said the final musician. "Trombone." He was thin and small-boned, with horn-rimmed glasses and thinning bowl-cut hair that gave him the look of an aging Prince Valiant. He had computer geek written all over him, although with his knee socks, leather breeches, and waistcoat, he and his fellow band members could probably do double duty as figures on the dancing platform of a cuckoo clock. "We've been playing together in our oompah band for going on a dozen years now. Astrid's the one who thought of the idea after her husband died. We call ourselves the Guten Tags, which means 'good day' in German, so we're the 'Good Days,' which is weird in English, but Astrid liked the sound of it, so that's what we went with."

"Astrid could be very persuasive," said Wendell.

"But in a nice way," Otis explained. "She was tact personified. Never bossy. Always putting everyone else first. Happy all the time." His lips started to quiver. "So . . . so willing to please." He swiped tears from his eyes and blew his nose into an oversized handkerchief.

"We entered kindergarten together over sixty years ago," sniffed Hetty. "I spilled milk all over my lunch, so Astrid offered to share hers. Peanut butter and grape jelly on white bread. From that moment on, we were like sisters. Right up until this morning." She inhaled a calming breath and blinked away tears. "I've lost so much more than the driving force of our band." Her voice swelled with emotion. "I've lost my best friend."

Otis draped his arm around her shoulders as she pressed a tissue to her eyes.

"So what's going to happen now?" called out another guest from the audience. "We've already missed our time slots at the Hofbräuhaus. Should we cancel the rest of our scheduled appearances?"

"That's a decision the remaining band members will have to make," said Wally. "We can continue with the present schedule, or if you think that might be too difficult emotionally, we can simply tour the rest of Germany and dispense with the musical element."

"It's going to be pretty hard for the Guten Tags to continue," admitted Wendell. "Without the accordion, we won't get the rich, full-bodied sound we're accustomed to. It'll throw everything off."

"We'll get booed off the stage," sobbed Hetty.

Another voice sang out from the audience. "If the Guten Tags don't play, I think it's only fair that the rest of us don't play either. Not the Little Bitte Band or Das Bier Band or the Brassed Off Band."

Gasps. Murmuring.

"Is that really fair?" asked a woman who was sitting two rows back. "We've been practicing for so long. Would Astrid have wanted all of us to throw in the towel because of her absence?"

"Astrid was the most unselfish person on the planet," asserted another man. "She would have wanted the show to go on no matter what."

"I disagree," said the woman with the

nasally voice. "We'll be disrespecting her memory if we march up on stage and act as if nothing happened back there on that street."

Harrumphing. Snorting.

Wally glanced at the audience and shrugged. "This isn't up to me, but I'm the one who'll have to make the phone calls if you decide to cancel, so I encourage you to arrive at some kind of consensus."

A hefty man in a red waistcoat stood up. "I say we cancel."

Head bobbing. Tepid clapping.

Another guy in a green vest and suspenders rose to his feet. "I say we continue."

Osmond shot out of his chair, arms raised in a V as he waved his forefingers to indicate the tally. "One yea, one nay. Do I hear two? We're at one, going for two. Who'll make it tw—"

Alice grabbed his belt and yanked him back down to his seat.

Oh, God.

Mom bent her head toward me, confiding under her breath, "Someone should tell Osmond to tone down this election silliness. He needs to understand that you and Etienne *don't* have time to humor every guest stricken with an obsessive-compulsive disorder." She patted my hand with moth-

58

erly affection. "By the way, there's a slew of guidebooks and magazines in our rooms, so if you'd like yours alphabetized, I'll be happy to oblige. It'll take me less than twenty seconds, and I guarantee the sense of order will leave you feeling even more tingly than a spa treatment." Her face glowed at the prospect.

My mom. Under the mistaken impression that the pot calling the kettle black actually referred to cookware.

"We should take a vote to see where the majority of us stand," suggested the man in the green vest.

Hetty held up a finger. "Hold that thought." She gathered Otis, Gilbert, and Wendell into a tight circle, and after a minute's worth of whispers, sighs, and grunts, they turned around to face the audience again.

"We've arrived at a compromise," she announced. "We knew Astrid better than any of you, so please believe me when I say she wouldn't have wanted you to miss out on the musical experience of a lifetime. That's why we think the rest of you should follow through with your appearances as scheduled."

"And what about you?" asked a man from the audience.

Otis swiped moisture from his cheeks with a beefy hand. "The Guten Tags are gonna sit this one out. And before you go getting all riled up about our decision, I've got two things to say. First: Hetty and us guys will pay all the respects necessary to Astrid's memory, so we don't want you thinking you're giving her short shrift. And second: the four of us can't perform without an accordionist, so that's all she wrote. We couldn't play even if we wanted to, but we'll be real happy to listen to the rest of you up there on stage."

Shocked silence filled the room, broken by a single clap of approval that was followed by another and another until all of us were on our feet, applauding the Guten Tags for the selflessness of their gesture. Otis's nose turned red with embarrassment. Hetty's eyes sparkled with unshed tears. Gilbert and Wendell clasped hands as if congratulating each other on the wisdom of their decision.

I had to hand it to them. Given their disappointing change of circumstances, they were being extraordinarily gracious. Back home we call that "Midwest nice."

"That settles it then," said Wally when the applause died down. "We'll continue our schedule as planned, and the only detail we'll change is that the three remaining bands will have more playing time. Is everyone agreed?"

"Hello?" A man in a navy blue business suit stepped into the room, accompanied by a man in an even more conservative black suit. "Please forgive the interruption. May we come in?"

The Guten Tags shuffled out of the way to allow the newcomers center stage. The suits shook hands with Wally before the navy suit addressed the audience. "Please allow me to introduce myself. My name is Dieter Dangler, and I am manager of this establishment." His words were clipped and precise, with barely a trace of an accent. "This is Egon Seiler." He nodded to the black suit. "Assistant to the mayor of Munich. He has come to deliver a message from the mayor."

Egon Seiler removed a paper from the inner pocket of his suit and snapped it open with a flick of his wrist. " 'To the guests of Destinations Travel: I am at a loss to find words to express my sorrow for the tragic incident that occurred earlier today. It is unconscionable that a visitor to our city should lose her life as a result of walking down one of our streets. Sadly, decades after the bombing of Munich, we continue to deal with the consequences. I only wish I

61

could reverse the outcome of today's misfortune.

" 'Sources have reported to me that despite the horror and confusion in the aftermath of the explosion, many Destinations Travel guests remained at the scene, offering assistance to the injured, with little concern for their own personal safety. There is no way the people of Munich can repay this act of generosity and courage, but we would like to try by offering you the key to our city. Wherever you travel in Munich, doors will be open to you. You will receive the best tables when you dine, upgraded hotel rooms, free admission to our museums and historic sights, and because I'm told that many of you are members of brass bands, we invite you to perform at whatever Oktoberfest tent you choose — the Schottenhamel, the Hippodrom, the Hofbrau-Festzelt, the Lowenbrau-Festzelt, or the Hacker-Festzelt.' "

Whoops of surprise. Gasps of delight.

" 'The city of Munich will accommodate you in whatever way we can, but there is truly no courtesy we can provide that will ever match the bravery you demonstrated today. The citizens of Munich remain forever in your debt.' Signed, Klaus Richter, Mayor of Munich." Egon looked up from the paper, businesslike and efficient. "I would like to add my own thanks to the words of the mayor. I'm admiring of your courage. You are true heroes."

A sea change descended upon the room. Smiles appeared. Eyes brightened. Spirits rose. All except for the four Guten Tags, who suddenly looked even more down in the mouth than they'd looked before. And why not? The other bands would be gearing up to play in the major leagues of all oompah bands — in an Oktoberfest tent — while the Guten Tags would get stuck watching. I'd be heartbroken too.

"If it would not be an intrusion," Egon continued, "would you object to giving interviews? Our local paper would like to run a feature story that showcases all of you."

Bernice bounced to her feet. "I'm the person they'll want to talk to. Zwerg. Bernice Zwerg." She brandished her phone in the air. "I got pictures of the whole thing, and for the right price, I'll be happy to share."

From somewhere in the hall, I heard a rhythmic squeaking sound that evoked images of the hated grocery store cart with the wonky wheel. What in the world? I glanced toward the open door, surprised when

Etienne crossed the threshold, his hand locked around the handle of —

"Astrid's accordion case!" wailed the woman with the nasally voice.

It was so encrusted with dried mud that its silver skin was camouflaged beneath what looked like a layer of beige stucco. But I saw no gaping holes. No obvious dents. No missing hinges. Other than the annoyingly squeaky wheel, it looked to be in pretty good shape.

The Guten Tags swarmed the case as if they were celebrating the return of Astrid herself, and in true flash mob tradition, their fellow band members leaped out of their folding chairs to join them, whooping, laughing, and high-fiving.

"Is her accordion damaged?" asked Otis.

"Let's check," said Hetty.

The band members circled it as if they were about to witness a rare surgical procedure in an operating theater. Etienne extricated himself to join Wally and the suits.

"A reporter will be contacting you about the interviews," Egon announced to the half of the room that wasn't huddled around the instrument case.

I heard several clicks, followed by a collective inhalation of breath and a hopeful "Ooooh."

"It's okay!" cried Hetty. "Good as new. Not a scratch on it."

Backslapping. Cheering. More high-fiving.

Having said apparently all he'd planned to say, Egon spoke briefly to both Wally and Etienne before he and the hotel manager underwent another round of handshaking and left. I could feel myself fading fast, so I hoped I could be next out the door.

"I have one final announcement," said Wally, directing his voice toward the musicians who'd become deaf to anything but the sounds of their own exuberance. Glancing toward me, he indicated that I should let loose with my signature whistle, but before I could even stretch my lips into position, the room exploded with the thunderous sounds of screeching tires, shattered glass, crumpling steel, and blaring horns.

Cries went up from the musicians as they spun in circles dodging invisible cars while my guys sat calmly in their chairs, rolling their eyes.

"I've got a new app on my phone," confessed Dick Teig in a sheepish tone. He held up the device. "Ear-Shattering Noises. That one's called Fifty-Car Pileup on I-95."

"Play 'em the one with the industrial-size leaf blowers," encouraged Dick Stolee. "No kidding. You need ear protectors to listen to it."

Wally flashed a droll smile. "We've heard enough. Thanks for sharing. So my final item of business is that dinner will be served in the hotel restaurant in an hour." He eyed Dick Teig. "And no Ear-Shattering Noises in the dining room."

"What about the rest of us?" asked the man in the red waistcoat. "When do we get to play the Oktoberfest tent?"

"I'll make those arrangements through the mayor's office. But when do you want to play? As early as tomorrow or later in the week?"

Otis fondled the handle of Astrid's case, his face glum. "If we could find another accordion player, the Guten Tags would be able to make an appearance too. I was all set to be happy about watching everyone else play, but now that her instrument has found its way back to us undamaged, I'm thinking it's some kind of sign from beyond the grave. I think Astrid *wants* us to play."

"I think so too," agreed Wendell. "Our other decision might have been premature."

"Do any of you musicians have expertise with more than one instrument?" I called out.

"I play the piano," said the woman with

the nasally voice. "But I couldn't learn the nuances of the accordion in time to be of any help."

Otis made a plea to the rest of the room. "Can you folks help us out? Do any of you play an instrument?"

Lucille Rasmussen raised her hand. "Are spoons considered an instrument? My Dick used to play the spoons on his bare belly, but he died on his very first trip to Europe with Emily, so we're spared the embarrassment of having to listen to him."

"Do you suppose we could rent a musician?" suggested Gilbert. "Maybe they have stores here that are like Ace Rental back home, only instead of renting out generators and power washers, they rent out accordionists."

That started a buzz that grew so loud, we nearly missed the voice from the back of the room. "I might be able to help you out."

Otis whipped his head around to ferret out the mystery voice. "What'd you say?"

"I said, I might be able to help you out."

I froze mid-breath, too stunned to finish inhaling.

Dad?

FOUR

"Why is your father offering to help?" asked Mom as she squinted toward the back of the room. "He doesn't even know how to whistle."

Dad stood up. "It's been a long time, but if you're in a bind, I might be able to pinch-hit for you."

Gasps. Hoots. Clapping.

"Hallelujah!" whooped Otis. "Come on up here and have a look at this thing, then. This is unbelievable. It's gonna happen, folks! Astrid is pulling strings from above."

"Good Lord," Mom wheezed as Dad marched to the front of the room. "What is he doing? He doesn't play the accordion."

"Are you sure?"

Her eyes narrowed to slits. "We've been married for forty-one years. If he played a musical instrument, don't you think he would have mentioned it by now?"

"Maybe he's been waiting for just the

right moment to spring it on you."

"Your father does *not* play the accordion." She buried her face in her hands and slumped forward over her lap. "He's going to make a fool of himself, and *I'll* be the one who'll have to bear the stigma and humiliation."

"C'mon, Mom. Nana has always preached that no one can embarrass us except ourselves."

"Your grandmother obviously told you all sorts of stupid things when you were growing up." She bowed her head lower. "I have to warn you, Emily, I'm praying for God to strike me dead, so if you don't see me in the morning, you'll know what happened."

I gave her shoulder a sympathetic pat. "Wouldn't you be better off praying for Dad to be granted the ability to play the accordion?"

She squeaked out a sound not dissimilar to the one Tosca might have made before she flung herself off the battlements of Castel Sant'Angelo.

Poor Mom. The anguish . . . the strain . . . the burden. No doubt about it: this would probably go down on record as the most exciting part of her trip.

I checked out the interactions up front: Otis lifting the accordion out of its case and handing it off to Dad. Dad hefting it in his arms.

I shifted in my chair for a better view. "Wow. You should see this baby, Mom. It's candy-apple red with a keyboard that looks like it's marbled with mother-of-pearl. And there's a big intricate diamond design on the bellows. And red marbled housing." I smiled in amazement. "And Dad actually looks pretty comfortable holding it."

Soft whimpering sounds escaped from Mom's throat as Wendell encouraged Dad to try it on for size. Dad slipped his arms through a set of wide straps and crushed the accordion to his chest. "Looks like we've got us a live one!" hooted Otis as the other musicians suddenly fell into each other snorting, laughing, and knee-slapping.

A befuddled look settled on Dad's face.

Hetty eased the instrument off Dad's chest and flipped it 180 degrees. "A small helpful hint, Bob. You'll find a piano accordion easier to play if you're not holding it upside down."

Play an accordion? He didn't even know how to *hold* an accordion.

Oh, God. I needed to get Mom out of here before the embarrassment became too crippling for her. "Would you like to go back to

70

your room to freshen up before dinner, Mom?"

Snatching her hands away from her eyes, she jackknifed upward, resolve stamped on her face. "I know what I'll do. I'll fly home. So if your father wants to continue this fool's errand, he won't be able to humiliate anyone but himself — and the musicians, and you, and Etienne, and the rest of the tour guests, and your tour company in general." She paused in reflection. "Maybe you'd like to fly home with me."

A frisson of alarm coiled in my stomach. Holy crap. She was serious. *How* could this be happening? I'd learned to contend with foul weather, feuding guests, unexpected death, and Bernice, but I had no idea how to contend with dissention between my parents. I couldn't even refer to the updated version of my *Escort's Manual* because I'd written it, and I hadn't included a section that dealt with parental discord.

OhGodohGodohGod. I had no other choice. I was going to have to initiate the nuclear option.

My throat started to close in protest. "What about me?" I gasped out in a hoarse breath.

The resolve on her face suddenly wilted.

"I thought you and I were going to be

71

joined at the hip until I started feeling like myself again."

I could see the war playing out in her eyes. Commitment or flight? Humiliation or duty? Good mother or bad mother?

She tucked in her lips, looking contrite. "I'm sorry, Emily. Your father has upset me so much that I completely forgot about you."

"No problem," I soothed. "I know it's been traumatic for you."

"You understand me so well." She patted my hand while Dad, in the front of the room, surrounded by a full complement of musicians, gawked at his marbled keyboard and chord buttons with a clueless look on his face.

Mom regarded him and winced. "So I'll stay with the tour until you're feeling better . . . and *then* I'll fly home. Do you have any idea how long you might need me? Another day? Maybe two?"

Okay, I hadn't solved the problem, but at least I'd gained a little breathing space to work things out.

Dad expanded the bellows, generating a mournful drone that sounded like ailing bagpipes. "That does it." Mom shot to her feet. "I've had enough. You stay right here. I'll get your key from Etienne and take you up to your room."

"Has the meeting been adjourned yet?" Osmond called out over the whining bellows.

"Meeting adjourned," announced Wally.

They vacated their seats in typical "mad dash" fashion, bumping into each other as they tried to cut each other off. "Watch where you're going!" I cautioned as they raced past me, monitoring the readout screens on their phones as they fled.

"How are you doing, Emily? Are you all right?" Zola Czarnecki paused in front of me, her freckled face creased with concern. "When I heard the explosion I feared the worst, so I can't begin to tell you how thankful I am that there weren't more casualties."

I grasped her hand and stared her straight in the eye, torn between disbelief and awe. "You knew." My voice caught in my throat like a fish bone. "You knew what was going to happen."

"Not exactly. I got spooked by a bad vibe that turned out to be more than just a vibe."

"But . . . how could you have sensed what was about to happen on that street? How is that possible?"

She shrugged. "It's a clairvoyant thing. I don't expect civilians to understand the

73

process, but what it boils down to is, I'm not wired the same as everyone else."

Guilt gnawed at my conscience, leaving a sour taste in my mouth. "I should have gotten the word out — warned the other guests. If I'd told them about your misgivings, maybe —"

Zola held up her other hand, cutting me off. "You think they would have believed me? Shoot, *you* didn't believe me. You thought I was a pain in the butt and a little nuts, and don't tell me otherwise because I could see it in your eyes. You started thinking the ole clairvoyant might prove herself to be not only annoying but a real financial drain on your whole operation. I dare you to tell me I'm wrong."

Wow. If she could see all that in my eyes, I needed to think about blinking more. "I — uh, I guess the financial implications did enter my mind . . . a little."

"Which is why when I get my twinges, I try not to shove them down anyone else's throat. But I'm not about to charge straight into the jaws of danger if my ears start humming and every hair on my body is standing on end."

"Is that what happens when you get one of your twinges?"

"Nah. That's the Hollywood version, but

it's as good as any. I've never been able to explain what happens exactly because I'm being bombarded by too many sensations when it hits me, but my ma used to say it was like getting zapped by a bolt of lightning, only on a smaller scale."

"Sounds a little scary."

"I don't recommend it to the general public. People think it would be so cool to be clairvoyant, but I'll let you in on a secret: it's highly overrated. Way too much grief involved."

Her words spurred two images. Zola standing in the plaza, head bowed, eyes closed, focusing all her energy on Astrid Peterson's hand, and Zola releasing Astrid's hand, looking completely unnerved. "You knew Astrid was going to die, didn't you? You saw it when you did your hand-holding thing."

"That's not true. I had no idea she only had minutes to live."

"Then what caused you to look so alarmed after you released her hand, remember? Your expression frightened her so much, she asked if you'd seen something horrible in her future, and you said no."

"I told her the truth."

"Then why did you look so rattled? If you

didn't see her imminent death, what *did* you see?"

"*That's* what frightened me. I can always predict something — something fun and harmless: a birthday party, a wedding, a vacation. It's never unclear." Her eyes grew haunted. She elevated her hands and stared at her palms. "But when I tried with Astrid, I felt as if my whole system had broken down. It was the first time anything like that had ever happened to me. It scared the bejeebers out of me. It was like looking into a black hole. When I was holding Astrid's hand, I didn't see the future."

She lifted her gaze to my face, fear rampant in her eyes. "I saw nothing at all."

Mom dropped me off at my door.

"Do you want me to come inside with you, Em? I could run a hot bath or rub your feet or get you a snack out of the minibar." A hint of excitement crept into her voice. "I don't know how the treats are organized in the minibar, but I'll bet no one takes the time to arrange them properly."

Our boutique hotel maintained a certain European charm by providing us with actual door keys rather than key cards, but the downside was, if we didn't return the hardware at the end of our stay, they'd tack an added fee onto our bill. I wasn't running the show here, but in this age of keyless ignitions and thumbprint entry locks, room keys seemed almost a little too retro to be practical.

As I inserted my key into the doorknob, Mom rubbed her hands together, champing at the bit to get inside. When I heard a click, I turned the knob and eased the door open.

"Thanks for the offer, Mom, but I'm good. Really. Why don't you take the rest of the night off? Dinner's in less than an hour, so go have a drink. Shmooze. Enjoy yourself. Etienne will be up in a few minutes, so I'll be just fine until tomorrow . . . when . . . when I'll look forward to hanging out with you" — I inhaled a steadying breath — "All. Day. Long."

She hesitated at the threshold. "You're sure? Because if you need me, I'll gladly miss supper."

I gave her a hug. "I'm fine. Thanks for all your help, and I'll see you in the morning. Okay?"

She craned her neck to peek inside the room. "If you'd like that stack of magazines on the desk organized, it wouldn't take me a minute to —"

"If you can hold out until tomorrow, I'll be happy to have you come in and organize to your heart's content. All right?"

"You bet." She shivered with delight. "Would you look at me?" She shoved her sleeve toward her elbow to show me her forearm. "I've got goose bumps just thinking about it. You run along and rest, then, and call if you need me for anything. Anything at all."

After closing the door, I headed immediately for the desk where Etienne's leather messenger bag was sitting. I unsnapped the main flap, removed a sheaf of documents from the first compartment, and found the page I was looking for on the very top. I scanned the sheet for the information I needed, repeated the information aloud to reinforce my memory, and headed back out the door and down the corridor until I arrived at the room I was looking for. It was pretty handy that we were on the same floor.

I knocked on the door and waited.

And waited.

I heard no telltale sounds indicating the room was occupied, but I knew for a fact that someone was inside and standing at the security peephole, looking out at me.

I knocked again. "Open up. I know you're in there. I can see your shadow at the base of the door."

Whispering. Shushing. Then silence.

I checked my watch. "If you don't head down to dinner within the next ten minutes, you'll probably have to wait in a really long line at the buffet station, so I'm going to stay right here and wait you out."

More whispers. Footsteps shuffling on the carpet. Heavy breathing. An odd crinkling sound.

I looked down to find a small rectangle of paper inching its way into the hall from beneath the door. I snatched it up. A personal check with my name listed as the payee. I rolled my eyes. "I don't want your money, Nana."

"But it's a million dollars."

"Open the door."

The lock clicked. The door opened.

Nana and Tilly stood on the other side — Nana looking physically diminished and shamefaced, Tilly looking tall and professorial. "I warned Marion that you wouldn't accept her blood money," said Tilly.

"You were right." I ripped the check in two and handed it back to Nana.

Nana's expression brightened. "How about two million? I got more checks."

"No! I will not ease your guilty conscience by taking your money."

"Three million?"

"Why'd you do it?" I regarded her sternly.

79

"You and I have always been on the same page when it comes to dealing with Mom — until today. Why'd you sell me out?"

She heaved a pathetic sigh. "It was one of them acts of desperation. I'm not proud of what I done, but when I seen an openin', I took it. I'm sorry for bein' a traitor, dear, but if your mother's plannin' to be a millstone around my neck for this whole trip, I'd rather go home."

"With the way things are starting to unravel, you'll probably end up sitting next to her on the flight back."

"What?"

"Mom is threatening to fly home early because of Dad. He's embarrassing her."

"No kiddin'?" Nana led me farther into the room while Tilly closed the door. "That could work. If Margaret goes, I'll stay."

I collapsed into the room's lone armchair. "Have you ever heard Dad play an accordion?"

"Your father don't play no instrument. He don't even hum."

"That's what Mom said." I closed my eyes and blew out a tired breath. "Lord, what a day."

"I imagine you'll be needin' this," said Nana as she dropped my shoulder bag onto my lap.

"My bag!" I gave it an affectionate squeeze before riffling through it to fish out my makeup mirror. Holding it in front of my face, I stared at my reflection . . . and screamed. My face was pockmarked with a half-dozen ulcerations that were big as peas and red with dried blood. "I look like I've been shot with beebees."

"Or been huntin' with Dick Cheney," said Nana.

I touched a particularly angry lesion on my cheek. "I can't be seen in public like this. I'll scare people."

"Tilly's got somethin' that'll heal them sores overnight, don't you, Til?"

Tilly walked over to her suitcase and removed a small jar from her toiletry bag. "This is a restorative compound that I stumbled upon in New Guinea on my first trip into the jungle. Shaman approved and a must-have among the headhunting set. Guaranteed to heal all types of weals, gashes, and wounds within twenty-four hours. When you're in the business of shrinking human heads, you're all about treatments that are strong and fast acting." She handed me the jar. "The witch doctor was kind enough to share his secret recipe with me, so I've been making it at home for decades."

I opened the jar and sniffed the contents, stunned by the pleasant fragrance. "You're able to find all the ingredients in Iowa?"

"Not exactly. The witch doctor's grandson sends me a shipment of special additives once a year. Mail service has improved so much from the Pacific Rim. Our postal service might be shutting down offices here in the States, but in New Guinea, FedEx is opening branch offices in strip malls all throughout the jungle."

"So . . . how do I use it?"

"Like a moisturizer, with a special concentration on the affected areas. One application should work. I guarantee positive results by morning."

It was worth a try. I figured it was either Tilly's cream or a paper sack with cutouts for my eyes.

"I got somethin' for you too," said Nana. She shuffled over to the closet, removed her wind jacket, and started rummaging inside the pockets. "George sneaked it to me when we was hikin' to the beer hall. He said I could use it to escape your mother." She seized the object, returned her jacket to its hanger, and hurried back across the room.

She pressed it into my palm. I stared at it, my confusion surpassed only by my alarm. "George is encouraging you to stab Mom with a Swiss army knife?"

"No. I was s'posed to use it to cut through the dang leash she slapped on my wrist. So here's the scoop. If she traps you tomorrow, wait 'til she's not lookin', then cut the cord and run. I hijacked the one she used on me today, but I don't know how many of the things she brung with her. She might have backups."

I lengthened my eyes to slits. "If you already had a plan in place to solve the problem, why did you go out of your way to sic her on *me*? Couldn't you have just carried out your scheme without dragging me into it?"

"There's only one thing important enough to stop your mother from fussin' over me, Emily, and that's you. It's a whole lot easier for you to stomach her 'cuz she don't treat you like you're a dotty relic what's in danger of goin' off the reservation. And you got your young man to swoop down and draw one a them lines in the sand if her fussin' goes over the top."

"Her fussing always goes over the top."

"I know, dear. That's why I handed the baton off to you. I been exposed to her a lot longer than you have, so I've reached the point of what you call critical mass."

My lips twitched involuntarily. I was trying to remain irritated, but it was a struggle. "Don't think for one minute that I've forgiven you, Nana."

She bowed her head and lowered her gaze in contrition. "I'm probably lookin' at extra time in Purgatory for what I done, so don't you worry. I'll have my day of reckonin'. I just hope the Good Lord'll take pity on me and postpone my punishment 'til after the trip." She looked up, an impish flicker in her eyes. "Now that I don't got your mother on my back no more, George and me can really let loose."

FIVE

"This is really nice of you folks to open up Astrid's room for me."

"We'd like to accommodate the hotel by vacating her room as quickly as possible," Etienne confided as he unlocked the door, "so it's no inconvenience. What is it you said you're looking for?"

"Just some silly . . . trifle," said Otis. He smoothed his hand over the bristly white hairs of his beard as if he were caressing a security blanket. "Something I lent her that I'd like to get back."

I'd skipped the group buffet dinner in favor of room service and quiet, and amazingly, after enjoying a hot meal and a long bath, I'd felt so restored that I'd volunteered to lend Etienne a hand while he packed up Astrid's belongings. Otis had knocked on our door before we left, asking if it would be possible for him to retrieve a personal item from Astrid's room, so since we were headed in that direction anyway, Etienne had invited him to join us.

Etienne pushed open the door and flipped on the wall switch, casting light into the far corners of a room that was an exact replica of ours — queen size bed, desk with rolling chair, mirrorless dresser, flat screen TV, upholstered barrel chair, floor lamp, glass-top side table. The only difference was that Astrid's room looked as if it had been upended by the *Wizard of Oz* tornado.

"Oh, my."

Clothing tumbled over the tops of opened drawers. Bedding hung to the floor down to the mattress cover. Underwear and nylon stockings lay scattered about the floor. An emptied suitcase sat atop the luggage rack. The closet door was halfway open, the hotel ironing board lying on the floor, the guest safe unused.

I gaped at the chaos. "Are we looking at the aftermath of a burglary?"

"Hell, no." Otis fisted his hands at his waist, his eyes hooded and unreadable. "Tidiness wasn't one of Astrid's virtues — or time management. When the two clashed, the result often looked like this." He shrugged. "The place actually looks pretty good if you consider she was running late this morning."

Etienne remained anchored to the spot, surveying the scene with doubt in his eye. "Was ripping her bed apart an integral step in her morning routine?"

"You bet. Bed bugs. She's been terrified of them ever since she got bitten on one of our overnight gigs a couple of years ago, so she's been a little obsessive about hunting them out no matter how nice the hotel. You wouldn't believe how long it took for those bites to disappear. She kept scratching them. They got infected. It was a mess."

"So you're saying that *this*" — Etienne gestured toward the disarray — "is perfectly normal?"

"No. I'm saying that in Astrid's world, *this*" — Otis tossed out his meaty hand in a gesture that mimicked Etienne's — "would be considered *House Beautiful.*"

Etienne arched his brows. "If you say so."

"I'll — uh . . . I'll pull up the bed covers so we can have a place to fold her clothes." I crossed the floor, snatching up her nylons and underwear as I went. "Have you spied your trifle yet, Otis?"

"Nope, but don't you folks pay any attention to me. I'll just snoop around the room for a minute and hope for the best."

"If you tell us what you're looking for, we might be able to help you find it," I insisted.

He slid the closet door all the way open and poked his head inside, moving hangers and sorting through the shelves. "It's kind of a book thing."

"A novel?"

"Uhhh . . . poetry."

Otis read poetry? Aww. Apparently there was a romantic disguised beneath that bushy beard of his. "What's the title?"

He stepped into the bathroom. "Title?" His voice echoed out to us.

"Of your book of poetry."

"Oh." I heard the *zzzzzt* of a zipper being opened and closed. "I — uh, I can't remember." He stepped back into the room. "I'm not very good with titles."

"Large book or small book?" asked Etienne as he removed clothing from the dresser drawers.

"Uhhh . . . average size."

I was beginning to think that Otis knew less about this book than Prissy knew about birthin' babies. I exchanged a curious look with Etienne. "It's not a library book, is it?"

Otis regarded me with bright eyes. "That's it exactly! A library book. So if I don't find it, I'll be looking at a pretty hefty fine."

Why did I feel as if I'd just given him an out? "When did you give it to her?" I asked as I began to fold the sweaters and tops that

Etienne placed on the bed.

Otis searched the drawers that Etienne had just finished emptying and scratched his head. "At the airport?"

I smiled. "Are you asking me or telling me?"

"I guess I gave it to her at the airport." He went down onto his knees to look under the bed.

"Maybe she stashed it in her handbag." I glanced around the room. "Has anyone seen it?"

"She was carrying it with her this morning, bella."

"I know. It was a huge high-end designer bag that probably cost a small fortune. Hard to hide something that big. So . . . where do you suppose it is?"

Etienne's voice grew soft. "Her accordion case is apparently indestructible, but the only personal item of Astrid's that the police could salvage from the explosion site was the badly damaged photo page of her passport. Her handbag didn't fare well in the blast. I'm afraid there was nothing left of it to recover."

"Oh." Obviously, my brain was still a little addled because I sure hadn't connected those dots. Of course her handbag had been obliterated; that's what bombs were built to do. Obliterate things.

"So if she was carrying my book with her, it's gone?" asked Otis. "Destroyed?" He pulled open the drawer of the nightstand to find it empty.

"That would be my guess," said Etienne.

Otis looked oddly pensive before heaving a disappointed sigh. "Maybe the librarian will go easy on me if I explain what happened."

"My mom works in a library. Would you like her to write you a note?"

"No, thanks. I'll wing it." He circled the bed, peeked behind the drapes, and checked under the barrel chair before scratching his head again. "Must have been in her pocketbook because it's sure not here. Okay, then. I'll get out of your hair now and let you finish up what you're doing. Thanks for helping me out."

"No problem," said Etienne as he escorted him to the door. "I just wish the outcome had been better for you."

"Me too. Me too. But at least I tried."

Etienne walked back to the bed with Astrid's lime green spinner suitcase in hand and set it on the mattress. "I know the man is grieving and might not be feeling himself, but did he seem a bit disingenuous to you?"

"A bit? What I'd like to know is, if he

wasn't actually looking for this book that he knew nothing about, what *was* he looking for?"

"Whatever it was, he didn't find it. I'll clean out the bathroom."

As I placed a couple of stacks of folded clothes into the suitcase, I noticed a bulge in a side pocket. Peeling the Velcro strips apart, I dug out a household storage bag filled with a dozen truffles that were so badly squished, the interior of the plastic was a dark smear of melted chocolate. "Astrid was a chocoholic," I called out to Etienne before depositing the bag in the wastebasket and heading for the closet.

Every hanger had something dangling from it. Ankle-length dresses in assorted colors for her beer hall performances. Crisply starched aprons. White blouses with short puffed sleeves and low-cut ruffled bodices. And at the end of the row, a frothy display of femininity in pastels as pale as butter mints. "Aww."

Etienne emerged from the bathroom with an armful of zippered toiletry bags. "*Aww* what?"

"Look at these nighties. They remind me of something TV housewives wore in the boudoir a few decades ago, in the days when they scrubbed floors and vacuumed carpets in high heels and pearls."

Lace. Silk. Nylon. Spaghetti straps. Ruffles. Feathers. Ankle-length confections with see-through cover-ups as delicate as gossamer. "Peignoirs. I didn't think women wore peignoirs anymore."

"Astrid Peterson obviously did."

I fingered the bodice of one nightgown, noting how the lace design was missing several strategic threads and the satin ribbon was frayed at the edge. "Do you suppose these were part of her wedding trousseau? Trousseaus and hope chests were a must with brides in my mom's generation. Women embroidered little flowers on pillowcases and collected pieces of their good china and bought provocative intimate apparel for their honeymoon. These days brides-to-be register at Home Depot and ask for gas grills and nail guns."

"Her lingerie does look a bit tattered."

"I remember my mom wearing a peignoir once when I was little. I thought she looked like a princess, so I asked her if she was going to a ball. I never saw her wear it again. I think she traded it in for flannel pajamas and wool socks." I grinned. "The closest thing I've come to a peignoir was one Halloween when I bought a French maid outfit. It had a flirty little short skirt, an apron, a lace choker and cuffs, and a lace garter belt with black fishnet stockings. I was the most popular girl at the party that year."

A slow, seductive smile worked its way across his mouth. "No doubt."

I removed her nightgowns from their hangers and returned to the bed, folding them neatly into her suitcase before emptying the closet of her folk costumes. When I'd compacted all her belongings into her spinner, Etienne made a final sweep of the room and gave me a thumbs-up. "I think that's everything."

I closed the lid, checked to make sure that none of her costumes were poking out the sides, and zipped it shut. After hoisting it to the floor, Etienne preceded me into the hall. "Would you get the light, bella?"

I cast a final look back before I flipped the switch. I had no logical reason to doubt Otis, but why couldn't I shake off the niggling feeling that the room hadn't been carelessly cluttered by Astrid? Why did I get the feeling it had been ransacked?

Once back in our room, I lingered in the bathroom, applying Tilly's shaman-approved restorative compound to the lesions on my face. I didn't expect miracles, so if the cream did nothing more than fade the redness, I'd be a happy camper.

By the time I finished, Etienne had returned Astrid's room key to the main desk and was already in bed. I crawled in beside him, snuggling against the sinewy contours of his body and tingling all over as he cocooned me in his arms. "You won't have to wake me up in the middle of the night to check my pupils or pulse or anything, will you?" I asked.

He pressed his mouth to my ear, his lips soft, his breath warm. "Should I wake you in the middle of the night, bella, it won't be to check your pulse."

I was so happy to be safe in bed beside him, I almost purred. I probably would have if a darker thought hadn't intruded. "What did you do when you heard the bomb blast today?"

His body stiffened involuntarily before he relaxed again. "I was disoriented initially. I couldn't pinpoint the location of the sound because it seemed to come from everywhere. But Zola didn't hesitate. She grabbed my arm and spun me around in the direction of the main boulevard. And she didn't mince words. She told me it was the street with the spooky sculpture and I should go find you." He paused. "You did say she's a practicing clairvoyant."

"She told me this evening that she had a bad vibe that something was going to happen on that street, but she didn't know that Astrid would be fatally injured."

"I'm not sure how this is going to play out, Emily. Depending on people's belief systems, a psychic among the guests could either prove to be a delightful novelty or a thorn in everyone's side. If she remains low-key, we should have no problem. If not . . ."

He let me fill in the blank.

"We'll work it out," I assured him. "She's a really nice person, so if she pushes the envelope a little too far and we're forced to ask her to tone it down, I'm sure she'll co-operate."

He responded by growling softly against my earlobe and giving it a playful nibble.

"And while we're discussing nice people, does my dad seem all right to you?"

"Define 'all right.' "

"He doesn't play the accordion."

"Yes, he does."

"No. He doesn't."

"All right: to be precise, he played in grammar school and gave it up, so he hasn't touched an accordion for decades. So what I should have said was, he *used* to play."

"Who told you that?"

"Your father."

"When?"

"I spoke to him briefly after the musicians dispersed this evening. He's never mentioned his musical ability to you?"

I racked my brain for occasions on which Dad had voluntarily uttered a complete sentence. "You do realize that conversation isn't Dad's strong point, right?"

"I'm not entirely convinced that your father is as taciturn as you make him out to be, Emily. He might turn out to be a regular chatterbox if someone would take the time to listen to what he has to say. I don't think he lacks verbal skills. I think he lacks an audience."

I swallowed slowly, enlightenment hitting me like a lightning bolt. "Omigod, you're right. The whole family does it. We ignore Dad — we talk over him, we forget he's there, we assume he has nothing to say, so we don't even try to engage him anymore." I pinched my eyes shut, mortified. "What if he's had tons of stuff to share all these years but kept it all to himself because the rest of us were talking so much, he couldn't get a word in edgewise?"

"Then you'll have a lot to look forward to when you give him your undivided attention and let him talk."

I fell into a kind of exhausted haze as he

feathered soft kisses along the curve of my ear, stirring fluttery sensations from my breastbone to my toes. "Umm . . . would this be a good time to tell you about Mom's threat to fly home early?"

"No." He tilted my face upward and placed a long, lingering kiss on my mouth, rendering me blissfully numb. "But I do have a question. The Halloween costume you mentioned — the French maid outfit?" He whispered the words against my lips, his voice low and throaty. "Do you still have it?"

Bam, bam, bam.

I opened one eye to find the room still dark and the nightstand clock aglow with red numerals indicating it was 4:54.

Bam, bam, bam. "Emily? Emily!" *Bam, bam, bam.*

The door.

Someone banging on the door.

I shot out of bed and raced across the room. I threw open the door to find Dad in his bare feet and pajamas.

"You gotta come quick. Your mother's had a stroke."

Six

"Transient global amnesia."

I stared at the same trauma specialist who'd treated me yesterday, my anxiety so crushing, my heart pounding so fiercely, that I could scarcely catch my breath. "Amnesia? Not . . . not a stroke?"

"Your mother's MRI and EEG show no neurological anomalies, Mrs. Miceli, so we've ruled out a stroke, as well as epilepsy."

"Amnesia?" questioned Etienne, who'd suffered his own bout with the affliction before we were married. "From the explosion yesterday?"

Dad continued to look as shell-shocked as he had when he'd pounded on my door five hours earlier. "She didn't know where she was when she woke up this morning, and she couldn't remember how she'd gotten here. So I told her, but five minutes later she asked me the same questions again."

"And five minutes after that, did she

repeat her questions?" asked Dr. Fischer.

Dad nodded. "That's when I ran down the hall to fetch Emily."

Dr. Fischer swept his hand toward the table in the center of the consultation room. "Why don't we sit down while I explain a little more about the condition."

Etienne pulled out a small notebook and pen as we seated ourselves. Dr. Fischer continued. "The type of amnesia Mrs. Andrew has can mimic the symptoms of a stroke, but unlike a stroke, the condition is harmless, has no lasting effects, and is usually short-lived."

"How short?" I asked.

"Typically, memory functions return to normal within twenty-four hours."

Dad was so juiced by the prognosis that his voice cracked like a twelve-year-old. "No kidding? Come tomorrow, she'll be her old self again?"

Dr. Fischer massaged the crown of his shaven skull. "Typically, that's the case, but there are always exceptions, and we don't know yet which category your wife will fall into. Trans-global amnesia is quite rare, so few cases ever cross our path."

"Then how can you be so sure that's what's wrong with her?" I asked.

"Because from what we *do* know of the

condition, your mother is exhibiting classic symptoms. The onset of her memory loss was sudden. She retains knowledge of her personal identity. She recognizes her family and familiar objects."

Etienne was jotting down notes as fast as the doctor was talking.

"She can follow simple directions. She has no limb paralysis, involuntary movement, or speech impairment. But she's unable to remember what happened yesterday or the day before or a year ago. And until the episode passes, she won't be able to form new memories and retain them, which means that every five minutes she'll be asking one of you how she came to be here and why. You can count on the exercise growing old very quickly."

"We can handle it," said Dad. "As long as we know Margaret'll be all right, we can handle anything."

"Have you any idea what caused the problem to begin with?" I inquired. "Etienne was asking about the explosion yesterday. Could the concussive wave from the blast have triggered the condition?"

"It could, but it's just as likely that the blast had nothing to do with it. Does Mrs. Andrew suffer from migraine headaches?"

Dad shook his head. "She never gets

headaches. But she's been known to cause a few."

"There's a notable link between migraines and this type of amnesia," Dr. Fischer continued, "but if Mrs. Andrew has no history of migraines . . ." He shrugged, palms up. "The singular underlying cause of the condition is still unknown, so I'm afraid we're left with a short list of anecdotal triggers."

"Which are?" asked Etienne, not looking up from his notebook.

He ticked them off on his fingers. "Invasive medical procedures. Strenuous physical activity. Sudden immersion in hot or cold water. Mild head trauma . . . which she certainly might have suffered yesterday at the blast site, but the trauma might have been so slight that it was undetectable at the time. The only other trigger that's been mentioned in the literature is acute emotional distress prompted by bad news, stress, or conflict. Has Mrs. Andrew been subjected to any undue emotional distress since she arrived?"

Dad scratched the bristles on his unshaven jaw and shook his head. "Nothing out of the ordinary . . . other than being caught in a bomb blast and thinking her daughter might be dead."

"Point taken," conceded Dr. Fischer. "Mrs. Andrew could well have escaped the concussion from the blast but suffered a delayed reaction from the emotional stress of the incident."

And that stress, coupled with her anxiety over Dad's musical delusions, might have been what pushed her over the edge. Poor Mom. A dream holiday in Bavaria and she'd return home with no memories of it. But on the flip side, if Dad's musical debut ended up being a total train wreck, at least she wouldn't be able to remember the humiliation.

Hmm. All things considered, this amnesia thing might turn out to be a blessing in disguise.

"Mrs. Andrew requires no further treatment," Dr. Fischer assured us, "but be mindful that losing one's memory can be extremely unsettling, so I encourage you to be as supportive and patient as humanly possible. Do you have any other questions?"

"If she doesn't make a full recovery within twenty-four hours, should we call you?" asked Etienne.

"She'll recover at her own pace," said Dr. Fischer. "Twenty-four hours is just an average, not a hard and fast time limit. So the answer to that is no."

"Last questions," said Etienne, referring to his notebook. "How do we prevent this from happening again, and should we expect any long-term complications?"

"Since we're not absolutely sure what caused it, I can't tell you how to prevent it from happening again, but according to the literature, the condition rarely manifests itself again. Erring on the side of caution, however, I would recommend that for the next few days you keep Mrs. Andrew's stress levels to a minimum. As to long-term complications? None."

Dr. Fischer pushed away from the table and stood up. "As soon as I sign her release forms, she'll be free to leave."

"Can't thank you enough," said Dad, rising to his feet and shaking Fischer's hand with the enthusiasm of a kid working a pitcher pump. When I extended my hand, Dr. Fischer clasped it politely, then tightened his grip as he studied my face with sudden interest.

"The lesions on your face, Mrs. Miceli." Disbelief in his voice. Incredulity in his eyes. "They've disappeared."

"They have?" I clapped my hand to my cheek, sampling the affected area with my fingertips. I'd been so freaked out about Mom, I'd never looked into a mirror before leaving the hotel this morning. Shoot, I hadn't even stopped to brush my teeth.

"How is this possible?" He tilted my chin toward the ceiling lights. "What did you do?"

"I slathered on some kind of compound that a friend gave me."

He turned my head left and right. "Developed by what pharmaceutical company?"

"She formulates it herself."

"Is she a chemist?"

"Retired anthropologist. She discovered it in New Guinea while living in the jungle. I guess it's a must-have with the folks who shrink heads for a living."

"I see." He took a step back, his eyebrows dipping to a V above his nose. "In other words, you'd prefer not to tell me."

"I just *did* tell you. Really! I don't know anything about the stuff other than it smells really good and apparently works like gangbusters."

He tipped his head politely, his expression skeptical. "I would invite the three of you to join Mrs. Andrew in her treatment room as soon as possible. Given her present condition, she'll feel more at ease if she's surrounded by familiar faces. Mr. Miceli." He extended his hand. "Pleasure."

My phone chimed an alert as he left the

room. I checked the readout. "Text message from Nana: *HOUSE MARGARET DUNE?*"

I flashed the screen toward Dad, whose brow furrowed in confusion when he saw the words with his own eyes. "Is that one of those coded messages?"

"I think it's supposed to read 'How's Margaret doing?' But Nana's voice text function tends to garble her diction. The little gizmo that transposes verbal commands apparently doesn't understand Iowan." I touched his arm. "Can I ask you about something before we go?"

He sidled a look at me, his expression as unsure as that of a child who'd just been called to the principal's office. "Sure."

"I'm heading down to Margaret's treatment room," Etienne announced as he removed his mobile phone from its holster. "And I'll give Wally a call to give him a heads-up about our ETA."

"Okay, sweetie. We'll join you in a minute." I narrowed my eyes at Dad. "Can you really play the accordion?"

"Don't know anymore."

"But you *used* to play? In grade school?" He nodded. "Yup."

"Why didn't you ever tell anyone?"

"No one ever asked."

"And you never thought to just throw it

105

into a conversation sometime?"

"Nope."

"What am I going to do with you?"

"Walk me down to see your mother, I suppose."

I gave him a peck on his cheek as we headed for the door. "So . . . why the accordion?"

"We had one in the house because your Grampa Andrew played, so it was available."

"Grampa Andrew played the accordion? We have authentic musical genes in the family?"

"Don't know that I'd go that far."

"Were you any good?"

"Depends on who you ask."

"Why'd you give it up?"

"My music teacher told me I was hopeless."

"Aww." I hugged his arm against me, worried that this didn't bode well for his comeback. "I'm sorry your musical career was cut short."

He lifted his shoulders noncommittally. "Guess I just wasn't cut from the same cloth as your grampa."

As we approached Treatment Room 3, Mom's voice drifted out into the hall. "How come I don't recognize this place?"

"Because it's an unfamiliar emergency

room," said Etienne.

"In Iowa?"

"Bavaria."

"It's quite a nice facility, isn't it? Very tidy." A pause. "How come I don't recognize this place?"

Dad fixed me with a woebegone look. "Ooh boy."

My phone chimed another text alert. Nana again: *EMILY, SHEETS KNOT DEAD, IS SHE?*

Nope. Mom wasn't dead, but if I was able to resolve this latest crisis the way I wanted, Nana might end up wanting to kill Mom herself.

"You want me to *what*?" Nana skewered me with her crinkly little eyes.

I was seated with Nana and Tilly in their newly upgraded room — a luxurious suite with kitchen facilities, floor-to-ceiling bay windows, a cozy living room with sofa, comfortable chairs, fresh flowers, and a minibar that was stocked with goodies that were free for the taking. But the best part of the room was — it was exactly like mine!

"I need you to help me with Mom." Knowing what an uphill battle this would be, I launched into the spiel I'd prepared on our taxi ride back from the hospital, when Mom had been asking where she was and where we were going every ninety seconds. "It should only be for twenty-four hours, until her short-term memory kicks back in. And I'll be with her every minute when I'm not needed someplace else, so we can be a kind of tag team. Dad volunteered to do it all himself, but if he does, he won't be able to practice with the band, and I can't have that. He'd be so disappointed. He really did play the accordion when he was a kid, so this is his big comeback."

Nana opened her mouth. I continued talking.

"I *know* she drives you crazy, Nana. I know you hate to be smothered, tethered, and made a fuss over, but she needs you. *I* need you. The doctor said it's not a good idea to leave her alone right now because she can't remember much, so she needs constant reassurance that she's where she's supposed to be and with the people she's supposed to be with. So I'm asking you to set aside your differences with Mom for twenty-four hours. I'm *beseeching* you to ignore her annoying habits, her obsessive-compulsive tendencies, her alphabet fixation, her —"

"Okay."

My spine straightened so fast, it made a

crack like a broken tree limb. "What?"

"Okay."

"Why are you saying okay?"

"Isn't that what you want me to say?"

"Well, yeah, but . . . why are you agreeing so quickly?"

She dropped her gaze and hung her head, causing all three of her chins to cascade onto her chest. "I've been known to say some awful critical things about your mother in years past, dear, and it's all comin' home to roost. The Lord's callin' in his chips. He's let me whine long enough, and now he's deliverin' my comeuppance. 'Marion,' he's sayin', 'it's time to pay the piper.' "

I'm not sure the Lord would use this many mixed metaphors, but who was I to judge divine grammar? "Sooo . . . what you're saying is . . ."

Tilly thumped the floor with her cane. "Your grandmother is feeling guilty about all the cynicism she's directed at Margaret, so she's convinced herself that this health scare is her personal wake-up call to start treating your mother with more kindness and less snark. Is that about right, Marion?"

"Pretty much."

"And if you'll allow me to submit the Lutheran translation," offered Tilly. "The

Good Lord just scared the snot out of Marion, so she's going to leave no stone unturned in a Herculean effort to turn over a new leaf and mend her wicked ways."

Okay, then. A Lutheran could screw up metaphors just as badly as a Catholic.

"The Lord's probably payin' me back for what I done to you, too, Emily. That was probably the last straw. He couldn't even wait 'til after my vacation to bust me. He decided to nail me today."

"So you'll help me out?"

"I don't see where I got no other choice. Margaret might drive me crazy, but she's still my kid, and . . . dang it" — she heaved a woeful sigh — "I love her." She peeked at me above her wire rims. "You never heard them words leave my mouth. Right?"

"Right." I stood up. "Would you like to see for yourself how mom's doing? Her room's at the end of the hall."

"I s'pose." She boosted herself to her feet. "Now's as good a time as any. But if she's got amnesia, how's she gonna know who I am?"

"She'll know you. It's not that kind of amnesia."

As we skirted around a freebie newspaper that was lying outside the door of a nearby suite, I was reminded of what the morning had held for everyone who hadn't been holed up in the emergency room. "Did the reporter from the newspaper stop by to conduct all the promised interviews?"

"Reporters," corrected Tilly. "They sent a battalion of them."

"And a photographer what took all kinds of pictures," Nana enthused. "Individual shots. Group shots. We're gonna be front page news tomorrow. Above the crease."

"And the interviews were quite in depth," added Tilly. "I was quite favorably impressed."

Arriving at Mom's room, I knocked on the door while Nana fidgeted nervously beside me.

"Your mother still looks the same, don't she?"

"Yup. Same Mom."

"She don't got a paralyzed face or twisted limbs or nuthin'?"

"She's suffering from a rare form of amnesia, Nana, not a session in Dr. Frankenstein's laboratory." I peered down at her, frowning. "Why do you want to know?"

" 'Cuz if she's all bent over and gnarly like that creature from *Beauty and the Beast,* I gotta prepare myself. I'm old. The fright could kill me."

Etienne opened the door and held it wide,

welcoming us into the room. "Come in, ladies. Margaret? You have guests."

Mom bustled across the floor to greet us. "Emily! You're here, too?" She crushed me against her bosom. "Isn't that funny how we're all here together? How did that happen?"

"Lots of planning, Mom."

She held me away from her and searched my face. "No, really, how *did* that happen? I don't know what I'm doing here. I don't even know where *here* is."

"We're in Germany," said Tilly, "touring the country with all our friends from Iowa, and you and Bob are traveling with us."

"Bob," Mom recited with confidence as she wheeled away from me to scan the room. "Where *is* Bob?"

"Band practice," said Etienne. "With the Guten Tags. You're on the Sounds of Music tour, Margaret."

"With all my friends." She looked suddenly perplexed. "But where *are* we?"

Nana shuffled up beside me and whispered out the side of her mouth, "She don't know where she is?"

I forced a stiff smile. "Did I forget to mention that?"

"Ladies?" Etienne pulled on his sports coat and headed for the door. "With Margaret in your capable hands, I'll excuse myself to attend to other duties. I'll send out an email alert after I've spoken to Wally about this afternoon's itinerary. And if you miss that, just check the whiteboard in the lobby."

"That man is so much more than a heart-throb," cooed Mom as she watched him leave. "Impeccable manners. Nurturing. Organized. The only thing that could possibly make him any more attractive is an eye patch. So!" She clapped her hands together and nodded toward the chairs surrounding the coffee table. "Sit down. Make yourselves comfortable. I'm sorry Bob isn't here to welcome you, but he's" — she spun in a slow circle, her eyes scrutinizing the room — "he seems to be missing at the moment. Bob?"

"He's practicing with the oompah band," I reminded her as I lowered myself into a barrel chair.

"Bob's in a band?" She seated herself opposite me, her eyes narrowing as she struggled to give the information some context. "Remind me what instrument he plays?"

"He don't play no instrument," said Nana as she sank down beside Tilly on the sofa. "So you don't need to remember nuthin', which is a blessin' considerin' what I'm seein'."

Just an observation, but I suspected that Nana's vow to lose the snark might require more practice than she realized.

Mom shifted her attention to Tilly, her little moon face a complete blank. "So Tilly, would you like to introduce me to your friend?"

Seven

"It's Nana, Mom. Nana? You know. Your mother?"

"My mother's still alive?"

Nana fisted her hands on her hips. "Do I look dead to you, Margaret?"

Mom cocked her head slowly left and right as she studied Nana's face. "How honest do you want me to be?"

Nana stiffened up like an arthritic joint, a clever comeback apparently trapped behind her clenched teeth. "Ohhh, I get it. You're havin' a little fun with your old mother. Pretendin' to remember everyone except me."

Mom continued to scrutinize Nana's face. "Uh-uh!"

"What's *that* s'posed to mean?" demanded Nana.

"Just a friendly observation, but if you don't stop smoking, your skin is going to look like a slab of beef jerky."

"I've never smoked no cigarettes."

Mom pulled a face. "You can fool some of the people some of the time."

"Don't make me come over there, Margaret," warned Nana, spearing Mom with a look that would have silenced any normal person whose filter hadn't been temporarily knocked out of order by amnesia.

"I'm sorry." Mom flashed a vacuous look. "What did you say your name was?"

The word exploded from Nana's mouth like a dart from a dart gun. *"MARION."*

"Oh! Like Marion the Librarian? Remember that old movie with Shirley Jones and Robert Preston?" Hands clasped over her bosom, Mom suddenly burst into song. "Marian . . . Madam Librarian, la-la-la, dum-de-dah, something something, Madam Librarian . . ."

Nana shot me a thorny look. "Not that kind of amnesia, huh?"

Okay. So the downside of the situation was that Mom couldn't recall Nana worth beans. But the upside was, she killed at almost remembering Academy Award-winning musicals from the sixties.

A symphony of text alerts echoed through the room. Nana, Tilly, and I went for our cell phones while Mom sprang out of her chair and rushed into the kitchen. "Is that the timer on the microwave?" She checked out the unit while we retrieved the message from Wally: *MEET IN LOBBY IN ONE-HALF HOUR TO BOARD COACH FOR OBERAMMERGAU.*

"The dinging isn't from the microwave, Mom. It's from our cell phones." I held up my unit. "Text alerts."

"Do I have a cell phone?"

"You bet. It's probably in your pocketbook."

"Where's my pocketbook?"

"Uh . . . wherever housekeeping stashed it when they moved your belongings to your new room. Nana can help you find it." I stood up, my mind racing at warp speed. "Okay, can you two ladies get Mom ready to go and have her downstairs in half an hour?"

Nana looked at me as if I'd invited her to sip a refreshing glass of bleach. "I don't wanna cause you no disappointment, dear, and I sure don't wanna give the Good Lord no reason to turn his back on me, but I'm not up to this. If I was a little more hard a hearin', I might have the stomach for it, but I don't got no copin' skills for listenin' to your mother ask me what my name is every two minutes. It's humiliatin'."

"You can count on us," Tilly spoke up. "We'll have Margaret there with time to spare, won't we, Marion?"

117

"Wasn't you listenin' to what I just told Emily?"

"You don't mean that."

"Yes, I do."

"I need to run down to my room and at least brush my teeth before I go anywhere," I said as I hurried into the kitchen to corral Mom. I looked into her eyes and spoke slowly and emphatically. "I'll see you in thirty minutes, okay? Tilly and Nana will take good care of you while I'm gone. Thirty minutes. Do everything they ask you. All right? Then we'll join the rest of the tour group."

"We're on a tour?"

"Jesus, Mary, and Joseph," muttered Nana.

As I headed out the door, I considered the irony of Nana's situation, from being smothered by the overreaching attentions of her daughter to becoming a nameless stranger.

If allowed a choice between the two now, I wondered which one she'd choose.

"In 1633, halfway through the Thirty Years' War, the Black Death swept through Germany, killing a quarter of a million people. But the village we're about to explore, Oberammergau, was spared total decimation.

Legend holds that only a handful of villagers became infected before the disease miraculously disappeared."

We were heading south on the A95, maintaining moderate speed while pricey, spit-polished cars in a festive range of colors from dark gray to black zoomed past us. Wally sat at the front of the bus, entertaining us with a little history about the town whose five-syllable name no one could pronounce. Etienne held down the front with him while I hung out in the back, sharing a seat with Mom.

"What stopped the plague dead in its tracks?" Wally asked rhetorically.

"D-Con," shouted Lucille Rasmussen, whose deceased husband had once run a successful pesticide company with the catchy motto *We get rid of what's bugging you.*

"Penicillin," called out Margi.

"Good guesses," said Wally. "Wrong century. Once again, legend has it that the people of Oberammergau made a solemn vow to the Almighty that if he saved their village, they'd perform a pious play commemorating his suffering and death every ten years for time immemorial. And whether you choose to believe it or not, once the vow was offered up, the plague petered out

119

and caused no more deaths. The first play was presented a year later in 1634, and the ten-year schedule has been maintained ever since 1680. Tickets are now on sale for the 2020 performance, so if you're in the market to attend a sixteen-act Passion play that takes five and a half hours to perform and features eight hundred actors on stage at the same time, buy your tickets now because they sell out fast."

"We should do that," Mom remarked as she gave my knee a friendly pat. "I'd be the envy of every parishioner at Holy Redeemer."

I got so excited, my voice sounded as if it had been shanghaied by Munchkins. "You know the name of our church?"

"Of course I know the name of our church. I've only been attending the same one all my married life."

"You've turned a corner, Mom. You're on the road to recovery!" I leaned toward the seatback in front of me and tapped the crown of Nana's head. "Mom remembers the name of our parish church."

Nana peeked over the top of her seat, doubt in her eyes as she squinted at Mom. "What's the name of the fella what got elected president last time?"

"Last time?" Mom's eyes darted wildly in

her sockets as she tapped her memory bank. "Uhhh . . ." She broke out in a sudden smile. "How badly do you need to know? Because if it's a real emergency, I bet Osmond could tell us."

"Not that kind of amnesia," grumbled Nana as she faced forward in her seat again. *"Pfffft."*

"This little wrinkled woman in front of us," Mom whispered in my ear. "She's very crabby. By any chance, is her name Bernice?"

Okay, so maybe I'd jumped the gun on the turning the corner thing.

"There's some great shopping in Ober-ammergau," Wally informed us as we exited the highway onto a secondary road. "A good majority of the villagers are famed wood-crafters, so if your taste runs toward intricate wood carvings, you've come to the right place: nativity scenes, Madonnas, crucifixes, cutting boards, kitchen utensils. And the Ammer Valley is a great area for hiking and sports, so you'll find some terrific deals on outdoor gear. For those of you who can never have your fill of Christmas and all its trimmings, there are two Käthe Wohlfahrt shops on the main street, selling everything from traditional German nutcrackers to incense smokers to music boxes. We'll be there in a few minutes, so I'd advise you to start drawing up those shopping lists."

"Astrid loved Christmas," Hetty lamented from the aisle seat across from me. "If she was here with us, she'd head straight for those Christmas shops and buy so many ornaments, she wouldn't have space in her suitcase to carry them all back."

"Would you have tagged along with her?" asked Zola, who occupied the window seat beside her. Wally had declared open seating on the bus today, so the guest pairings were all over the place.

"I didn't enjoy shopping as much as Astrid did. It was a recreational sport for her. But I would have tagged along anyway because Astrid was just a fun person to be around. She had Miss Congeniality written all over her."

"She was an extrovert, huh?"

"I don't know about that, but she always wanted to include everyone in what she was doing and never shut anyone out." Hetty's voice sounded accusatory as she directed this comment to the seatback in front of her, where Otis Erickson and Gilbert Graves were sitting.

"Oh, she was an extrovert all right," said Zola. "I knew that the moment I laid eyes on her. I bet those stage performances of yours really energized her while they leave you feeling completely drained."

Hetty grew quiet. "They do. The noise, the people, playing my clarinet all night — it's exhausting. It takes me forever to recharge my batteries. But how do you know that? You've never seen us play, have you?"

"I don't need to see you play. The proof is in a person's eyes — the energy, the animation. Introverts lack the firecracker spark that's always twinkling in an extrovert's eyes."

Hetty jutted her chin into the air in a defensive gesture and coaxed a strand of her hair behind her ear. "You make introverts sound like duds. We're not duds. We're simply more cerebral and less vocal than other folks, which seems to be highly underrated in some circles." She glared at the seatbacks in front of her again.

"I'm not knocking introverts," chuckled Zola. "What I'm saying metaphorically is that if you're a leopard, I can identify you by your spots."

Clairvoyants seemed to have a much better grasp of symbolic speech than either Catholics or Lutherans.

Hetty shot a look across the aisle at me. "So what's Emily?"

Zola leaned forward, winking at me as she cracked a smile. "Big-time extrovert. I'm surprised you even have to ask. Can you see the vitality in her eyes? That's what I'm talking about."

Zola might call it vitality. I called it acute ocular bleariness due to lack of sleep.

Otis angled around in his seat, his cheeks flushed beneath his Santa Claus beard. "Is it true you read Astrid's fortune before she died?"

"I tried, but —" she paused. "There was too much noise and not enough time, so . . . I couldn't tell her anything. I suggested we try again later when we weren't standing in the middle of the city plaza."

Gilbert craned his neck to peer over his seatback. "If you were a real psychic, wouldn't you have known there'd never be a later for her?"

"Real psychics aren't in the business of frightening people. You might find this surprising, but if I'd sensed she was going to die, I wouldn't have told her. I may be many things, but I'm not heartless."

"How about you show us what you've got?" suggested Otis. "Do your fortunetelling routine with Gil right here."

"I don't want my fortune told," protested Gilbert, looking as if he's just been slapped.

"C'mon, Gil." Otis egged him on. "Be a sport."

"*You* be a sport. I don't want her messing with my personal karma."

Otis's booming voice took on an edge. "Got something to hide?"

A vibe so toxic passed between the two men that I swore I heard the hiss of a light saber slashing through the air.

"If you're so gung-ho to see Zola in action, *you* be the guinea pig," spat Gilbert. He scrunched up his nostrils and sniffed, a gesture that seemed to autocorrect the position of his glasses on the bridge of his nose.

Zola looked from one man to the other. "Any takers? I'm anxious to get back up on my horse after my epic fail yesterday, so I'll be more than happy to oblige. What do you say, Otis?"

"Me?" His Adam's apple bobbed uncomfortably. "Nah. Not my thing."

"Why not?" taunted Gilbert. "Got something to hide?"

Zzzzzzzt went the tension between the two musicians again.

Zola turned to Hetty. "How 'bout you? Are you game?"

"No!" Hetty looked more terrified than a shopaholic whose credit cards were about to be shredded. "Why should I let you dig

125

into my life when the guys aren't man enough to let you dig into theirs? But why doesn't that surprise me? Par for the course for them." The look she fired at Gilbert and Otis caused their expressions to stiffen with what could only be described as extreme discomfort.

"I'll volunteer," offered Mom, breaking into the conversation with bubbly enthusiasm. "Maybe she can tell me where I am."

Zola tossed me a look across the aisle. "Are you all right with that?"

"Go for it." Mom had nothing to lose, actually. If the reading turned out to be apocalyptic, she'd probably be distraught for all of a minute. Two minutes, tops.

While Mom and Hetty exchanged seats, Wally resumed his announcements. "We'll be in Oberammergau for four hours. Please take note of the murals painted on the façades of the houses because it's one of the features that make the local architecture so unique. The majority of murals depict religious scenes, but if you take a stroll down Ettaler Strasse, off the central plaza, you'll be treated to whimsical scenes from Little Red Riding Hood and Hansel and Gretel. Visit the museum on the main street if you'd like to be wowed by 350 years of local art, and if you're in the mood for an afternoon snack, I'd recommend the Hafner Stub'n. The food is great, but the exterior is so spectacular, you might want to devote your time to picture-taking rather than eating. The bus will drop us off at the Passion Play House. From there it's a short two-minute walk to the main street."

Zola clasped Mom's hand, pinched her eyes shut, and in a matter of minutes unearthed her first tidbit.

"I see bookshelves with many, many books. Do you work in a bookstore, Mrs. Andrew?"

"Beats the hell out of me," said Mom.

"She works in a public library," I advised.

"Of course," said Zola. "I can see it now. And you need to upgrade your technology because you're still in the Dark Ages, using the Dewey decimal system."

"That's right," I said, duly impressed. But how did she know that?

"And I see soup cans in some kind of kitchen pantry . . . and they're all in alphabetical order. Dozens and dozens of soup cans."

Otis and Gilbert glanced at me, apparently awaiting an opinion. "She's good, guys. Really good."

While Zola continued to entertain us by outing Mom's eccentricities, we followed the course of a meandering river and soon entered a wide valley that was flanked by sprawling mountains whose sloped shoulders were nearly black with forest. Unlike Norway, there were no waterfalls cascading from crags and niches. Unlike Switzerland, there was no snow capping the highest peaks. But given the valley's lushness and isolation, I felt as if we were in Scotland, about to enter the fictional world of Brigadoon, minus the Broadway set and the musical soundtrack by Lerner and Loewe.

"And you're about to witness some serious limelight," Zola predicted as the bus slowed to a crawl. "A once in a lifetime event. So put a smile on your face and enjoy."

To our left, a tidy expanse of green space beckoned visitors with shade trees, walking paths, and an intriguing array of statuary. To our right, a building that could only be the Passion Play Theater stretched the length of a football field. Mostly windowless, it resembled an updated warehouse with a soaring roof and horizontal stripes that alternated between basic white and a color that Crayola would refer to as Desert Sand.

"Are we done?" Mom asked her.

"That's all I've got."

"Oh, good." Mom looked across the aisle at me. "I'm not quite remembering, but did she happen to mention where we are?"

We coasted to a stop in front of the theater, which was our cue to gather up our belongings and perch on the edge of our seats until the doors opened. I could feel the excitement begin to build. Shoes scraping the floor. Cell phones at the ready.

Wally threw out a few final instructions. "We'll meet at this exact location in four hours. We couldn't arrange a tour of the Passion Play House, but I suggest you stroll around the outside to get an idea of how enormous the theater is. The last renovation was completed in 1999, which enlarged the seating capacity to 4,720, allowing it to accommodate more patrons than either the Metropolitan or Sydney Opera Houses."

The doors whooshed open.

"And one more thing before I cut you loose. I told you about Mrs. Andrew's health issue before we left, so let me reiterate. If you should see her wandering around the streets of Oberammergau without a companion, I would ask you to take personal responsibility and take her under your wing. She's going to be a little disoriented for a couple of days, so we all need to pitch in to make sure she stays safe."

129

"Did you hear that?" Mom said in a stage whisper. "There's another Mrs. Andrew on the bus." She cast a long look down the length of the vehicle as if trying to pick the woman out of the crowd. "Do you think we're related?"

"Okay, then," said Wally. "Have a good time."

And the race was on.

Everyone sprang from their seats and bunched into the center aisle, the log jam thinning out only as guests reached the exits.

"Which venue is first on our list?" Tilly asked into her phone, initializing a verbal text.

Seconds later, a flurry of tings rang out on the bus. Nana scanned the message that Tilly had just sent and spoke into her phone to reply. "We might wanna try out that restaurant what Wally told us about."

Ting. Ting. Ting.

"Head for the nearest restaurant," Dick Teig yelled out from somewhere in front of us. "Marion wants to try out the walleye."

I rolled my eyes. Great new feature, this words-to-text thing. No possibility at all for miscommunication.

I took hold of Mom's arm and guided her toward the stepwell.

"Where's your father, Emily? He didn't go and get himself lost, did he?"

"Dad stayed behind at the hotel to practice the accordion for his big musical debut."

"Your father doesn't play the accordion."

At least she remembered that much.

EIGHT

"What happened to your face?"

My hand flew to my cheek. "Why? What's wrong?"

"Nothing," said Bernice. "That's why I'm asking. How'd you get rid of the crud?" She pushed her face close to mine, squinting at me one-eyed. "Are you wearing some kind of new industrial-strength concealer?"

We were standing on the intricately designed brick walkway of the main street, perusing a building above whose storefront windows were painted the words *Anno Domini 1635*. To the right of the date, a scene depicting the Crucifixion of Christ rose two stories, from the overhang above the ground floor to the third-story roof. To the left of the crucifix, a handful of people wearing white hose and academic robes raised their right hands toward the heavens, flashing what looked like peace signs. To the far right, a dozen men in flowing cloaks and floppy wide-brimmed hats huddled around a table, listening to a bearded gent read a decree from a scroll. I didn't know if this was a modern interpretation of the Last Supper or an updated version of Pontius Pilate rendering his judgment, but the mural left me a little confused both historically and geographically because to my untutored eyes everyone looked like a pilgrim.

"It's not concealer," I told Bernice, unable to hide my continued amazement. "Tilly lent me a jar of homemade corrective cream, and this was the result after only one application. Pretty amazing, huh?"

She tested my cheek with her fingertip, as if expecting to find telltale signs of theatrical makeup. When her finger came back clean, she arched her brows. "She makes it herself?"

"Yup. With secret ingredients flown in from New Guinea."

"And it repairs skin . . . overnight?"

"It sure did in my case."

She turned away from me to scan the street. "She's got a lot of nerve keeping this to herself. Where is she? We gotta talk."

The main street of Oberammergau flaunted its alpine heritage with equal parts pride and charm. Merchant shops boasted the chalet-style architecture that had been perfected by the Swiss and recreated by Department 56 snow villages. Roofs were steeply pitched. Painted shutters framed every window. Decorative balconies clung to every upper-story landing. Summer flowers tumbled from window boxes, spilled from balcony rails, flowed from curbside planters, and hung from every lamppost. I knew we were in Bavaria, but everything about this place screamed Switzerland. All that was missing was the sound of cow bells ringing from high alpine meadows and a few ornery mountain goats.

"There she is." I pointed to a clump of people gathered on the sidewalk a block farther down the street. Tilly was easy to find in a crowd not only because of her signature beret, pleated skirt, and walking stick, but because she was half a head taller than the other ladies and built like Olive Oyl.

"Come on," ordered Bernice as she struck out in that direction. "You're my witness."

"For what?" I fell in beside her as a double-decker Asiana tour bus roared past us, spewing diesel fumes in its wake.

"For the scoop about the miracle cream. If you're there, she can't tell me she doesn't know what I'm talking about."

I had to walk double-time to keep up with her. "How come you're not eating lunch in the restaurant like all of you planned?"

"Too crowded. We're going later."

The gang and other guests were congregated outside Käthe Wohlfahrt's Christmas store, wielding their phones like bidding paddles at an auction: snapping pictures, sending texts, and shooting video. They'd formed a queue curbside, waiting their turn to have their photo taken in front of the Humpty Dumpty figure that was perched on a toy chest near the store entrance. At least, I assumed it was Humpty. If not, it was simply an oversized egg with a mustache, alpine hat, short pants, and clown's feet.

"Time's up!" yelled Dick Stolee as he regarded his smartphone. Dick's favorite feature on his device was the stopwatch function, so he enjoyed setting strict time limits on completely irrelevant activities. "Okay, folks, let's keep moving. We've only got three hours and forty minutes left." He shooed Osmond away from the statue and motioned to Dick Teig to release the next person in line.

Bernice parked herself in front of Tilly, who'd ended up at the back of the line with Nana and Mom. "That cream you lent Em-

135

ily to get rid of the crud on her face? I want some."

Tilly braced her hands on her walking stick, leaned forward, and stared at Bernice down the length of her nose. "Can't help you. I've depleted my supply."

"It's gone?" Bernice fired an accusing look at me. "This is all *your* fault. You have a heck of a lot of nerve using all the stuff up before Tilly can hand out free samples."

"Emily had crud on her face?" said Mom, her eyes swimming in their sockets as if trying to retrieve the image.

"She looked like she'd been blasted with buckshot," said Bernice, "but Tilly's cream cleared it up overnight. So if one application can do *that* to the bride of Frankenstein here, there's no telling what it can do for someone like me, whose only imperfections are a couple of insignificant laugh lines around my mouth."

It was apparent now that the more immediate problem with Bernice wasn't with her face but with her eyesight.

Mom inched closer to Bernice for a better look. "Those laugh lines aren't your only imperfections, dear, but look at the bright side: you're not half as wrinkled as some other folks around here." Eyebrows waggling like Groucho Marx, Mom bobbed her head toward Nana.

I hung my head and winced. *Oh, God.* Life had been so much less stressful when Mom had been predictable . . . and unfailingly polite.

"What's that smell?" asked Mom, suddenly distracted.

Nana wriggled her nose as she inhaled. "Exhaust fumes."

Mom shook her head. "This is a good smell."

"Bernice," I spoke up, "if you want to sample the cream, I'll give you the jar. There's still a lot left."

"*You've* got the jar?"

"Not with me. It's back at the hotel."

"Excellent. You can hand it over when we get back." She ran a knuckle down her cheek. "I can apply my first treatment before we hit the beer tent tonight. Doesn't hurt to freshen up the complexion a little. You never know who might be there, just waiting to introduce himself."

"It smells like apple pie," said Mom, chin elevated as she sniffed the air.

Having inherited Mom's olfactory genes, I could smell it too. "Maybe there's a pastry shop nearby." In which case, I could look into my own future and predict that I was about to succumb to that most dreaded of all temptations: the three-thousand calorie dessert.

The woman ahead of us in line turned around, smoke billowing around her head like a low-lying cloud. "It's not pie. It's Cinnamon Apple Crumble. Isn't it divine?" Securing her cigarette between her middle- and forefingers, she held it up as if she were showcasing exhibit A in a criminal trial and swept her other hand through the smoke to steer it in our direction. "Best innovation since sliced bread. And it comes in an assortment of other scrumptious flavors: Tahitian Punch, Caramel Macchiato, Cherry Crush, Peach Schnapps, and my all-time favorite, Piña Colada."

Nana eyed it suspiciously. "I never seen no cigarette what smelled like that before."

"That's because, technically, it's not a real cigarette. It's what's called an electronic cigarette."

Her name tag identified her as Maisie Barnes, but I recognized her as the nasally voiced woman who'd sung Astrid Peterson's praises at the gathering last night — the one who'd suggested that business as usual for the remaining bands would be disrespectful of Astrid's memory. She stood about my height, boasted curves in all the right places, had mesmerizing blue-green eyes, and wore her graying hair in a perky short-clipped style that would negate her ever having to buy conditioner, curling gel, elastic texturizer, shine mist, anti-frizz serum, hair spray, or mousse.

I eyed her maintenance-free hairdo with envy, but I feared that if I ever followed suit I'd put the entire hair product industry in jeopardy. I guess it said a lot about the manageability of my hair when a change in my buying habits could bring down a whole sector of the market.

"I've been trying to break the habit for years," Maisie chattered on, "but couldn't get over the hump. Gum. Pills. Patches. Hypnosis. Nothing worked — until I tried this little beauty. I started making the substitution about a month ago, and I think I'm doing a kickass job. Isn't that right, Stretch?" She thwacked the man in front of her on the shoulder.

I recognized him from the group meeting last night, too. The actual name on his badge read Ralph Doozey, but he obviously preferred his nickname. And in an irony that so often happens with nicknames, Stretch was about the same height as Nana.

"Yup. We're real proud of Maisie." He circled his arm around her waist with casual familiarity. His voice was a surprise because it was so high-pitched, he could have shared the lead singer role with Alvin and the Chipmunks. "In another couple of months, she'll be living a tobacco-free life . . . with a hefty raise in her paycheck to show for it."

Maisie nodded agreement. "Wendell and everyone else at work have been busting my chops for two years to give up the crutch, and I'm finally coming through for them."

"Wendell?" I asked. "The Guten Tags' trumpet player? You work with him?"

"He's my boss. And Stretch's boss. He's everyone's boss: the Guten Tags, the Little Bittes, the Das Biers, the Brassed Offs. You ever heard of Newton Lock and Key outside Boone? We all work there. Wendell owns the company."

"Time's up," barked Dick Stolee. "Next!"

We shuffled a half-step ahead as Lucille Rasmussen hurried toward Humpty.

"I had no idea you all worked at the same place," I confessed. Our new travel question-naires asked guests to disclose everything about their health history and nothing about their work history.

"We're one big happy work family," admitted Stretch, which made me wonder how well acquainted he was with Otis and Gilbert. "Of course, we don't all work in the same department. We're divvied up between production, sales, shipping, and accounting, but we work under the same roof, so we've known each other for eons."

"And you're all musical," said Tilly. "Is that a requirement of the job?"

Maisie shook her head. "It just kind of worked out that way. Once Astrid started the Guten Tags, we discovered that every one of us had had some kind of musical training when we were kids, so we blew the dust off our instruments and decided to join the fun. Stretch and me, we're part of the Little Bitte Band, and not to brag or anything, but folks tell us that of the four company bands, we're the best." She took a drag on her cigarette and released a stream of cinnamon apple smoke into the air.

Her fake cigarette might not be real, but it sure bore a striking resemblance to a real cigarette, right down to the fiery tip. "Exactly how does that thing work?" I asked.

"Uh, well, without getting too technical, there's a cartridge, an atomizer, and a battery, and the mechanism heats up the liquid in the cartridge and turns it into vapor. So the stuff that looks like smoke, isn't; it's water vapor. The device is actually nothing more than a little vaporizer disguised as a cigarette, so I'm not really smoking. I'm vaping."

141

Mom tsked with disapproval.

"What?" asked Maisie.

"Save your complexion while you still can." She lowered her voice and bobbed her head in Nana's direction again. "Look what decades of smoking has done to the woman at the end of the line."

Nana puffed out her cheeks, eyes snapping, voice rising. "I can hear you, Margaret, on account of I'm *old,* not deaf. And since I told you I never took no puff of no cigarette in my entire life, you can't go blamin' my wrinkles on no tobacco products."

"Then how do you explain them?" challenged Mom.

Nana narrowed her eyes. "It's part of a continuin' natural disaster."

"Time's up," announced Dick Stolee. "Next!"

Alice Tjarks raced toward Humpty. The rest of us moved up in line.

"How about we take a group photo for the society page of the *Gazette*?" Alice suggested as she posed in front of the egg.

Dick Stolee nodded agreement. "Good idea. Hey, everyone, gather around Alice so we can take a group shot."

They hurried away from the sidewalk spinners displaying postcards, key chains, and personalized mugs to huddle around Alice — Margi, Lucille, and Helen filling in one side while Grace, Osmond, and George filled in the other. The two Dicks left their posts to kneel in front, which was pretty gutsy of them considering they might never be able to get back up again. George motioned for us to join them. "Come on, girls."

Nana shook her head. "Can't. I don't wanna give up my place in line."

"You do realize you're at the back of the line, right?" scoffed Bernice. Breaking ranks with us, she crab-walked toward the group and planted herself in front of the Dicks.

"Do you want me to take the photo?" I asked as I fished my phone out of my shoulder bag.

"Nope," said Dick Stolee. "We're good."

I frowned. "Well, Bernice needs to shift either left or right because she's completely blocking the Dicks."

Bernice shrugged. "Is that a problem?"

"Okay, everyone," announced Dick Stolee. "On my count. One . . ."

Like members of a drum corps color guard, they shot into action. Up went their phones.

"Two . . ."

Synchronizing their smiles, they gazed into their personal devices.

"Three!"

Ten thumbs hit their touchscreens, producing ten individual selfies.

I shook my head. "Hel*lo*? I thought you wanted a group photo. You know? A picture of all of you standing together *in a group*?"

"I thought we *were* standing together in a group," fretted Margi.

"The Dicks weren't standing," Alice pointed out. "They were kneeling."

Helen Teig leaned toward her husband and bellowed, "Stand up, Dick! You just ruined the group shot."

"Group shot, take two," Dick Stolee gasped out as he struggled upward. "On my count."

Not needing to witness any more of their antics, I excused myself from Maisie and Stretch and turned to the girls. "I want to shoot a few pictures of the Hafner Stub'n, so I'm heading out. I'll catch up with you in the Christmas store."

Mom glanced at her surroundings, suddenly mystified. "Where are we?"

"Disneyworld," said Nana.

"Is Bob here, too?"

Nana nodded. "You bet. You see that craggy peak pokin' outta them hills over there?" She motioned toward a pinnacle of rock that towered above the village like a

144

pinheaded giant who'd been turned into solid granite. "He's over there."

"Oh." Mom studied the odd formation. "What is that thing?"

Nana smiled. "Space Mountain."

NINE

The Hafner Stub'n was a short block away.

While crossing to the other side of the street, I dug out my phone and texted Etienne, telling him where he could find me when he finished speaking to Astrid Peterson's sister. He'd received her call just as we'd been exiting the bus, so he and Wally had retired to a café so they could address her questions in relative quiet.

As I strode toward the restaurant, I passed not only the typical souvenir shops with their sweatshirts, placemats, yodeling teddy bears, and beer steins, but stores whose display windows showcased the magnificent carvings that Wally had told us about. Madonnas as tall as real people. Angels with spreading wings and golden trumpets. Nativity figures accompanied by sheep and oxen so big, they could have doubled as carousel animals. Owls. Balladeers. Monks. Kings. Deftly carved, brilliantly painted, and jaw-droppingly expensive. I suspected Nana might be tempted to buy a life-size nativity scene for our parish church, but by the time she included necessary add-ons like shepherds, camels, wise men, and a small flock of sheep, the shipping costs would be so astronomical, she'd be too shell-shocked to spring for even small-ticket items like gold, frankincense, and myrrh.

Arriving at the intersection of the main street and Othmar-Weis-Strasse, I lingered by a street lamp at the corner, unable to take my eyes off the building directly across from me. As a structure, the Restaurant Hafner Stub'n was less than unique — two stories of white stucco with a double bank of green shuttered windows. What elevated it to the level of spellbinding were the dark-timbered top story, whose front alcove dripped with tiers of pink and red flowers, and the wraparound balcony, whose railings disappeared beneath cascades of blossoms that wreathed the entire building in a dazzling riot of blood red and pale pink. Flowers were everywhere: overflowing their window boxes, tumbling onto overhanging canopies, flanking the front door.

Wally sure wasn't kidding with his earlier prediction. The exterior of the restaurant was so spectacular, I imagined most tourists spent all their time on this very corner gawking rather than venturing inside.

I whipped out my phone and began snapping pictures.

"Sorry to interrupt, Emily, but have you run into any of the other Guten Tags? They seem to have disappeared."

If not for his signature handlebar mustache, I wouldn't have recognized Wendell beneath his bucket hat and dark glasses. Squarely built and dressed in casual clothes that bespoke afternoons on the golf course, he looked more like a well-to-do German native than a Midwest import, especially since he was missing the one item that would have pegged him as a tourist: his name tag.

"The last time I saw Otis, Gilbert, and Hetty, they were plowing through a crush of people to exit our bus. But some of the other band members are in a line outside the Christmas store" — I pointed down the street — "waiting to take selfies with Humpty Dumpty. In fact, I just had a very informative chat with Maisie Barnes. I had no idea you owned a company that employed every band member on the tour."

"Newton Lock and Key," Wendell said proudly. "Family owned and operated since 1888. You probably own one of our locks and don't even know it. We're the Midwest's premier manufacturers of padlocks, dead bolts, knob locks, lever-handle locks, cam locks, and mortise locks. And every lock we produce comes with a lifetime guarantee. Not many companies can afford to do *that* anymore. We produce a quality product. Our competitors produce crap."

"Well, Maisie and Stretch sure sound like two happy employees. Maisie even told us that if she quits smoking, you'll give her a raise. Talk about incentive."

Wendell chuckled. "When Maisie finally quits, *everyone* gets a raise. If the company can earn smoke-free status, we'll get a substantial break on our health insurance premiums, so I'll pass the savings on to my employees in the form of a raise. Maisie's our last holdout, so we're all rooting her on. If she succeeds, everyone wins. And I know she can do it. Maisie's about as special as they come." His voice softened with the kind of warmth one reserves for a dearest friend . . . or lover. "She won't let us down. Maisie's my go-to person." He seemed to smile involuntarily every time he said her name. "She always follows through and never disappoints. Never ever."

"No pressure there."

"I'm even thinking about making her a

special gold key on the day she retires the habit for good." He dug his hand into his pants pocket, producing a few foreign coins and a silver key that resembled the one to the front door of my house. He held it up. "All my employees get one of these." Beneath the keychain hole appeared the word "Newton" with the company's address. Flipping it over, he showed me where his name and phone number were stamped onto the metal. "It's not an official form of ID, but the employees think they're kind of fun. When they retire, I upgrade them to gold and add their dates of employment."

Right. Kinda like a portable tombstone.

"I haven't had to give out too many gold keys since I've been in charge. We don't have a mandatory retirement age, so people tend to stay. They like the workplace environment. They like the folks who work beside them. They like the wages. Why quit?"

"I guess when you go home, you'll have the sad task of finding someone to replace Astrid Peterson."

"Yeah." He gave his head a somber nod. "I'm not looking forward to that. I might be able to find someone to fill her shoes in the office, but I'll never find anyone to replace her sunny disposition. Astrid was always up;

150

never moody. Always trying to find ways to give people a lift and make them feel good about themselves. That's a rare gift."

Sure was. Just ask Bernice.

"In the summer she'd bring in vases of cut flowers from her garden and place them all over the plant. And let's face it: who can honestly admit that their day isn't made better with flowers?"

Bernice?

"Her husband was a horticulturalist, so they were real garden people. Flowers. Herbs. Vegetables. They even had some kind of specialty garden in their hothouse. They never let on what they were growing, but everyone suspected it was probably marijuana. I figured that's why Astrid was so happy all the time: high-grade weed. But that was her business, not mine, and it never affected her work, so what the hell."

He paused, his voice strained. "I can tell you one thing. I'm not looking forward to her funeral. That'll be a day when a lot of grown men will be shedding tears." He slid his sunglasses off his face to dry his eyes, which seemed an opportune time to suggest a change of both scenery and topic.

"I'm heading down to the Christmas store. You wanna tag along? If the Guten Tags aren't there, I can guarantee that some of your other employees will be."

"Sure. Thanks for asking."

"Did you want to get a picture of the restaurant before we leave?"

"Yeah, thanks for the reminder." He dug a thin, streamlined camera out of his front pocket and snapped a few shots. "My wife was in charge of picture-taking duty when I was married, but now that I'm divorced I have to do it myself, and I don't always remember."

"That's the tiniest camera I've ever seen."

"That's what I like about it. Expensive as hell, but real cutting edge. Fits in my pocket. Comes with its own tripod. Takes really high-resolution photos and even better video — movie quality, cinema ready. I've posted some short videos of our band performances on YouTube. You should check them out." He laughed. "I sometimes feel like a wannabe movie director who sacrificed his ultimate dream to enter the family business. Talk about pie in the sky, huh? But I'm not knocking the family business. It's my bread and butter. So even though I'll never be recognized as the next Otto Preminger, even though I'd like to, I tinker with my own video stuff enough to keep me happy."

By the time the Käthe Wohlfahrt store

came into view, the shutterbug queue in front of Humpty had disappeared. The only people loitering by Humpty now were Zola and the Dicks, who were apparently so averse to the thought of Christmas shopping, they'd agreed to have their fortunes told. As we approached, Dick Teig was rocking back and forth on his heels, looking bored and impatient as Zola meditated over his hand. Dick Stolee, on the other hand, was so hyped up he was bouncing all over the sidewalk. I hoped he was careful not to collide with Humpty. If he cracked this particular egg, he wouldn't be getting an assist from all the king's horses and all the king's men.

He ran to meet me and Wendell as we crossed the street. "Guess who you're looking at?"

I prayed this was a jest rather than an indication that he couldn't actually remember who he was.

"Dick Stolee," Wendell said matter-of-factly as he read the name off Dick's ID badge.

Dick's mouth slid into a cheesy grin. "Okay, I'll tell you. You're looking at Windsor City's next gazillionaire!"

Wow. "No kidding?"

He nodded like a turbocharged bobble-head doll, a motion that threatened to provoke a major concussive event. "Zola sees a financial windfall in my future. And we're not talking small potatoes, we're talking big bucks. Mi*llll*ions and mi*llll*ions. I'm going to be stinking rich!"

I didn't know what percentage of Zola's predictions panned out, but from what I'd witnessed so far, she displayed an uncanny ability to be spot-on. "Did she tell you where the windfall would come from?"

"Windows."

Wendell looked intrigued. "Do you own a window manufacturing company?"

"Nope. But her reference is so obvious, any idiot could figure it out. Windows, as in Microsoft? Internet access? Online gaming? I'm going to strike it rich on one of those casino gambling sites." He cradled his phone in his palm and eyed it adoringly. "I just have to decide which site has the highest payout and duck Grace while I'm — how should I phrase this — doing my investing."

Uh-oh. No matter Zola's track record, this sounded like a disaster waiting to happen. "Okay, but . . . what if Zola's windows don't have anything to do with Microsoft? What if she's referring to something more subtle, like a window of opportunity or something like that?"

"You don't want to get carried away with online gaming," cautioned Wendell. "You can get sucked into that stuff and lose your house, car, and family pet in less time than it takes to read the daily paper. Hey, I've seen it happen. My former brother-in-law is still trying to claw his way out of the financial hole he landed himself in. Do yourself a favor. Buy a lottery ticket and hope for the best."

"Hey, like the Bible says, 'One must lose a minnow to catch a salmon.' "

I frowned. "I don't think that's in the Bible, Dick."

"Are you sure? Grace might not go so ballistic if I tell her I have the backing of scripture."

I rolled my eyes. Dick Stolee, biblical scholar.

"How much longer?" Dick Teig whined to Zola, his attention span apparently at its limit.

"You're not concentrating," scolded Zola.

"What am I supposed to concentrate on?" asked Dick.

"Being still."

"I'll tell you what," he countered. "Tell me what you've got so far and we'll call it a day."

With a snort of disgust, Zola released his hand. "You want to see what I have so far?" She rounded her thumb and forefinger into a circle and stuck it in front of his face. "It's called a goose egg."

"All the time I've been standing here and this is what you come up with?" sputtered Dick. "Nothin'?"

My knees went suddenly weak. She'd seen nothing? Omigod. Was Dick Teig about to meet the same fate as Astrid Peterson?

"I defy *anyone* to predict *anything* about your future," snapped Zola. "The energy you give off is all" — she made a stirring motion with her hand — "haywire. Frenzied. It squirms around too much for me to read it with any accuracy. Besides which, your signal is weak."

"I've got a signal?"

"We all have signals. They're like the bars on a cell phone. Unfortunately, yours are practically nonexistent."

"So what does that mean?"

"In layman's terms? It means you're extremely shallow."

"Well, shoot," scoffed Dick Stolee. "I could've told you that ten minutes ago. C'mon, bud." He tore Dick away from Zola and steered him in the direction of a nearby bench. "If my winning streak doesn't kick

156

in right away, how would you feel about lending me your credit card?"

Eyes wild, Zola clamped her hands around her head and squeezed, mimicking the same motion I use when testing cantaloupe for ripeness. "I think Dick number two just blew all my circuits."

"I'm not out to criticize," hedged Wendell as he slid his sunglasses off his face, "but don't you think it's kind of irresponsible of you to put people on the path of financial ruin by promising them imaginary pots of gold? That man could go through his entire savings before he sees one red cent of your predicted windfall."

"Just what I need. A doubting Thomas, otherwise known as the guy who denies anything he can't understand — religious dogma, mortgage derivatives, climate change, psychic ability. I can hardly wait to hear your solutions for the impending crises of our times, like who's going to man the twenty-four-hour cable news stations during the zombie apocalypse and what'll happen to our two-party system if the undead demand their own political party."

I obviously needed to brush up on current events because I thought that had already happened.

Wendell's voice grew louder and more

defensive. "Hey, I pride myself on being able to spot a fraud when I see one."

"You want to see what kind of fraud I am?" Zola bristled. "Gimme your hand . . ."

"Knock yourself out." He thrust out his right hand. She smothered it between hers.

"Don't talk," Zola instructed. "Just stand there and keep your mouth shut." She bowed her head and pressed her eyes shut.

Wendell sidled a look in my direction and winked.

"And no winking."

Whoa! She'd seen him with her eyes closed? That was a little creepy. I could tell Wendell was creeped out too because he suddenly looked a whole lot less self-assured than he'd seemed a minute ago.

Zola concentrated. Wendell waited. I eyed the merchandise in the display window of Käthe Wohlfahrt's store, itching to leave the drama behind so I could attempt some serious shopping but hesitant to appear impolite by making a mad dash for the front door. Lucky for me, Wendell Newton was apparently less shallow than Dick Teig, because Zola was ready with her prediction in three minutes flat. She stared him straight in the eye, her gaze flinty and unapologetic.

"Your future holds great disappointment."

"Been there, done that. It's called a cheating wife."

"I'm not talking about your ex-wife, although I suspect she had a legitimate beef. You never paid attention to her. You were always too busy making money to be the kind of husband she'd hoped you'd be."

"She milked my devotion to my company for every cent it was worth. I didn't hear her complain about the in-ground pool or the tennis court or the Hummer she just *had* to have."

Zola looked taken aback. "She wanted a Hummer? What was she planning to do, invade a neighboring state?"

"No, she liked sitting high off the road so she could see into everyone else's car. Made her feel like she was above everyone else."

"You starved her emotionally."

"Oh, yeah? Well, what about me? I invited her to attend my musical gigs, but did she ever show up? Nooo. Mrs. Newton said she could spend a more stimulating evening by staying home and washing her hai—" He paused, his eyes lengthening with suspicion. "Why am I telling you about my personal life? I'm just feeding you information that you can twist into some sordid fictional tale. You got anything else for me or are we through here?"

"You're in a relationship that's destined to

end badly, so be prepared."

The smirk faded from his lips. "I'm not in any kind of relationship." But the sheen of sweat that popped out on his forehead suggested otherwise.

Zola grinned. "That's a lie, and you know it."

"I'm not in a relationship! You better check your crystal ball, lady, because I hate to tell you, but it's all fogged up."

"But the good news is, once the relationship is over, at least you'll be able to stop sneaking around, trying to pretend to the world that you're *not* in a relationship."

"Hey, I'm the most successful businessman in my hometown. I don't have to sneak around for anything."

Hoping to smooth over the situation, I decided to add my two cents. "Wendell, if you're divorced, what's the big deal about being in another relationship? Isn't that why online dating services are so popular? Aren't people always wanting to replace the relationship that's gone sour with a new one that works?"

He skewered me with a look that hinted I should mind my own business.

"Newton. Wendell Newton," Zola chimed, her voice suddenly animated. She snapped her fingers. "I knew that name sounded familiar, but I couldn't quite place it. Newton Lock and Key in Boone, right?"

"What of it?"

"My accounting firm just signed a contract with your company. You've hired us to perform your next internal audit. Small world, eh? I'm afraid you're going to be seeing a lot more of me than you ever bargained for."

"You think so, huh? Well, I wouldn't count on it." He took a half-dozen steps down the sidewalk, only to return with a final barrage. "Stay away from me, lady. People like you are dangerous." Then to me, "If I'd known I'd be traveling with nut jobs like her, I never would have signed up for this tour."

He stormed off like a two-year-old who'd been kicked out of the sandbox for biting. "Later, gator," Zola called to his retreating figure, obviously having mastered the art of letting blatant incivility roll off her back. She regarded me and smiled. "People with temperaments like his do much better with fortune cookies."

A warning should have been posted outside Käthe Wohlfahrt's Christmas store that read Entry Not Recommended for Shoppers with Claustrophobia because tourists were squeezed into every inch of real estate, reaching over each other in wild haste to grab at the displays. Christmas mugs. Figurines of snowmen and angels. Nutcrackers of Bavarian beer drinkers, policemen, chimney sweeps, and soldiers. Incense smokers of santas, dwarves, hikers, and reindeer. Beer steins. Cuckoo clocks. And signs every three feet that read No Photography Allowed.

I bumped into Nana and Mom inside. While they were going back and forth with their now-typical banter, I removed a snow globe from the shelf and gave it a shake, releasing a blinding snowstorm onto a miniature alpine village.

"If I *knew* where I was, I wouldn't have to ask, would I? So, would you *please* tell me where I am?"

"The North Pole," said Nana.

Mom cupped her hands over her mouth to muffle a gasp. "Oh, my stars. Are we in Santa's workshop?"

"You bet," said Nana.

Mom frowned as she peered out the storefront window. "If we're in the North Pole, how come there's no snow?"

"Global warmin'," said Nana. "It melted."

Oh, God.

Muscling my way toward the next room, I

162

crossed the threshold and stepped into wonderland.

Christmas trees of every height and color forested the room. White trees hung with red ornaments, draped with velvet ribbon, and lit with twinkling lights. Blue trees with white ornaments and miniature candles. Gold trees with silver ornaments and glittered fruit. Pink trees with icicle lights and strands of alabaster pearls. Mauve trees. Silver trees. Perched on display tables. Brightening dark corners. Lining the long walls.

I circled around the ceiling-high tree that occupied the center of the floor and wandered into the next room, where I made my way toward a toy soldier nutcracker that stood as tall as a man. It guarded a wall of specialty ornaments in the shapes of medallions, hearts, bratwursts, bears, and musical instruments, so I wasn't surprised to find Hetty Munk standing in front of it, gazing at the selections.

"Looking for clarinets?" I asked as I came up beside her.

"Accordions." She indicated two that hung at eye level. "I can't decide between porcelain or glass. I thought I might buy a couple to bring back to Astrid's family."

"That's really nice of you."

163

"Mementos. They might appreciate them."

"I'm sure they will. You're lucky the musical ornaments are still here. I would have thought you musicians would have bought them all up by now."

"I'm safe. The guys have better things to do with their time than shop for Christmas ornaments."

"Speaking of the guys, do you know what's going on with Otis and Gilbert?"

She paused just long enough to make me wonder if I was trespassing on forbidden territory. "I don't know what you mean."

"On the bus, did they seem a little at odds with each other?"

"They seemed fine to me," she hedged. "No different than normal."

"Oh. So the Guten Tags aren't breaking up or anything?"

She stared at me, wide-eyed. "Why? Have you heard we are?"

"No. I was just trying to figure out what would cause the tension between the two men and thought it might have something to do with whether your band is going to stay together or not. You've said yourselves that Astrid's absence is a huge problem for you."

"We're not breaking up," she said forcefully.

"Well, that's good to hear."

A noisy ruckus behind us sent us both spinning around to observe a mob of guests from the Asiana tour bus flocking through the room, armed with cameras and over-sized designer bags. They deployed as if they were on military maneuvers, bulldozing straight through browsing shoppers toward the merchandise in the back rooms, pausing along the way to snap photos of each other beneath the nutcrackers and No Photography Allowed signs.

"Have you packed up Astrid's belongings yet?" Hetty asked a bit self-consciously when the commotion had passed.

I nodded. "Last night. But I hope you won't mind my saying, I wasn't prepared for the shock."

"What shock?"

"Her room. You were best friends, so you'd be familiar with her habits, but I was a little surprised by the clutter. I guess she was a teenager at heart."

Hetty regarded me as if I'd sprouted another head. "Astrid was the most detail-oriented, the most organized, the most obsessively tidy person I've ever known. What do you mean her room was cluttered?"

"Clothes on the floor. Clothes hanging out

165

of drawers." I narrowed my eyes. "So . . . that wasn't typical?"

"Certainly not for Astrid."

Then why had Otis told us it was?

"Did you pack her journal?" she questioned. "I'm sure her family will want that, too, although —" She bobbed her head, allowing the statement to go unfinished. "When we were twelve years old, we bought our first journals together at the five and dime store. Only back then we called them diaries, and they came with little locks and keys. I gave up after a couple of weeks. It was way too much work. But Astrid never missed a day. It was her thing. She's been journaling ever since."

"I don't remember seeing a journal." But then again, I was suffering from a minor head trauma, so maybe my memory was more faulty than I was willing to admit. "Otis was with us, looking for a library book he'd lent her, but we didn't find that either."

Her brows slanted upward with surprise. "Otis went with you?"

"I believe his potential library fine was looming large in his mind."

"Library fine? Otis?" Her voice took on an edge that hadn't been there before. "Yes. He must be watching his pennies if he felt compelled to beat a path to her room so

166

quickly."

"Could Astrid have been carrying her journal in her handbag?"

"I'm not sure where she kept it when she was traveling."

"Let's pray it wasn't in her handbag because if it was, it may be lost to her family forever." I softened my voice as I delivered the bad news. "The police informed Etienne that her bag and all its contents were destroyed in the bomb blast."

"Really? I'm very sorry to hear that." But the sudden lilt in her voice seemed to belie the sentiment. "Very sorry indeed."

TEN

"Do you recall seeing a journal when we packed Astrid's belongings?"

We'd gotten stuck in traffic on the way back to Munich, so by the time we reached our hotel, we were staring at a scant half hour to freshen up and dress for our big night at Oktoberfest. While we were still on the bus, the mayor's office had phoned Wally with the unexpected news that all four Iowa oompah bands would have time slots in the Hippodrom beer tent this evening. And since the Hippodrom hosted the unofficial red carpet for celebrity guests, the group shouldn't be surprised if their appearance spurred something of a media circus.

The bus had gone wild when Wally made the announcement. Not only would the event be a dream come true for the musicians, but the whole group would be recognized for their humanitarian efforts after the explosion, which was a tribute to what kind of people they really were beneath all their contrarian banter. "This will be your time in the spotlight," Wally told everyone. "You'll be among the glitterati this evening, so dress the part. Remember, your photos might be splashed across newspapers all through Europe."

That we had so little time to plan our ensembles for such an important night was discouraging, but my afterburners were on overdrive as I raced between the closet and the bathroom, dithering over shoe and makeup options.

"There was no journal in her room," Etienne replied as he slipped into his sports jacket. "Why are you asking?"

"Because Hetty Munk told me that Astrid wrote in a journal every day of her life. So if she brought her journal with her, where is it?" I presented my back to him for assistance with my zipper.

"Could it have been in her handbag with Otis's elusive book of poetry?" He fastened the hook and eye at the top of my little black dress and planted a kiss at the nape of my neck.

"And that's something else that's weird." I dashed into the bathroom. "Hetty implied that Astrid was almost pathologically neat, so why did Otis tell us that tidiness wasn't one of her virtues?"

Knock. Knock. Knock.

"Perhaps because of the condition of her bedroom?" he suggested on his way to answer the door.

"Can I speak to Emily real quick?" Nana's voice. Anxiety-ridden. Breathy.

"She's in the bathroom creating magic with her lipstick wand. Feel free to poke your head in, Marion. The door's open."

She skidded into the bathroom like a surfer riding a wave, her sneakers squeaking on the tiled floor. "Has Bernice been 'round to pick up Tilly's miracle cream yet?"

"Not yet. Why?"

She held out a small plastic travel jar. "You reckon I could borrow a glop before she takes off with it? I usually don't pay your mother no mind, dear, but I took a long look in the mirror when we got back, and she's right. I been in denial. I got so many wrinkles, I could audition to be one a them California raisins what we seen on TV ads years ago. So I need help, and fast. I figure if I use Tilly's cream before we hit the festival grounds, maybe it'll do for my face what it done for yours. By the time we walk down the red carpet, them media folks could be takin' pictures of a whole new me."

"I hope not. I'm pretty fond of the old you."

From the outer room, Etienne reminded us, "Ten minutes 'til showtime, ladies."

BAM. BAM. BAM.

"Hurry up." Nana slapped her jar down next to the sink. "That's probably her now."

"Bernice," Etienne announced as he answered the door. "How can I help you?"

"I'm here for my miracle cream. Where's Emily?"

I whipped the lid off Tilly's jar, dug in with my forefinger, and slopped several ounces into Nana's container. "Remember, apply lightly," I whispered as I watched her cap the jar and stuff it inside the pocket of her Minnesota Vikings wind jacket. I gave her a conspiratorial wink and nudged her out the door.

"Where's my cream?" demanded Bernice, eyeing Nana with suspicion.

"Got it right here," I said, popping back into the bathroom and returning with Tilly's jar. I handed it over.

"So tell me, Marion," Bernice asked as she unscrewed the lid, "what pressing reason brings you to Emily's room minutes before we're supposed to leave?"

"I'm kin," said Nana. "Kin don't need to make up no reason to visit."

171

Bernice lifted the jar to her nose to sniff the contents. "It better all be here or — hey, how come this stuff doesn't stink? Anything that works usually smells like pigeon poop, but this smells pretty good. So how thick do I need to pile it on?"

"Lightly," said Nana in a helpful tone, stiffening up like an old washboard when she realized she'd said something.

Bernice slatted her eyes. "How do you know that?"

I felt a moment's panic before inspiration struck. "Nana's only repeating what she heard Tilly tell me last night."

"Sure, sure," sniped Bernice. She drilled Nana with an accusing look. "You took some of my cream, didn't you?"

"She most certainly did not," I defended. Nana didn't take anything; I gave it to her. There was a huge difference. "So, ladies, I don't want to be rude, but you'd better scoot back to your rooms so you can change your clothes before we head out." I herded them toward the door.

"I already changed," said Nana, her wind-suit swishing as she walked. "You think I need to kick it up a notch? I s'pose I could wear my World's Best Gramma sweatshirt, but I didn't want no one accusin' me of puttin' on airs 'cuz of the glitter on the let-

172

terin'. It's pretty dazzlin'."

"It doesn't matter what you wear," Bernice declared, reaching the door a step ahead of Nana. "I'm wearing sequins tonight, so all eyes will be on Bernice Zwerg, former magazine model, making her much-anticipated comeback. Trust me, Marion, if we appear on the red carpet together, you could be buck naked and no one would notice."

"Takes too long to get naked. These new bloomers what I'm wearin's got so much spandex in 'em, they'd be rollin' up the carpet before I'd have time to get 'em off."

When Etienne and I reached the lobby ten minutes later, the place was in an uproar. Laughter. Backslapping. Excited whispers. Either the musicians were suffering performance jitters or the whole tour group was giddy at the prospect of spending an entire evening getting hammered on dark beer. "What's up?" I asked George, who was standing beside a potted plant with a goofy smile on his face.

"Dick just struck it rich."

"Which Dick?"

"Stolee. Now everyone wants in on the action."

"Omigod." I grabbed Etienne's forearm. "Zola predicted a windfall in Dick's future just a few hours ago."

George nodded. "Five hundred big ones from some kind of gambling thing."

"Dollars?" asked Etienne.

"Euros. That's even more than dollars, depending on the conversion rate. Lookit 'im." He bobbed his head toward where Dick was holding court with Zola, surrounded by a throng of well-wishers. "Folks are saying that redhead can really predict the future."

"For what it's worth," I said somewhat reluctantly, "she's been right more than she's been wrong."

"She's been practicing on other folks?"

I nodded. "She told Dick Teig he was shallow."

"Dang," George reflected. "She's good."

A shrill whistle shot through the room, silencing the chatter. It sounded a lot like my signature whistle, only it wasn't. This one belonged to Maisie Barnes. "Hey, everyone, I've got an idea. How about after a night of music and beer, we come back here for a fortunetelling marathon with Zola? Maybe she'll find quick cash in all our futures!"

Nods. Shrugs. Murmurs of assent.

"Everyone's already guaranteed extra cash in their future once you stop smoking,"

Stretch called out.

Maisie grinned. "Okay. Maybe she can tell me if my latest push is going to succeed. What do you say, Zola? Are you up for it?"

Zola fluffed her hair and smiled, appearing deliriously happy to be appreciated. "I'm game if the rest of you are."

"All right, then," said Maisie. "We'll meet back here after our gig is over. And let's all be good sports. Let's have a hundred percent participation."

"Is she calling for a vote?" asked Osmond.

I spied Wendell loitering by the elevator, arms folded tightly across his chest, jaw locked, looking as if he were sucking on the world's sourest lemon.

Uh-oh. I was getting a bad feeling about this.

Wally made his presence known by thrusting his umbrella into the air. "It's about a ten-minute walk to the Oktoberfest grounds and it'll be crowded on the sidewalks, so watch where you're going and stick together. I'll also warn you to mind your handbags and wallets because this kind of a crowd means open season for pickpockets. If you should get separated from the group, when you reach the fairgrounds, aim for the tent with the red and gold Ringling Brothers-style façade. It only seats forty-two hundred people, so it's one of the smaller venues. Do all the musicians have their instruments?"

"YOU BET," they shouted, as if responding to a football cheer. "Let's go, then," said Wally, charging forward with his umbrella held high.

"We can't go yet." Osmond threw a desperate look at the mass of humanity parading for the exit. "We haven't voted."

"I bet she pulled one of those unanimous consent deals," said Alice Tjarks as she looped her arm through his and marched him toward the door. "I think we voted. We just didn't realize it."

Walking through the gates of the beerfest grounds, beneath the Willkommen Zum Oktoberfest sign, I felt the kind of adrenaline rush a kid feels at the prospect of spending the day riding the Scrambler and Caterpillar while pigging out on candy apples and cotton candy.

Oktoberfest in Munich wasn't just a beer-drinking event. It was the Iowa State Fair on steroids . . . minus the six-hundred-pound cow sculpted from pure dairy butter.

The midway opened up before us in an exuberant chaos of fright-filled screams and flashing lights. Giant swings umbrellaed outward from a column that seemed to reach the stratosphere. A quintuple-looping rollercoaster tore shrieks from the throats of people who enjoyed their beer with a g-force chaser. Something called the Toboggan sluiced fairgoers down a mammoth wooden slide like logs down a flume. A ferris wheel that vied for height with London's Millennium Wheel rose high above the midway. Bumper cars. Carousels. A haunted house. Pony rides. Gravity-defying rides with catchy names like Topspin and Free Fall. A towering contraption that looked like a handheld blender with a propeller stuck on the end that turned people upside down, inside out, and end over end while swooping a hundred feet off the ground. If this ride had been available in medieval times, it would have been labeled a torture device — and the price of admission would have been free rather than a whopping four euros.

The press of revelers was claustrophobic as we muscled our way through the crowd. We passed arcades where patrons could hammer nails, shoot rifles, or launch darts to win a purple elephant or helium balloon. We passed concessions selling the best of wurst: bratwurst, blutwurst, bockwurst, knackwurst, and weisswurst, served on sticks or in buns, with or without sauerkraut. We smelled the heavy scent of cooking oil as vendors deep-fried such culinary delights as cheese curds, corndogs, cabbage rolls, mushrooms, onion rings, pickles, funnel cakes, and Oreo cookies. They were probably still trying to perfect the process for candy apples and Peeps.

As we approached the area of beer tents, I realized my perception of the word *tent* had been completely out of whack because these structures were the size of airplane hangars, with solid sides and decorative exteriors. The Hippodrom's façade was a wild splash of red that was gilded with curlicues and swirls reminiscent of a circus parade wagon. On the rooftop above the front entrance, a trio of carousel horses reared their wooden hooves as they stared down at those of us waiting in line to pass through the security check. But they didn't stare at us for long because Wally spoke to an official at the door who escorted us directly to a reserved seating area, bypassing the long queue, bag checks, No Smoking signs, and the much-touted red carpet. I'd probably get an earful from Bernice about the omission, but the noise level inside the tent was so high, I suspected I might not be able to hear a word she said.

Yes!

Music blared from the speakers perched

on the raised bandstand in front of us, filling the tent with a foot-stomping, knee-slapping polka that prompted a spontaneous sing-along. Voices rose to the rafters in a roar of drunken abandon. Dancing broke out in the aisles. Patrons hopped onto benches, heads bobbing, arms flopping, elbows flying, in a synchronized performance of what was either a Jane Fonda aerobic workout or the German version of the Chicken Dance. Swaying. Chanting. Clapping. The six-person brass band onstage played louder and louder, faster and faster. Beer flew. Froth spattered. The floor shook with an intensity that might have registered a magnitude 4 on the Richter scale. "Zicke, zacke, zicke, zacke, oi, oi, oi," they hollered in unison. "ZICKE, ZACKE, ZICKE, ZACKE, OI, OI, OI. PROST!" The atmosphere was so festive, I felt like a member of the Wisconsin student body again, watching "Jump Around" being performed by every fan in the football stadium.

We occupied three tables in a section of prime real estate that was cordoned off by wooden partitions and located directly beneath the bandstand. The tables-for-ten were narrower than a diving board, but since the Hippodrom was known for hosting a more gentile crowd, our impossibly narrow tables sported a touch of elegance that was missing from all the other beer tents: plastic tablecloths.

We were shoehorned together five on a bench, with no space left for arm movements that might include eating or drinking, so I now understood the *other* reason why so many people were standing in the aisles and on top of their benches: the illusion of breathing space.

I sat at the first table with all the ladies, Etienne sat at table two with the Guten Tags and the guys, and Wally sat at table three with the rest of the musicians and Zola, although he couldn't really sit because there was no room left on the benches so he kind of floated between all three. When the polka ended, the sounds of pandemonium still rumbled through the tent, but at least I could hear myself think a little better.

"Why are we at the circus?" Mom shouted into my ear as she eyed the green, gold, and red streamers that ribboned the ceiling.

"Forget that!" yelled Bernice from the opposite side of the table. "Why do we have our butts parked here when we should be posing on the red —"

The band struck up another tune, drowning her out completely. I poked a finger at my ear, shook my head, and flashed one of those "I can't hear a word you're saying" looks. She made a megaphone of her hands and continued yelling, but I really *couldn't* hear a thing, so I had no choice but to offer her a sympathetic smile and a shrug. It was freaking awesome.

A troop of official-looking men in white shirts and red vests entered the partitioned area, and after speaking to Wally, they collected all the instrument cases that were scattered on the floor and carried them to what looked like a holding area near the bandstand. Next to arrive were barmaids in official costume, flaunting smiles, cleavage, and comically oversized beer mugs brimming with ale that was dark as axle grease. They slammed a mug down in front of each of us.

"What am I s'posed to do with this?" Nana shouted into my other ear.

"Drink it," I shouted back at her.

She made a face as she sniffed the contents. "This one's spoiled. It smells like dirt."

"Probably from the kind of yeast they use in the brewing process."

She drew her brows together in a frown as she pondered the liter mug. "Would you flag down one of them waitresses when she heads back our way? If I gotta drink this thing, it's gonna need cherries."

When the music ended again, a man in lederhosen and a feathered hat took up a center stage position on the bandstand and commandeered a microphone. I might have been able to understand him if he'd been speaking English, but his announcement was in German so I didn't have a clue. Except I did hear him utter the word "Iowa," after which he swept his hand in a grand gesture to indicate our tables in the reserved section.

I was suddenly forced to squint as the spotlight caught us in its glare.

The tent erupted with thunderous applause, followed by whistles, hoots, and table-pounding. The area around our partition filled with Germans clamoring to photograph us. They even directed the poses they wanted us to strike: standing, sitting, smiling, waving. Wally took pictures. Etienne took pictures. Dad fired up his camcorder and filmed the Germans shooting pictures of us with their camera phones. Bernice managed to end up front and center for nearly every shot, showing off her sequined jacket. She especially liked close-ups and delivered a wide spectrum of emotions ranging from pouty to surprised, like a Gloria

Swanson wannabe stepping onto the set of *Sunset Boulevard.*

I had to admit she looked sensational. The silver sequins softened the bulge of her dowager's hump. Whatever product she'd used on her hair made it appear less like a wire whisk. And her nicotine- and smoke-damaged complexion was suddenly glowing with health and vitality. Was that even possible with a single application of Tilly's cream?

I peeked at Nana, whose face was still cross-hatched with fine wrinkles that were offset by liver spots and senile plaque.

Nana still looked the same, but given Bernice's transformation, maybe we'd be looking at a dermatological miracle as early as tomorrow!

We continued circulating between tables, posing for photos, until a conga line of barmaids laden with heavy trays paraded toward us. Platters of meat landed on our tables: roast chicken, roast pork, a chunk of bone-in fat as big as my head, grilled fish on a stick, six different kinds of sausages. A smorgasbord of side dishes followed: jumbo pretzels with pots of mustard, cheese noodles, potato pancakes, potato salad, sauerkraut, red cabbage, and a mysterious veggie that looked like a foam rubber golf ball.

"Did we budget for all this?" I asked Etienne against the competing background racket of "ZICKE, ZACKE, ZICKE, ZACKE, OI, OI, OI."

"Compliments of the house," he assured me. "With unlimited beer. Bon appétit."

We'd no sooner returned to our original tables to start dishing out the food than the man at the microphone announced the three words that our musicians had been waiting to hear since we entered the tent. "Little Bitte Band!"

Not wasting a moment, Maisie, Stretch, and their trombonist, Arlin Foote, clambered off their benches and ran toward the bandstand.

Applause. Whistles. Foot-stomping.

I handed out empty plates to the ladies and watched as they perused the overwhelming selection of entrees.

"I've never seen a sausage this white before," Lucille commented with distaste. "It looks like a . . . well, I'm not going to say what it looks like because I have more dignity than that." She gave it a poke with her finger. "What would I have to do to get an all-beef hot dog with ketchup and onions?"

"What can I get you, Mom?" I figured she might need a little assistance as she looked a bit dazed with all the overstimulation.

She glanced at the carousel horses suspended from the ceiling and asked rather dreamily, "Are we at the circus?"

"It's not a traditional circus, but it has a circus atmosphere."

"Oh, good." She clasped her hands with excitement before freezing up with alarm. "But there's no room in here. Where are the elephants going to perform?"

"What *is* this thing?" asked Grace, grimacing at the chunk of fat that sat directly in front of her.

"I suspect it's the joint between the tibia and metatarsal of an artiodactyl's foot," said Tilly, her professorial explanation effecting a few seconds of stunned silence from all of us.

"A what?" asked Alice.

"She just said it's some kind of dinosaur, you morons," snapped Bernice.

"I'm not eating any dinosaur," vowed Helen. "Even if it was canned, it's way past its expiration date."

"In layman's terms," continued Tilly, "it's a pig's knuckle, also known as a ham hock. Happily, Iowa swine are raised for their thick-cut chops rather than their tarsal joints."

Grace set her plate down. "I think I'll just wait for dessert."

A cheer went up as Maisie, Stretch, and Arlin walked out on the bandstand, brandishing their instruments above their heads. After basking in the limelight for a full minute of bowing, smiling, and waving, they formed a semicircle around the standing microphone. Maisie poised her bow on her fiddle, Stretch raised his trumpet to his lips, and on Arlin's downbeat, they began playing a rousing rendition of an obscure beer song that caused the entire tent to go wild.

Swaying. Clapping. Hooting. Singing.

I was so impressed with their talent that I simply sat like a dunce, gawking at them with my mouth hanging open. *Wow.* The only German word I could think to describe their performance was *wunderbar.* Maisie never missed a beat. She made that fiddle of hers sing as if she were dueling with the devil for possession of her soul. Stretch pumped out notes with the lung power of Louie Armstrong. And Arlin worked his trombone slide with such vigor, I half expected it to shoot off into the audience. They were so exhilarating to listen to, we really got into the spirit of things by swaying, clapping, and bouncing up and down to the rhythm of the music and shouting out an occasional "ZICKE, ZACKE, ZICKE, ZACKE, OI, OI, OI."

At the end of fifteen minutes, the Little Bittes departed the stage to the roar of applause, and the master of ceremonies called for the Brassed Off Band, which sent Wally's table scrambling. The Little Bittes returned to the reserved seating area like conquering heroes, red-faced and breathless, as if they'd just crossed the finish line of the Boston Marathon. They gave each other a group hug and high-fived everyone before returning to their table, clinking their mugs together, and tossing back several gulps of ale. As the Brassed Offs took their place on stage, Maisie hurried over to me with Zola in tow, acting as if they were new best friends.

"Do you have any idea where the restroom facilities are?"

"Look for a sign that says Toilette," I suggested as I craned my neck left and right, finding a telltale clue at the rear of the building: a line of women that snaked halfway around the tent. "Over there." I pointed her in the right direction. "But it looks like you're in for a long wait."

"It's only going to get worse as the night progresses," predicted Zola, "so now's as good a time as any."

"Are they goin' to the potty?" Nana asked as she watched them leave.

"Yup. But the line's a monster. Are you in desperate need to use the facilities?"

"Nope." She slid off the bench. "But folks what's my age have gotta do some strategic plannin'. So if I get in line now, by the time I reach the stall, I'll have to go for sure. You need to use the potty, Til?"

When the rest of the girls learned where Nana and Tilly were headed, they began peeling off in twos in a reenactment of the buddy system first employed by animals boarding the ark. Why women needed a companion to visit a place that guys always visited solo remained a mystery to me, but by the time the Brassed Off Band started to play, my table was empty except for me and Mom, whose internal plumbing had sometimes been compared to that of a desert camel.

If the Little Bitte Band had been spectacular, the Brassed Offs were even more spectacular, if that was possible. Playing a French horn, banjo, and clarinet, they produced a full-bodied sound that filled every corner of the tent. Their opening piece was so frolicsome, their notes so crisp and spirited, that even Mom and I leaped off our bench to execute some fancy footwork. At the end of the song, a round of feverish applause nearly blew the roof off the tent, and shouts of "OI, OI, OI!" sent the trio cue-ing up their second offering at warp speed.

The gleeful strains of "Beer Barrel Polka" started almost immediately. As patrons clogged the aisles with their dancing, I noticed Maisie and Zola plowing their way through the masses in an attempt to return to their seats. *Back already?* But the line to the restroom was even longer than it had been five minutes ago. How had they pulled that off?

Maisie caught my eye as she pressed against the partition to let the barmaids pass.

"That didn't take long!" I shouted at her.

"We used the men's room! No line at all there."

Nana and the girls had obviously nixed that option because even after the Brassed Offs and Das Bier Band finished their sets a half-hour later, they still weren't back.

"Are we at the circus?" asked Mom as the Guten Tags made their way to the stage. My heart was in my mouth as I watched Dad lumber forward behind the other band members.

Why fight it? "Yup. We're at the circus."

"Where are the elephants?"

"No elephants."

"Clowns?"

"No clowns."

She crooked her mouth to the side. "Not much of a circus." She looked up as Dad walked stiffly onto the stage, Astrid's ruby-red piano accordion strapped to his chest. "Jesus, Mary, and Joseph." She seized my forearm. "Is that Bob?"

"Sure is."

"What's he doing up there?"

"He's about to play the accordion."

"He doesn't play the accordion."

"He used to play when he was a kid."

"He did not."

"Yes, he did. He just forgot to mention it. How 'bout a sausage?"

She perused the meat selections before us. "They're all shriveled up. They remind me of that little midget woman who keeps following me around. I don't even know who she is."

"She's your mother, Mom."

"My mother's still alive?"

Wendell stepped up to the microphone, trumpet in hand. "Evening, folks. I don't know how many of you can understand me, but for those of you who speak English, I just want you to know that we're dedicating our performance to our former accordion player, Astrid Peterson, who was killed in that bomb blast yesterday. She was the heart

190

and soul of our group, but this fella, Bob Andrew" — he gestured to Dad — "has generously offered to step into her shoes. He might be suffering a few opening night jitters, so I'd ask you to give him a big round of applause to ease his nerves."

I heard only scattered applause until the master of ceremonies translated what Wendell had said, then the applause became deafening — which I suspected didn't help Dad's nerves at all.

"The first song on our playlist was Astrid's favorite," Wendell announced to the crowd. "So we play it in her honor. We give you the penultimate beer song, 'The Maine Stein Song'!" And on the downbeat, Otis's tuba, Gilbert's trombone, Hetty's clarinet, and Wendell's trumpet struck a lively chord.

Dad's accordion squealed out a discordant noise.

Oh, God.

Luckily, many of the beer drinkers in the tent knew the lyrics, so they began to sing along, enhancing the song's famous refrain with their German accents and slurred words. Otis pumped out deep, resonating bass notes on his tuba. Trombone, trumpet, and clarinet rendered the melody.

Dad stared at his sheet music and played a screechy chord that mashed way too many notes together.

"Does that sound right to you, Emily?" asked Mom.

"It'll get better. I think Dad's just warming up."

The Germans sang louder and louder. They cheered. They laughed. They clapped their hands to the beat of the music. Either they were really into the song or they were trying to protect their eardrums by drowning out the accordion.

Dad's fingers slipped on the button board, sending a sliding scale of chords and bass notes into hair-raising tones that caused me to cringe.

Mom leaned toward me. "I know the reason your father never mentioned his musical talent, Em. He doesn't have any."

Nana returned from the restroom and sat down beside me on the bench. "I was hopin' the song what them folks is playin' wouldn't sound as bad out here as it does in the potty."

"And?" I asked.

"It's worse."

"We need to get Dad off the stage."

"How?" Nana winced as he hit another dissonant chord. "Dang, this is brutal."

"We've gotta do something before he embarrasses himself any more."

"You s'pose they got a fire alarm around here someplace?" asked Nana.

Mom grabbed my forearm again. "Jesus, Mary, and Joseph, is that your father up on stage, Emily? Why is he playing the accordion? He can't play the accordion."

Tell me about it.

A half-second later, the music faded mid-note as a terrified scream pierced the rising din.

"HELP! Somebody help! She's not breathing!"

Eleven

Etienne and Wally performed CPR until the ambulance arrived and the paramedics could take over, which was a matter of mere minutes since the ambulance was already on the festival grounds. Etienne volunteered to accompany the ambulance to the hospital and promised to call us the minute he had a status report. The commotion brought the Guten Tags' performance to an abrupt end, but as soon as the medics left and the dust cleared, another oompah band took the stage and the festivities in the Hippodrom resumed in earnest — minus the participation of our tour group. We were all pretty shaken up, and the musicians were spent both physically and emotionally, so we opted to cut the evening short and return to the hotel.

Etienne called me on the walk back.

Zola Czarnecki hadn't made it.

She was dead.

I passed the information on to Wally, who made an immediate decision to conduct a group meeting as soon as we reached the hotel. We gathered in the Prince Ludwig room once again, but this time, instead of sitting in the audience, I stood in the front of the room with Wally. As soon as he completed a cell phone call to Etienne, he opened the meeting with our grim tidings.

"I'm afraid the news isn't good, folks. Zola Czarnecki has died."

Gasps. Murmurs. A cry of "Oh, God," from Maisie Barnes, whose piercing scream had sounded the initial alarm about Zola. And while the majority of faces in the audience registered shock, Wendell remained stone-faced, as if forcing himself to register no emotion at all.

"She's dead?" sobbed Maisie. "But . . . but . . . she was fine until she collapsed."

"She showed no signs of physical distress before then?" asked Wally.

Maisie lifted one shoulder. "She said she had a little buzz on, so she was feeling a little dizzy. But she'd just polished off a liter of beer, so why wouldn't she feel dizzy? I felt dizzy, too. But then she started blinking really fast and twitching and gasping for air. And before I could even ask her what was wrong, she crumpled like a rag doll. I've never seen anyone go down that fast in my life." She paused to suck in a calming breath. "Do the docs have any idea what happened to her?"

"Etienne tells me that an autopsy is being scheduled, so we won't know anything definitive until the results are back. But, since this will eventually become public information, I *can* tell you that Ms. Czarnecki was taking medication to treat a chronic heart condition. I know from your medical histories that some others of you are suffering from mild heart conditions, so given what's happened to Zola, I'd caution you to watch your alcohol intake. I'm not suggesting that her beer consumption caused her death, but until we hear otherwise, I'm asking you to play it safe."

"Is this going to force you to cancel the rest of the tour?" asked Wendell.

The gang already knew the answer to that, so they began shaking their heads in unison like a display of metronomes. "We've set a precedent of never canceling the tour no matter how many guests die," said Tilly, prompting the rest of the gang to nod in agreement.

Silence settled over the room as the musicians exchanged uncomfortable glances.

"How many guests normally die?" asked Otis.

Dick Teig scratched his jaw. "Do you want exact numbers or would an average be okay?"

"WHAT?" barked Wendell.

"What Dick means to say," I interrupted, "is that since our tours are geared toward older adults, the law of averages sometimes catches up with us, so we've had to deal with a few instances where guests were . . . unable to complete the trip."

"How many is a few?" questioned Gilbert.

"I think the body count is up to eight," said Margi.

"Eight?" Dick Stolee guffawed. "Hell, it's twice that number." He leveled a look at Margi. "Guests were dropping like flies long before you came aboard."

Nervous grumbles. Shifting eyes.

"What kind of trips are you people offering?" demanded Wendell. "Shouldn't a Sounds of Music tour include some selections other than funeral marches and requiems?"

"You should have been on the last tour," droned Bernice. "Black plague. Mass graves. Wall-to-wall undertakers. It was a real knee-slapper."

"Your brochure never mentioned anything

about guests dropping like flies," Stretch accused.

"Please allow me to reiterate," Wally said in a loud voice. "It's the policy of our travel agency to complete our tour no matter what happens. Our responsibility is to our remaining guests — the ones who put down no small amount of money to experience what our brochure promised."

Arlin Foote, the Little Bitte's trombonist, stood up. "I'm only speaking for myself here, but I think the tour is great. I'm sorry we lost Astrid in that freak accident and I wish Zola was still with us because it would have been fun to have our fortunes told, but Emily's not responsible for any of the bad stuff that's happened. We had stage time at one of the Oktoberfest tents, people. How amazing is that? And the audience loved us. When have we ever heard applause that loud? It was the opportunity of a lifetime. And if we weren't on this tour, it never would have happened. So I think we should be grateful that folks are clamoring to listen to us and stop complaining about things none of us have any control over." He gave an emphatic nod of his head and sat down. "That's all I have to say."

Bernice let out a derisive snort as she caught my eye. "How much did you have to pay him to say that?"

Arlin stood back up. "My previous statement was unsolicited and expressed no one's view except my own."

Silence. Soul-searching. Head-bobbing.

"Despite everything that's happened, I'm having a great time too," admitted Maisie.

"Ditto for me," echoed Stretch.

Nods. Smiles. Hapless shrugging.

Osmond sprang to his feet. "Show of hands. How many guests are having —"

"No voting!" I fired a look at him that sent him sinking back down onto his seat.

"Well, I'm glad our oompah band members are having a good experience," Wally continued, "because unbeknownst to you, you're suddenly in great demand."

"We're getting requests for appearances?" asked Wendell, with more than a little surprise in his voice.

"And how." Wally pulled up the calendar on his phone. "Your reputation precedes you. Tomorrow we're scheduled to visit Neuschwanstein Castle, and the restaurant near the entrance has requested that you entertain the lunch crowd."

"They want all *four* bands?" asked Otis with some hesitation.

"All four bands," said Wally. "And tomorrow night you've been invited to entertain

199

the dinner crowd at one of the premier Bavarian beer halls in the heart of Old Town Munich. You're gaining quite a name for yourselves."

The Guten Tags crossed uneasy glances with each other. "Here's the thing," offered Otis, his cheeks bright pink above his beard, "after our performance tonight, I'm not sure we're ready to —"

"Could I say something?" asked Dad as he heaved himself slowly to his feet. Head bent, shoulders slumped, he looked so demoralized, I felt an aching need to run over and hug him. "I'm sorry about flubbing up tonight and being such a disappointment to you, but if you give me one more chance, I think I can do a whole lot better. I won't blame you if you decide to can me, though. I was an awful embarrassment."

"I didn't think you were so bad," soothed Alice Tjarks. "I bet you played some chords no one ever attempted before. That's pretty gutsy."

"I enjoyed every note I heard," said Osmond.

"That's because you turned off your hearing aids after about three notes," scoffed Bernice.

Osmond shot her a dour look. "I was trying to preserve the memory."

"I used to get so nervous when I first started performing," Hetty confessed, "that I always ended up with hiccups and couldn't play the first songs anyway. But no one ever scolded me for it. They just let me join in when I was able. And after my confidence got built up, I never had a problem again. So I know what Bob went through tonight, and I vote to give him another chance."

Gilbert nodded agreement. "Hetty's right. It's not brain surgery, so no one's life is in the balance if one of us hits a wrong note."

"Hell," snorted Otis. "That Hippodrom crowd was so rowdy, they probably never even noticed that Bob was playing a different tune altogether."

"I guess that says it all," Wendell concluded. "We'll give you another shot at it, Bob. And in the meantime, if you have any questions about the music or need any help, let one of us know, and we'll be there for you."

Dad gave a nod of thanks. "Appreciate the second chance. I think I know what I did wrong, though, so I'm pretty sure I can fix it. I won't disappoint you again."

He sat back down next to Mom, who grabbed his shirt sleeve in alarm. "What are you going to fix?"

"My accordion playing."

"You don't play the accordion."

"She's got that right," crowed Bernice.

Hisses. Boos. Razzberries.

Wally called for order. "Before I let you go, I'll remind you that the schedule for tomorrow will be wake-up calls at seven, breakfast beginning at seven thirty, and departure for the castle at nine, so get a good night's sleep. You've had a busy day today, and tomorrow might even surpass it."

Chairs scraped and creaked as the group rose en masse. While the musicians retrieved their instrument cases from alongside the wall, the gang gathered around Dad, bolstering his confidence with claps on the back and a flurry of thumbs-up.

"Chin up," Lucille encouraged him. "I've heard worse. Not *much* worse, but definitely worse."

Margi slapped a travel-size bottle of pink hand sanitizer into his hand. "You might want to use this on your accordion. If your keyboard was sticky, maybe that's what caused all those notes to play at the same time."

The Dicks hurried over to me, Dick Stolee's expression signaling he was still hyped up about his recent windfall. "With Zola

202

gone, I guess there won't be any fortune-telling in the lobby tonight, huh?"

"Good assumption."

He scanned the room. "No one willing to take her place?"

I regarded him with amusement. "Are you looking to add to your windfall?"

"You bet," he tittered, removing a violet-colored banknote from his wallet for show and tell. "See this? It's the highest currency available in euros."

"Zola really nailed that, huh? But I had no idea online gaming paid out in actual cash."

Dick Teig puffed his face up like a chipmunk whose cheeks had exceeded the maximum limit for nuts. "It doesn't. He won it off a scratch game at the corner market down the street, and he has *me* to thank. If I hadn't had a sudden craving for ice cream, he'd be maxing out another credit card on those stupid online slots."

I winced. "You maxed out a credit card?"

"Yeah, but it only had a five-thousand-dollar limit."

"WHAT?"

"Shh," they warned in unison.

My voice rose to a high-pitched whisper. "You lost *five thousand dollars* in order to win *five hundred*?"

"Yeah, but it's euros, so I figure I'm only out about four grand."

"Geez, Dick."

"It was the windows clue that threw me off." He held his five hundred euro banknote up, indicating the tall windowed building imprinted on the front of the bill. "See the windows on this building? I figure that's what Zola was seeing when she told my fortune. So my windfall didn't have anything to do with Microsoft or casino gambling. She saw an image of my actual payout."

"You are in such deep doo-doo."

"You think I should buy more scratch cards?"

"NO!" I dropped my voice as they proceeded to shush me again. "No more scratch cards. No more online gaming. Just . . . just . . . pray Grace doesn't want to make any large purchases before you get that card paid off. If she finds out what you've done, she'll kill you."

"I think I'm good on that," he said with confidence. "Zola didn't predict anything about an untimely death for me."

"She didn't predict an untimely death for herself either," Dick Teig pointed out. "But guess what happened?"

I watched Dick Stolee's complexion drain of color as Nana shuffled over to me. "We're headin' up, dear. Tilly and your mother've already gone on ahead with your father."

"I'm coming too," I said, more than anxious to call it a day.

There was a log jam of Iowans, instrument cases, and other hotel guests at the elevator when we arrived. Since Nana was looking a little flushed, I suggested we have a seat in the lobby because it looked as if it might take a while for the crowd to clear. As we waited she began blinking, wriggling her nose, sniffing, and scratching her eyebrows, mimicking facial expressions reminiscent of the ones she'd used in Scotland in her unsuccessful attempt to put a hex on Bernice.

"Are you okay?"

"I think it's them flowers." She directed an evil look at the overflowing floral arrangement on the display table. "My allergies must be kickin' in."

"I didn't know you had allergies."

"Seems I do now."

"How about we find other seats?"

We moved as far away from the flowers and the elevator as possible, to a secluded alcove with a direct line of vision to another alcove where Otis, Gilbert, Wendell, and Hetty were involved in what looked to be a heated discussion. They were all talking at once, and to say they didn't look happy would have been an understatement. Finger-pointing. Fist-shaking. Eye-rolling. Arm-folding.

"Whaddaya s'pose them folks are havin' words about?" asked Nana as she nodded toward the alcove.

"I hope they're not fighting about Dad. Maybe they're not as willing as they initially appeared about keeping him in the group."

"It'd be a blessin' if they'd can him." She rubbed the heel of her palm against her cheek.

"Don't give up on him yet, Nana. We need to have faith in him."

She gave her nose a long, slow scratch. "You got any musical ability that you know of, dear?"

"None whatsoever."

Nana nodded sagely. "You get that from your father."

We hit the elevator as soon as the crowd cleared. Etienne still wasn't back from the hospital, so I sent him a quick text before I stripped off my clothes, grabbed my nightie out of the dresser, and headed for our luxuriously upgraded bathroom, noticing something odd about Astrid's lime green spinner as I walked by the place where Etienne had stowed it.

I paused, my gaze lingering on the wad of material that was poking out from the spot where the dual zippers met beneath the top handle.

Wait a sec. Hadn't I double-checked to see that all her clothing was completely tucked inside last night? Head trauma or not, I remembered that much. So why was something sticking out now?

I flipped the suitcase onto its side and opened it up. Her clothes remained in neat stacks, the way I'd folded them, but that didn't explain how the corner of her blouse had worked its way through the zipper. Did Etienne have cause to open her suitcase today? Was this his doing or someone else's?

Uncomfortable with the turn my mind had taken, I walked to the bed and picked up the phone.

"Hallo. Front desk."

"This is Emily Miceli in 728. Are there surveillance cameras operating in this hotel?"

"We are a boutique hotel, Mrs. Miceli. I'm happy to report there are no surveillance cameras on the premises. It's our policy not to spy on our guests."

"I'm sorry to hear that. Thanks anyway."

Surveillance footage might have revealed who'd entered our room besides the maid, because I had a sneaking suspicion that someone other than Etienne had tampered with Astrid's suitcase. The question was, who?

I took a quick shower and crawled into bed with every intention of waiting up for Etienne, but sometime during my wait I inadvertently closed my eyes, and that was all she wrote.

The desperate knock on our door jarred me from a sound sleep and sent my internal alarm system into high alert. My heart flew into my throat. My stomach sank to my knees. I felt Etienne's hand on my arm, soothing me. "Stay here, bella. I'll get it."

When the door clicked open, Tilly's voice exploded into the silence.

"It's Marion. I think she's got leprosy."

TWELVE

"Contact urticaria."

I stared at Dr. Fischer. I wasn't sure what the words meant, but I sure hoped they weren't Latin for leprosy or German for something even worse. Etienne might have been able to translate, but I'd insisted that he hang out in the waiting room and attempt to catch forty winks before the sun rose. He hadn't slept all night, so he was running on fumes.

"I'm sorry. Contact *what?*"

It was 4:13 AM, and we seemed to be stuck in the middle of the Munich version of *Groundhog Day.* Same emergency ward. Same treatment room. Same attending physician, who was apparently on duty 24/7 at the hospital. The only difference was the patient, who was sporting a grisly rash on her face and hands that included irregular swelling, inflammation, scaly patches, and welts the size of jawbreakers.

"Your grandmother appears to be suffering from a severe reaction to an allergen."

"It's not leprosy?"

He slatted his eyes behind his rimless specs. "Are you aware that leprosy has been virtually eradicated in Europe, Mrs. Miceli?"

"I guess I'm not up to speed with the world's current infectious disease maps."

"Obviously." He nearly broke a smile, but not quite. "Why would you think leprosy?"

Not wanting to disparage Tilly and her decades of anthropological research, I opted for ambiguousness. "Hearsay?"

Refocusing his attention on Nana, who was sitting on the edge of the gurney with her feet dangling over the side, he grabbed a penlight and tongue depressor and asked her to open her mouth and say *ahhh*. "Any trouble breathing?" he asked her.

"Nope."

"Your throat doesn't feel as if it's closing on you?"

"Nope."

He disposed of the tongue depressor and placed the penlight back in the pocket of his lab coat. Nana peered at him through the tiny slits that remained open beneath her swollen eyelids.

"You s'pose it was them flowers in the

lobby what done me in, Doc?"

"Your reaction indicates exposure of a more direct nature, Mrs. Sippel. Have you applied anything unusual to your face recently?"

"Just the beauty cream what Emily give me."

"I see." He turned humorless eyes on me. "Would that be the same cream that was developed by your retired anthropologist friend who was shrinking heads in New Guinea?"

"I don't think she participated in any of the actual shrinking. She was just there to kind of . . . take notes."

"Is this the same compound that eliminated your lesions overnight?"

Wow. Good memory. "Yup."

"It might have performed a small miracle on you, but it's toxic to your grandmother." He turned back to Nana. "Stop using the compound immediately, Mrs. Sippel. If you bring the jar in for analysis, we might be able to determine which ingredient is causing your reaction, but I suspect your granddaughter might be averse to any type of analysis."

"I don't care if you analyze it," I objected, "but I don't have any left. I gave it all away."

"I'm sure." He elevated Nana's chin to

211

examine her face one last time. "The good thing about contact urticaria, Mrs. Sippel, is that once the offending allergen is removed, the symptoms usually disappear within twenty-four to forty-eight hours. So, stop using the face cream, and you should be back to normal in a couple of days."

"You don't need to give me no shots or transfusions or nuthin'?"

"I can prescribe a mild antihistamine for the itching. You can pick it up at the hospital pharmacy, but the best remedy for your condition is to do nothing at all."

I worried my lip as a niggling thought gnawed at a far corner of my brain. If the cream had proved to be toxic for Nana, could it be toxic for other people as well?

Holy crap.

Bernice.

Taptaptaptaptap.

I rapped on her door with the gentlest of knocks, hoping it was loud enough to get her attention but quiet enough not to disturb her neighbors. Five thirty AM. She was a native Iowan. She'd probably already been up for an hour.

Taptaptaptaptap.

Ten seconds passed.

Twenty.

212

"Bernice," I whispered close to the door. "Are you awake?"

The door flew open. Bernice stood before me, glaring. "This better be good. Whaddaya want?"

She was a rumpled mess with her short satin robe twisted haphazardly around her body and her hair sticking out like the wire bristles on a pot scrubber. But despite that, she looked . . .

I blinked to clear my vision.

Geez. She looked good. No irregular swelling. No inflammation. No scaly patches. No welts the size of jawbreakers. Her complexion looked as creamy as 30 percent butterfat. Flawless texture, luminous, rose-petal soft — and free of the wrinkles that usually cross-hatched her cheeks and forehead.

Correction: she didn't look good, she looked like a million bucks. Like . . . like she was wearing a Hollywood starlet's head on her body. Like . . . like her whole face had been photoshopped.

"Well, spit it out," she crabbed, "or are you just planning to stand there gawking at me?"

"No . . . sorry, I . . ." I squinted for a better look. "The thing is, I was just wondering if . . . if . . . how are you feeling this morning, Bernice?"

Eyes snapping, brows set at an angry slant, she flashed a sneer that sent me back a full step. "Lemme get this straight. You woke me out of a dead sleep to inquire how I'm feeling?"

"I know it's early, but we *are* a full-service tour company, which means our highest priority is the well-being of our gue—"

The door swung shut in my face.

"You'll be hearing about this on your evaluation!" she bellowed from behind the door.

I exhaled a relieved breath. Bernice wasn't allergic. Thank *God.* Catastrophe averted.

But she was starting to exhibit signs of memory loss.

We'd eliminated the evaluation forms a couple of years ago.

Back at the room Etienne greeted me dressed in a towel and nothing else. I wrapped my arms around his waist and snuggled against his chest. "Did you get Nana settled in her room again?" I leaned into him, willing my emotional stress to melt away.

He kissed the crown of my head. "She's a trooper. No whining. No drama. If I weren't already happily married to a member of her family, I'd cut off George at the pass and propose to her myself."

"Are you headed for the shower?"

He inched my chin upward and pressed a soft kiss on my mouth. "I am . . . unless you have a more inviting suggestion."

"Have you opened Astrid's suitcase since it's been in our room?"

"No. I'm not sure when I would have had time. Why?"

"Because I swear someone's monkeyed with it. I noticed some clothing poking out from the zipper earlier tonight that wasn't there yesterday. I called the front desk to inquire about surveillance cameras, but just our luck: boutique hotels in Munich have a strict policy about not spying on their guests."

"Housekeeping might have had a need to open it, although that seems highly un-likely."

"I think there's something fishy going on with everything connected to Astrid: her room, her suitcase, the Guten Tags, her missing books . . ."

"Could we postpone further discussion of Astrid until later?" Slipping the towel off his waist, he looped it around my neck and drew me against him. "We have an hour and fifteen minutes before our wake-up call,

Mrs. Miceli."

I slanted a look at the bedside clock and shook my head. "An hour and seventeen minutes, actually."

His breathing quickened as he twined his fingers in my hair. "Even better."

THIRTEEN

"Ludwig II ascended the Bavarian throne in 1864, following the death of his father, King Maximilian," Wally informed us as we neared Hohenschwangau later that morning. "He was eighteen years old, introverted, and very much a dreamer who imagined himself as the Swan King of operatic lore, but he was more often referred to as Mad King Ludwig. Obsessed with chivalry, knights, and legends, he undertook an ill-advised building project that resulted in the construction of the fairy-tale castle of Neuschwanstein. But there were unfortunate repercussions because his extravagance and excesses drained the family coffers of nearly all its capital — fourteen million marks, which in today's economy would equal three and a half billion euros."

The countryside through which we were driving was green, lush, and flatter than an Iowa cornfield, with an occasional copse of trees to break up the monotony. But unlike Iowa, the terrain was ringed by a chain of saw-toothed, snow-capped mountain peaks that stretched toward infinity. According to my map, we were approaching the foothills of the Bavarian Alps.

"Seventeen years after the building projects began, the king's finance ministers assembled a panel of doctors to analyze the monarch's mental health, and without ever examining him, they declared him insane. He was carted off to a nearby castle, where a day later he was found floating in the lake along with the panel's lead doctor. The circumstances surrounding Ludwig's death remain a mystery to this day."

"I'll tell you what happened to him," Bernice called out. "Someone whacked him. Probably those finance ministers of his. You'd have to be pretty ignorant to let that one stump you."

Bernice was her usual cantankerous self this morning and appeared to be suffering no signs of sleep deprivation from my early morning intrusion. I, on the other hand, was dragging. All the amazing sights and sounds in Bavaria, and the only thing I would kill to have right now was a night of uninterrupted sleep. Not that I was complaining about my pre-dawn aerobic activity. I felt all warm and shiny inside just thinking about it. But I was so tired, I could swear I was beginning to see double.

Mom tapped my arm. "Why are we on this bus?"

"We're going to visit the most iconic castle ever built, Mom. It's the one that Walt Disney used as inspiration for Sleeping Beauty's castle at Disneyland."

"We're going to Disneyland? Ooh!" She clapped her hands as she peered out the window. "Look how green California is, Emily. They must have gotten rain."

"We're in Germany, Mom." Dr. Fischer had indicated that Mom's symptoms would disappear within twenty-four hours, but I wasn't seeing any sign of it yet — just one more concern that was wearing me down.

"Germany?" Mom's voice was distraught. "Why are we in Germany?"

"We're here to visit Sleeping Beauty's castle."

"That should be fun. Did you know she has a castle in Disneyland, too?"

Nothing like a circular conversation to start the morning out right.

"When we reach the parking lot," Wally continued, "please remain on the bus until I give you the okay to exit. It's quite a hike to the castle, all uphill, but since our musi-

219

cians need to conserve their energy for their performances this afternoon, we're going to treat you to a surprise."

"I bet he's planning to give us tickets to ride the teacups," Mom gushed in a burst of enthusiasm. "Emily, will you take a picture of me spinning around in one of those adorable little cups and saucers? Of course, if I end up hurling my breakfast, you might want to use some discretion."

I nodded dutifully. "You got it."

She tapped my arm again and leaned toward my ear, saying in an undertone, "Have you noticed that three-chinned dwarf with the boils all over her face? Do you know who she is?"

Oh, God.

The castle appeared in the distance — a gleaming white confection nestled in a tangle of woodland, its turrets rising like gigantic birthday candles above multilayers of whipped cream frosting. "Thar she blows, Mom. Neuschwanstein Castle. Look out the window."

"Will you at least tell me if she's contagious?" Mom persisted. "Because she looks contagious." She boosted herself up in her seat and craned her neck, searching. "Where's Margi Swanson? In a case of dire emergency, would she ever consider hand-

220

ing out bottles of her sanitizer free of charge?"

Wally picked up where he'd left off with his instructions. "We'll have an in-depth guided tour of the castle that'll keep you occupied for a couple of hours, and then we'll have lunch at the restaurant, where our bands are scheduled to play after we finish our meal. I'll caution you to stick together for the tour and not wander off because if we lose one of you, it'll throw off our entire schedule. Do not attempt to enter rooms that are not open to the public. Any questions?"

"Where'd you say we're headed?" tossed out Dick Stolee, who apparently remained so rattled by his credit card fiasco that his listening skills had deteriorated to the level of his finances.

Upon arrival at the car park, we remained on the coach until Wally made a few official inquiries. When he returned, we off-loaded into the parking lot and followed him and his oversized umbrella to a ticket kiosk near the entrance, where five horse-drawn wagons with overhead canopies were waiting to transport us up the long road to the castle.

"It doesn't matter which vehicle you ride in," Wally instructed as guests gathered around the lead wagon. "They're all going to the same place."

To my amazement, and perhaps influenced by the presence of the castle that loomed high above us, the men tapped into their chivalrous roots and undertook a policy of women first. I helped Mom get situated between Tilly and Nana, and when the seats were full, the driver wasted no time barking a verbal command to his team and jiggling his reins to send them forward.

"What's wrong with your grandmother? Is she contagious?"

Bernice appeared at my side, her voice as abrasive as ever, but her face looked even better than it had at five thirty this morning. Supermodel ready. Inexplicably stunning. "Allergies," I lied, unable to tear my gaze away from her. "And she's not contagious."

"What's she allergic to?"

"You know. Just . . . stuff."

"What stuff?"

"The — uh . . . the doctors weren't sure."

"Morons. They've never heard of allergy skin tests?"

"Maybe they approach skin conditions differently in Germany."

She slatted her eyes with suspicion. "Funny how it's isolated to only two parts of her body. Like she applied something to her face with her hands and *poof!* She starts looking like a troll."

"Nana does *not* look like a troll, Bernice."

"Yeah? Well, I wouldn't be asking Osmond to take a vote on it anytime soon. And will you quit staring at me! You're giving me the creeps. Have I got a bug stuck between my teeth or something?"

"Let me help you into the wagon, Bernice," Wally offered as he directed the remaining guests toward the waiting vehicles.

"I've got this," said Wendell, appearing out of nowhere to extend his arm to her.

Otis, who was already seated, reached out his hand to help her up. "Here you go, beautiful. I've saved a place for you right beside me."

Bernice fluttered her eyelashes and reverted to Scarlett O'Hara mode, cooing demurely as the men fussed over her.

"Are you sure you want to sit between those two sourpusses?" Gilbert teased as he slid onto the bench in front of her. "The place next to me is free."

"I've got a spot next to me too," added Arlin from the front seat.

Like worker bees to the queen, they buzzed around her. Nothing like a pretty face to turn a man's head. I wasn't going to fault them for their testosterone highs, but I wondered if they realized this gorgeous ingénue was *not* a misplaced tourist but a refurbished version of Bernice Zwerg.

Etienne and I piled onto the last seat in the last wagon, where for the next several minutes we could huddle intimately together, linking fingers and touching thighs. As the wagon jerked forward, he placed a kiss on my forehead. "How are you holding up?"

My mouth widened into a shameless yawn. "I could use one of two things: either a catnap or caffeine."

"I'm told the horses can be notoriously slow hauling their load, so you might have time to squeeze in that catnap."

"But I'll miss out on the scenery on the way up to the castle."

"There's no scenery other than trees. Acre upon acre of trees."

"Really?" I pressed my cheek to his shoulder and closed my eyes. "Talked me into it."

The rocking motion of the wagon in combination with the rhythmic clop of horse hooves created a soothing calm that washed over me like a cradlesong, lulling me toward sluggishness . . . dr*owww*siness . . . *sleee*—

224

Etienne's phone began vibrating against my hip like an electric blender. "I'm sorry, bella."

Blinking awake, I sat up arrow straight as he retrieved his phone.

"Miceli."

I knew the call was official when the person on the other end of the line did most of the talking, allowing Etienne to utter only a handful of *uh-huhs* to go along with an occasional *I see.* By the time we approached our drop-off point near the top of the mountain, I realized Etienne had been right about the sameness of the scenery. I also realized that something was drastically wrong because when he ended his conversation, his expression took on a dark, introspective quality, as if he were trying to gauge how to deal with a burden that had been unceremoniously placed on his shoulders.

"What's wrong, sweetie?"

"That was the medical examiner's office. The preliminary results of Zola's autopsy are in. Her heart condition wasn't the cause of her death." He regarded me, baffled. "She died from what, at first blush, is consistent with nicotine poisoning."

"Nicotine poisoning? But . . . she didn't smoke, did she?"

"Long-term smoking wasn't the culprit.

She either absorbed a lethal dose of nicotine through her skin or she ingested it — a dose so large, it apparently killed her within minutes."

"So it . . . it happened at the Hippodrom?"

"That's the current thinking."

"But how could something like that happen when there was no smoking allowed in the tent?"

"I don't know, but according to the official I spoke with, acute nicotine poisoning isn't that common in adults. It's more common among children who mistake nicotine gum for chewing gum, or toddlers who stick those smoking cessation patches in their mouths."

I racked my brain for probable scenarios. "Could there have been a mishap in the kitchen? A tin of someone's chewing tobacco getting upended into the food — into the pots of mustard or the potato pancakes?"

"If that were the case, shouldn't we have ended up with more victims?"

"Maybe she ate more than everyone else."

"I should think that a clump of chewing tobacco in either mustard *or* potato pancakes would render the food completely unpalatable."

I arched an eyebrow. "There were a few people at my table who thought the entire *meal* was unpalatable."

"Whatever Zola did or didn't eat, she was exposed to a deadly dose of nicotine in the period between when we arrived at the tent and the moment she collapsed. That's the timeline."

"Did your contact indicate how her death is being classified?"

"We won't know until after the medical examiner completes his final analysis, but they've promised to keep me in the loop. We'll need to be prepared, though, because if her death is ruled a homicide, we'll be looking at the kind of police investigation that will change our itinerary rather drastically."

"Nooo." I hung my head in despair. Everything that had gone wrong already, and now this? I heaved a sigh. "Do you ever get the feeling we're in the wrong line of work?"

"It's too soon to jump to conclusions, Emily. The medical examiner may yet decide that her death was accidental."

Oh, sure. That was as likely to happen as Margi Swanson scarfing down a pig's head sandwich on marble rye. "How does a medical examiner determine if someone's death is accidental or deliberate?"

"I don't know. I'm not the medical examiner."

Our driver halted the team short of the castle gate, near a building whose hexagonal turret and half-timbered accents smacked of Old World Bavaria and storybook charm. "Schlossrestaurant," I read aloud as Etienne helped me to the ground. A stone fence surrounded the patio where an array of blue table umbrellas lured guests to dine alfresco. "Is this the restaurant where the bands will be playing?" The place was so enchanting in its alpine setting that I wouldn't have been surprised to find Hansel and Gretel dining at one of the tables, playing host to Goldilocks and the Gingerbread Man.

"I wish. Our restaurant is the large structure off the car park, at the bottom of the hill."

We made our way toward Wally, who was rounding everyone up to begin the last leg of the hike. "It's about a fifteen-minute walk to the entrance," he announced, "and you might find it a bit steep, so we're going to proceed at a leisurely pace. There's a waiting area outside the castle walls with an electronic sign board that posts tour numbers. When our tour is posted, we'll proceed to the gatehouse and into the courtyard to await the final posting of our tour, which should happen about five minutes before the tour is set to begin. If there are no questions, let's start the hike."

As the group surged forward, Etienne and I hung back to keep a lookout from the rear. Given the pitch of the pathway, no one in the gang seemed inclined to race to the castle gate, so there was no jockeying for position or accidental tripping, which made me long to locate all our sightseeing venues at the tops of mountains.

"Hypothetically speaking, what would motivate someone to kill Zola?" I asked Etienne as we slogged up the path. I felt as if we were following the Yellow Brick Road around the outer edge of the Big Rock Candy Mountain.

He shook his head. "I have no idea. She was the one guest who had no prior connection to either the musicians or the Windsor City gang before she signed up for that final spot. So if someone did indeed kill her, they had to have developed an exceedingly strong dislike of her almost instantly."

"Her predictions were pretty unsettling for a couple of guests." Like the fact that Dick Teig was shallow. Although the only person who was shocked by the revelation of that bombshell was Dick Teig himself.

"But she was remarkably on target. Could someone have killed her out of fear of what she might reveal?"

"It's certainly a possibility. If plans had worked out as scheduled last night, Zola would have ended up telling *everyone's* fortune."

Holy crap. If Zola's death was ruled a homicide, Maisie's innocent suggestion could certainly become more significant.

Without meaning to, Maisie might have goaded someone into committing murder.

FOURTEEN

Our tour number was already posted when we reached the waiting area, so we kept on trucking.

After leaning over a guardrail of perfectly chiseled stone to peer into the depths of a wooded ravine that thundered with the sounds of rushing water, we huffed and puffed the last few yards to walk beneath the raised portcullis of the Grand Entrance gate — a wide arching portal flanked by a façade of red brick and bookended by cylindrical twin towers that looked taller than Dad's grain silos. Bypassing the requisite gift shop, we emerged into a courtyard that boasted a theme park ambiance with its electronic scanners, turnstiles, monitors, and rope barriers.

The castle soared around us like a Hollywood sound stage enhanced by special effects — turrets and towers, witch-hatted roofs and balconies, parapets and crenelated moldings. It was more delicate than Harry Potter's Hogwarts and grander than Tolkien's Minas Tirith. But its design was so whimsical, it cultivated the impression of an architectural theater rather than a fortress.

We followed Wally's umbrella toward the electronic sign board at the far end of the courtyard and realized that by dillydallying on the walkway, we'd probably knocked a huge chunk of time off our wait. According to the number posted on the monitor, our tour would be up next.

Sometime during our ascent Bernice had gained more male admirers, who now formed an impenetrable circle around her, teasing, laughing, flirting, snapping photos. Even the two Dicks were sniffing around the perimeter, wanting, no doubt, to ogle the eye candy without drawing the ire of their wives. The rest of the gang were actually making use of their camera phones, but instead of shooting pictures of the lofty towers that spiraled to near impossible heights, they were extending their arms, saying cheese, and taking selfies.

"Are any of you planning to take a picture of the castle?" I asked as I wandered into their midst. "I can guarantee a space in our brochure for the best shot."

"Maybe you should buy a postcard," suggested Helen as she mugged for a selfie with Lucille and Grace. "They probably sell really nice ones in the gift shop."

I leveled a flinty look on the bunch of them. "Does the idea of a post-tour photo exchange hold no appeal for anyone anymore?"

Silence. Shrugs. Downcast eyes.

"Have you taken *any* pictures of the places we've visited so far?" I admonished. "What are you planning to put in your photo albums?"

"We don't bother with albums anymore," Alice Tjarks spoke up. "We download content to our computers and iPads and burn CDs so we don't have to fuss with paper."

"Okay, but . . . how are you going to remember what you've seen if you have no visual reminders of where you've been?"

Osmond raised his hand. "Is that a trick question?"

"We can remember what we've seen," Margi assured me.

I crossed my arms and raised questioning brows. "Oh, yeah? Prove it."

They gathered around me, flipping through the photo galleries on their screens at warp speed. "Here we go," cried Margi as she thrust her phone toward me. "This is the big plaza in Munich where we stood around looking at that glockenspiel thing."

I eyed the image. "That's a close-up of your face."

"Right. That's me watching those little figures go 'round. See how amused I look?"

"I don't think you look amused," countered Helen as she perused the screen. "I think you look bored."

"No, I don't."

"Yes, you do."

"I think she looks bewildered," said Lucille.

"I do not," snapped Margi. "*This* is bewildered." She bunched her brows over her nose, rounded her eyes, and pursed her lips. "My bewildered look in no way resembles my amused look."

George glanced from Margi's phone to her face. "Look the same to me."

"I've got one," said Osmond as he pushed toward me, waving his phone. "This is the Little Red Riding Hood House in Oberga — Obarm — that town with the Humpty Dumpty sculpture."

His eyes, nose, and forehead filled the screen. I sighed. "So where's the house?"

"Right in front of me, on the other side of the street. This is when I'm looking at it."

"Are you sure that was the Little Red Riding Hood House?" asked Grace as she flipped madly through her gallery. "I have a picture exactly like that of the Passion Play House." She held up her own half-headed shot. "See?" She hesitated. "Or is this the Hippodrom? Shoot, I might have to label these."

"That must be the Hippodrom," insisted Helen. "See how blurry it is? Looks like *someone* drank a little too much beer last night."

"Does this place look familiar to anyone?" asked George as he flashed a headshot of himself around. "I don't look amused, bewildered, bored, or drunk, so I don't know where the hell I was."

"That's our number," announced Wally, gesturing toward the monitor. "Okay, everyone. We're up."

We merged together in a disorganized clump before queuing up to run our tickets through the scanners. Mom came up beside me, ushered by Dad. "Em, do you know —"

"We're in Germany, Mom. At the most visited fairy-tale castle in the world."

"I know. Your father just told me." She inched closer and lowered her voice to a whisper. "Do you know who that woman over there is? The one who's attracting attention from all the men. Is she famous or something?"

"That's Bernice Zwerg, Mom."

"No."

"Yes."

She stretched her neck for a better look, giving Bernice a thorough once-over. "Seriously. Who is it?"

I noticed that Hetty Munk was also giving Bernice the eye, but unlike Mom, she didn't look as if she were being motivated by curiosity.

Hetty Munk was throwing daggers.

So what was up with that?

At the far end of the courtyard we were greeted by an attendant who directed us through a door and into a foyer that felt as cramped as a lighthouse tower. "Where's the elevator?" demanded Bernice when she saw the staircase that spiraled upward in front of us. "I'm not climbing all those stairs. What is this? The Leaning Tower of Pisa?"

"I'll give you a hand," offered Arlin Foote.

"I've got this," said Wendell as he took possession of her arm.

We climbed around and around and around. I don't know how many stories we racked up, but it was enough to leave us all winded as we exited into an interminably long corridor where our guide awaited us.

He introduced himself as Sepp, a gray-haired pensioner whose thick German accent was going to make listening a challenge.

Well, maybe not so much listening as understanding.

"Velcome to Neuschwanstein Castle, or New Shvon Stone Castle as vee sometimes refer to it, former home of King Ludvig II of Bavaria. The castle vas constructed between the years 1869 and 1892, and as I valk you tru the halls, you vill note that the shvon symbol is prevalent everyvair you look."

Margi raised her hand. "What's a shvon?"

"Shvon, madam? You do not know vot shvon is?" He spread his arms as if they were wings and began flapping them like a prehistoric bird. "Shvon?"

"Sepp is referring to a swan," Wally informed us. "It was Ludwig's heraldic animal."

"We need to be on the English tour," hollered Bernice.

"Dis *is* the English tour," corrected Sepp.

"Sure it is," she muttered. "And I'm Daffy Duck."

"Neuschwanstein Castle is a mythical knight's castle," Sepp continued, "combining operatic lore, chivalric legends, and the romanticism of the Middle Ages."

I wasn't sure that the era best known for the Black Plague, open sewers, and non-pillowtop mattresses could be considered romantic, but hey, this wasn't my gig.

"As vee proceed into the palace, I ask you to alvays remain on the carpet, behind the rope barriers. Photography is strictly forbidden. Please to follow me."

The Dicks tracked me down as we climbed the unpolished marble risers of the main staircase, falling in step on either side of me. Dick Teig cradled his phone in his palm and flashed it surreptitiously to show me the photo on his screen. "Emily, who's the babe?"

"Is she with us?" pressed Dick Stolee. "Where'd she come from?"

I rolled my eyes. "She came from Windsor City, guys. That's Bernice."

"No way," snorted Dick Teig.

"Way," I shot back as we entered a long cavernous hall. It was narrower on one end than the other and mimicked the shape of a blunt-ended cake server. The room was dominated by a vaulted ceiling and colorful wall murals that depicted a sword blade being whacked by a mallet-wielding blacksmith, a knight gasping his last breath, and an ancient king having intense discourse on what might have been vital issues of the day, like undocumented barbarians or feudal-care health options.

"Dis room is the Lower Hall, or westibule," Sepp began. "It separates the Throne Hall on our right vit the king's apartments on our left. The vall paintings represent scenes from the Nordic Sigurd saga, and . . ."

"Bernice doesn't look anything like this," Dick Stolee rasped in my ear.

I gave him a palms up. "She does now."

The guys gawked at each other in disbelief. "What'd she do?" asked Dick Teig.

"Beauty cream. She found one that really works."

"Are you sure that's her?" Dick Stolee persisted.

"Is she wearing glittery *Wizard of Oz* ruby slippers?"

They danced left and right and bobbed their heads for a look-see.

"Yup," said Dick Stolee.

"Shoot," groaned Dick Teig. "That *is* Bernice."

"You vill kindly proceed into the Throne Hall," Sepp instructed, reminding us again to stay within the rope barriers. Dick Teig shuffled along beside me as I followed the group.

"Emily," he asked in a pleading tone, "do you know where she bought the stuff? I need to get some for Helen."

"Dis hall vas intended to velcome Ludvig's subjects vit their petitions to the King, but no subjects ever wizited the castle. Ludvig vas, how you say, a flaming introwert."

Sepp's voice echoed in the vast emptiness of the chamber, floating up to the cupola that rose two stories above the marble floor and swirling around the lapis lazuli colonnades that flanked the upper gallery. The room resembled an Eastern Orthodox church with its white marble altar and gleaming splashes of gold. Religious images festooned the side walls while St. George undertook the task of slaying the dragon on the wall opposite the altar.

"The chandelier above is shaped like a Byzantine crown," Sepp explained, prompting us to look up. "It veighs somesing close to thirteen hundred pounds, is made of gilded brass, and holds ninety-six candles."

I drifted backward as I gaped up at the chandelier, hooking my foot on something that caused me to do a little stutter step to regain my balance.

Tilly's cane.

"Careful!" cried Tilly as she grabbed my forearm to right me. Nana stood beside her, looking uncharacteristically glum, her *Iowa: It's Pretty Corny* sweatshirt splattered with a mysterious substance that left a trail of stains from her neckline to the rib-knit hem. It looked as if a migratory flock of birds had used her sweatshirt for target practice.

I flickered a finger at the blotches. "Are those . . . ?"

"Bird droppin's?" She looked down her nose at her chest. "Nope. This is your mother's doin'."

"What'd she spill?"

"She didn't spill nuthin'. She's been squirtin' me with them dang bottles of hand sanitizer what Margi give her on account of she thinks I'm contagious. Every time I get within two feet of her, she blasts me."

This is what happens when your mother spends a lifetime shunning all things science fiction. She nurtures the mistaken impression that a glob of hand gel will provide the same safeguard as a deflector shield. "I'm sorry, Nana. Do you want me to speak to her?"

"Won't do no good on account of she won't remember nuthin' you tell her." She scrunched up her face as she studied the splotches. "Only good thing is, the stuff what Margi gave her don't smell too bad." She pointed to a stain near her shoulder.

"This one smells like strawberry jam, and this one" — she touched a place over her bosom — "smells like chocolate fudge. The more I inhale, the hungrier I get. By the time we get to our restaurant, I should have a pretty good appetite."

We filed out of the Throne Hall and across the floor of the vestibule again, where we entered an oak-paneled room whose main purpose seemed to be that of a foyer.

"Dis is the anteroom to Ludvig's private apartments," said Sepp. "A servant vas alvays on duty here to answer the call of the king. Many hours of boredom ver probably spent in dis chamber. The first room vee vill wizit vill be Ludvig's dining room."

As we crowded into the room with its scarlet and gold textiles, parquet flooring, and paintings of long-haired kings, Etienne pulled me aside. "This happened more quickly than I imagined. The medical examiner's office must have a German-engineered mass spectrometer. They just sent me this text." He handed me his phone.

The message was short and to the point. RE: ZOLA CZARNECKI. DEATH CAUSED BY NICOTINE INGESTION. HOMICIDE INVESTIGATION WILL ENSUE.

"Oh, no." I exhaled a discouraged breath

and handed him back his phone. "What now?"

"We'll finish the day's activities as planned, then travel back to Munich to see what awaits us. I'll give Wally a heads-up."

"Are we sharing the information with the group?"

"Not yet. I'd prefer not to alert anyone to what lies ahead. Better our killer is lulled into a false sense of security before the hammer drops."

"So . . . it's an absolute certainty that someone on the tour killed Zola?"

"It appears that way." He scrutinized the group with unyielding eyes. "I believe one of our musicians wanted Zola dead . . . and found a way to do it."

I blended back into the group as Etienne sought out Wally. We trooped into Ludwig's bedroom and listened to Sepp explain the monastic scheme of the chamber, with its dark wood and canopied state bed whose gothic-inspired massiveness looked like an oversized confessional that might collapse beneath its own weight. Golden embroidery threads showcased lions, crowns, lilies, and swans on the bedcover and curtains, and another swan squatted on the washstand, silver-plated and gleaming, looking as if it were about to take a header into the silver basin below. Ludwig might have found the room restful, but I would have found it as warm and fuzzy as a sleepover in the side chapel of a British cathedral.

"I need a word with you, Mom." I caught up to her and Dad as the people ahead of us poked their heads through the door of the tiny chapel off the bedroom.

"Isn't this exciting, Em?" She splayed her hand over her chest. "I've always wanted to tour this place."

Omigod! I grabbed her upper arms. "Do you know where you are?"

"I'm hoping it's St. Peter's Basilica because I'd love to run into the new pope."

Nuts. But on a brighter note, she was current with the recent papal upheaval, so that *had* to be a positive sign, didn't it?

"Okay, Mom, here's the scoop. Stop squirting Nana with hand sanitizer."

She gave me a blank look.

"Nana," I repeated.

More blankness from Mom. Dad dropped his head to his chest and sighed.

"The short woman with the boils all over her face," I prompted.

"Oh, her." She cast a surreptitious look around us and drew me close. "Emily, do you happen to know the symptoms for Ebola?"

"Nana doesn't have Ebola. She's suffering from an allergic reaction that's specific to her and her alone. It's impossible for you to catch what she has, so stop trying to sanitize her. You've made an absolute mess of her sweatshirt."

Dad nodded. "What'd I tell you, Margaret? You've made your poor mother look like she decided to wear her last meal instead of eat it."

"It's soap," complained Mom. "It washes out."

I narrowed my eyes. "How many bottles do you have left?"

"She blew her wad in her last attack," said Dad, "so they're all empty."

"Good. Don't even *think* about asking Margi for replacement bottles. We're cutting you off."

Mom trained a quizzical look on me and Dad before shrugging agreeably. "Okay." She grabbed Dad's hand. "C'mon, Bob. I'm sure the Pieta's around here somewhere."

We breezed through the remaining staterooms in Ludwig's apartments, bombarded by more wood paneling, fanciful chandeliers, ornate columns, billboard-sized murals, gilded brass, and extraneous swans. We ended the tour on the fourth floor in the Singer's Hall, where a mural of a magical forest peeked out from behind three flamboyant arcades. It was a room where the ceiling panels were painted with signs of the zodiac, where branched candlesticks as tall as light posts stood at military attention, and where not a single musical note ever rang out to entertain welcoming ears. "King Ludvig preferred his solitude," Sepp reiterated, "so the hall, vit its fine acoustics, vas never used in his lifetime."

By the time Sepp led us to the cafeteria and restrooms on the second floor, I had Neuschwanstein Castle all figured out. It wasn't so much a real residence as it was a theatrical set: a backdrop for an operatic production. A dwelling that owed its existence to pure make-believe, kind of like the pink condo I used to have for my Barbie doll. It was long on show but really short on comfort.

Wally gathered us around him after we bade *auf wiedersehen* to Sepp.

"We have forty minutes to kill before we head down to the restaurant for lunch, so I suggest you visit the museum shop, watch the multivision show that chronicles the life of King Ludwig, or use the comfort station. If you feel like snacking, go ahead, but pace yourself. You'll be scarfing down Wiener schnitzel in less than an hour."

The group scattered like marbles. Bernice sashayed to the food counter, where her persistent admirers argued over which one of them would buy her coffee or tea or whatever other overpriced beverage she desired. Nana and Tilly won the footrace to the restroom, emerging long minutes later to announce that it was only a two-seater so the ladies in the group had better think about lining up now, which prompted the expected stampede.

I browsed through the museum shop while keeping one eye on the queue and stopped to talk to Gilbert Graves, who was thumbing through a photographic book of the castle that must have weighed ten pounds. "So what was your reaction to the Singer's Hall? Can you believe it's never been used for anything musical?"

He adjusted his horn-rims on the bridge of his nose. "What a waste. Did you notice the acoustics in that room? They were incredible. Man, if we ever had a chance to play in a room like that, we wouldn't even need a sound system."

"I guess it's too much to expect today's restaurant to have great acoustics."

"Restaurants usually have lousy acoustics, but I'm not knocking the gig. We're happy to be playing. Hell, this is what we've dreamed about ever since we formed the band." He hesitated. "Ever since Astrid formed the band. I just wish she could be here to enjoy the fruits of her labor. It's not fair."

"Are you sure you're still okay with my dad taking her place?" I hedged, recalling the band's seeming dissention in the lobby last night.

"He's doing us a favor, and we appreciate it. I bet your dad's problem at the Hippodrom last night was what Hetty said: nerves. Today's venue will be a lot smaller, so I think he'll be able to show us what he's got. I feel bad for him, though. It's no cakewalk being out there in the limelight. Kudos to him for even wanting to get back up on his horse. I know a lot of musicians who'd never be able to live down the shame. They'd walk into the sunset, never to be seen again."

My stomach bubbled into a stew of acid as I fretted over the outcome of today's performance. *Please don't let him screw up. Please don't let him screw up.*

"You in the market to buy any books?" asked Gilbert as he perused the shelves. "Chivalric knight's tales? Neuschwanstein Castle guidebooks? Epic poems and sagas from the Norse?"

"Not me, but you might want to bring this to Otis's attention. Epic poems are probably right up his alley."

Gilbert snorted derisively. "Otis Erickson? Epic poems? I don't think so."

"Otis reads poetry."

"Who told you that?"

"*He* did. He lent a book of poetry to Astrid for this trip."

"Not in a million years did Otis Erickson give Astrid a book of poetry."

"He didn't *buy* it. He lent it. It was a library book."

"Sure it was." He let out a whoop of laughter. "Not only does Otis not read, he doesn't own a library card."

I gave him a hard look. "Are you sure?"

"We've only been buds for decades. Blimpie's reward card, yes. Ace Hardware reward card, yes. Library card, no."

"Then how —" I swallowed the end of my question. If there was no library card, there was no library *book.* So if Otis hadn't been looking for his fictitious volume of poetry, what *had* he been looking for? Her journal? Is that what he'd been searching for all along? But what reason would he have to steal such a personal item?

"Why'd Otis tell you about his adventures in poetry in the first place?"

"He needed the book back to avoid having to pay the library fine, so Etienne and I let him search for it the night we packed up Astrid's belongings."

"Otis was in her room?"

"For a short time."

"What about his book? Did he find it?"

"How could he? From what you're telling me, there *was* no book."

"So he left empty-handed?"

"As far as I know."

"Good." Gilbert allowed a half-smile to play across his lips. "That sonofa—" He caught himself mid-epithet, replacing his sudden ill humor with forced cheerfulness. "Thanks for the laugh, Emily. Otis and poetry." A shadow passed over his face, making his eyes hard. "Some guys are just full of surprises."

Peering toward the ladies' room to find the queue gone, I left Gilbert to shoot across the floor and take my turn. I was freshening my lip gloss when the door opened to admit one last straggler.

Bernice.

She glided into the room and struck a pose against the door, the back of her hand angled against her forehead as if she were a Southern belle executing a swoon. "I'd forgotten how exhausting it is to be the designated hottie in the group. Thank God the restroom isn't unisex or they'd be chasing me inside here too. I need some me time."

I eyed her reflection in the mirror. "Too much of a good thing, huh?"

"It's too bad that psychic bit the dust. I would love to have told her to her face how wrong she was."

"Wrong? You're reaping the benefits of her prediction, aren't you? Didn't she tell you that you'd meet a handsome stranger?"

"Her prediction was too limited." She sighed melodramatically and primped her hair. "The tall, dark, handsome ones are getting overrun by the short, fat, homely ones. It's getting unmanageable. How can I vet the princes with the toads always in the picture?"

"Are things moving so quickly that you're already at the vetting stage?" Considering she'd been the "It" girl for all of ten minutes, she might be jumping the gun a bit.

She stared at me in the mirror. "Sometimes I'm surprised you're able to walk and chew gum at the same time. It's *never* too soon to check for financial assets. Here's the deal: no hefty portfolio, no private date with Bernice Zwerg. I have standards to maintain." She slipped into a stall and shut the door. "Hey, you're the one who's supposed to know all the confidential stuff about us guests. What do you know about these musicians? What do they do besides hop up on a stage and play dorky polka music?"

I didn't think I'd be betraying any confidences to repeat the basics. "Have you ever heard of Newton Lock and Key in Boone?"

"Nope."

"Well, every musician on the tour works there in some capacity."

"My stable of admirers are all blue-collar factory workers?"

"Everyone but Wendell. He owns the company."

She flushed the toilet in response.

"Which one's Wendell?" She opened the door and joined me at the sink.

"Handlebar mustache? Square build? Plays trumpet with the Guten Tags? Doesn't wear his name tag?"

"Oh, him." She cupped her palm beneath the automatic soap dispenser before flashing her hand in front of the sensor on the faucet. "He needs more hair."

"The shaved-head look is pretty trendy for guys these days."

"Balding guys may be fond of shaved heads. I'm not. Besides which, your Wendell

252

comes with baggage attached."

"What kind of baggage?"

"Romantic baggage. When I went to refill my ice bucket the first night we were here, I saw him sneaking out of someone's room in the wee hours of the morning."

Omigod. Zola was right. He *was* in a relationship. He *was* sneaking around.

"Of course he finds me utterly irresistible, so I expect he'll dump the other broad and try to wow me with a full court press, but I'm not sure I want to waste my time on secondhand goods."

"You're absolutely sure about this, Bernice? I mean, how do you know he wasn't leaving his own room?"

She shook excess water off her hands and waved her forearm in front of the towel dispenser. "He was wearing his bathrobe, his slippers, and a goofy grin on his face. I recognized the grin. It wasn't from binge-watching Sunday football. He was floating back to his own room, happy as a tick on a fat hound." When no towel appeared, she glowered at the dispenser and waved both hands in front of it.

"No chance he was headed to get ice?"

"Without an ice bucket? Oh, sure. Maybe he was planning to stash it in his pockets." She glared at the paper towel dispenser and gave it a thwack. "What's wrong with this thing?"

I seized the corners of a towel that was poking out from beneath the dispenser and yanked down, releasing the needed sheet. I ripped it off and handed it to her. "It's not motion-activated."

Lucille poked her head through the door. "Restroom check! Wally's starting the two-minute countdown, so you'd better move it because we're getting ready to leave."

We exited the castle after Wally performed his mandatory head count and began the downhill hike to the place where the horse-drawn wagons would pick us up. "I'm glad we're going down and not up," Osmond remarked. "Too bad they couldn't find a way to make everything downhill."

"It'd sure be easier on people," insisted Alice.

"Not necessarily," objected Tilly. "Trying to decrease forward motion on a downhill slope can be just as taxing on a person's knees and hips as climbing an incline can be on someone's heart and lungs. The acceleration created by gravitational pull can be a bear to stop. Why, it's thought that among the ancient cliff dwellers of the Mesa Verde —"

"Dammit all!"

I swiveled my head to find Maisie several paces behind me, looking apoplectic as she dropped to her knees beside the scattered contents of what appeared to be a broken shoulder bag. "My stuff! It's — it's getting away."

Tilly stopped in her tracks to look uphill. "Aha. See there?" She waggled her cane at a tube of lip balm that was rolling downhill past her. "This is precisely what I'm talking about. If you watch closely, you'll notice that gravitational pull will cause that object to reach its terminal velocity in approximately —"

Etienne scooped it into his hand.

"Well," Tilly huffed. "I guess we can scratch that."

"I've got your Lifesavers," shouted Dick Stolee, blocking them with his foot.

We all pitched in, rescuing whatever items went tumbling past us. Dad retrieved a travel-size bottle of aspirin. Dick Teig gathered up a few rogue Tic Tacs that were no longer fit for human consumption. Prescription bottle here. Penlight there. I chased down a nasal inhaler and a mini bottle of what looked like contact lens re-wetting solution — until I picked it up and read the label.

Atomized Liquid: E-Cigarette Nicotine Refill.

A tingling sensation slithered down my spine.

Maisie refilled her e-cigarette cartridges manually? From a bottle of liquid nicotine that she carried around in her shoulder bag?

I clutched the bottle in my fist.

Oh. My. God.

Maisie hadn't accidentally goaded anyone into killing Zola.

She'd done it herself.

FIFTEEN

"Maisie did it," I said in a breathless rush.

"Maisie did what?"

I gave Etienne's arm a tug, prompting him to bend his head closer to hear me. "She killed Zola."

After we'd seen the group seated at their assigned tables, I'd dragged him into the hallway off the restaurant's foyer where the restrooms were located. With the dining room packed with noisy tourists, this was the only place I could find that was even halfway private.

Glancing both ways, Etienne lowered his voice and, in the same way Clark Kent swapped his suit and hat for a cape and tights, he became Etienne Miceli, former Swiss police inspector. "How do you know?"

"Incriminating evidence." I handed him the plastic refill bottle.

"Liquid nicotine? Where did you get this?"

"It rolled out of Maisie's shoulder bag and

straight past me on its way to terminal velocity."

"Why is she carrying liquid nicotine?"

"To fill her e-cigarette. She's trying to break her smoking habit, so she's going the e-cigarette route. She's the last holdout in the whole company. Once she quits, everyone gets a bonus because of lower healthcare costs."

He muttered something in either French, Italian, or a combination of the two before nodding. "Does she know you have this?"

"Nope. You saw for yourself. The contents of her shoulder bag scattered all over the place after the strap broke, so I suspect she doesn't know where a lot of her stuff ended up."

He paused. "I don't need to remind you that this could either be something or nothing at all, correct?"

"Oh, it's something, all right."

He held the bottle up to the light, his features hardening into a frown. "If Maisie *did* kill Zola, she didn't use the contents of this particular bottle to carry out the deed."

"But she's the only guest on the tour who smokes, or vapes, or whatever she calls it. She *has* to be the killer."

"This bottle's full."

"Of course *this* one's full. She emptied

258

the one she was carrying last night into Zola's egg noodles or mustard or beer. She probably has a whole slew of them in her suitcase."

"I'm not discrediting your find, Emily. I'm merely pointing out that the Munich police will need more evidence than this to file charges against her. Even if she was carrying a bottle in her purse, it doesn't mean she actually used it."

"Yeah, but —"

"I assume these nicotine refills are available to the general public and can be purchased at convenience stores everywhere?"

"Well, probably, but —"

"There you two are." Wally jaunted toward us. "They've begun to serve, so you'd better take your seats before the serving staff thinks you're no-shows." He raised a curious eyebrow as he glanced from Etienne to me. "What's up? Or is this one of those marital things that's none of my business?"

Etienne clapped him on the back before herding us toward the dining area. "I'll get you up to speed later. Meanwhile, let's enjoy the schnitzel, shall we?"

We filled five tables in the dining area — a vast grange-hall type room with space set for staging small performance events. I was playing hostess to Margi, Nana, George, and the Dicks, and I occupied a chair with an unobstructed view of the table where Maisie Barnes sat with her fellow Little Bitte band members and the Brassed Offs. In my checkered career as a reluctant sleuth, I'd gained a reputation for being wrong at just about every turn, but this time was different. *This* time, I'd caught the killer red-handed.

Kinda.

"This isn't the main course, is it?" asked Margi as she trained a sour look on the dinner plate in front of her. "I was expecting hot dogs."

"Me too." Dick Teig glanced around at the other tables to see what everyone else had been served. "But I'm not seeing wieners on anyone's plate."

Dick Stolee poked his flat breaded cutlet with his fork. "Maybe they ran out of wieners and decided to substitute some kind of German mystery meat. Does anyone know what this is?"

"I think that's the schnitzel," said George.

"What kind of animal is a schnitzel?" asked Margi, her eyes widening as she answered her own question. "Omigod. Is that like a . . . a neutered schnauzer? Eww. Hey, I'm not eating dog no matter how light the breading is."

"It's veal," said Nana as she speared a parslied potato. "The Food Network done a whole afternoon series on cuts of meat what can give PETA a notion to hold a demonstration right in front of your very own home."

"Veal?" Dick Teig squinted at the cutlet. "Isn't that like . . . the bovine equivalent of Bambi?"

Margi froze as she regarded the meat in horror. She pushed her plate away. "This is going from bad to worse. Flag down our waitress. I'd like to order take-out from another restaurant."

I studied Maisie as she attacked her meal with the same enthusiasm with which she played her fiddle. I knew she'd killed Zola. I knew how she'd done it. I just didn't know why. I mean, she and Zola had been friends for a shorter time than it took my fingernail polish to dry. That wasn't long enough for her to start despising what she'd first liked about her, was it?

"I brung a bunch of earplugs with me today if anyone needs 'em," Nana announced to the table. "But you gotta do it on the Q-T."

"Why do we need earplugs?" asked Dick Stolee.

"The oompah band?" razzed Dick Teig. "Emily's father on the accordion? Potential damage to healthy eardrums? I think they're gonna be first up today."

There followed a moment of reflective silence before four hands flew toward Nana, palms up.

I returned to my ruminations as I toyed with my food. Had Maisie been alarmed by what Zola might find if she allowed the clairvoyant to look into her future? Could her private life bear the scrutiny of a fortune-teller? Was she trying to protect some deeply hidden, unsavory secret?

But if that were the case, why would she have suggested that Zola tell *everyone's* fortune after the Oktoberfest performance? That wouldn't be a logical move if she was afraid to have her own fortune told. Unless . . .

Unless it was a ploy to divert suspicion away from herself. Could she have convinced everyone to participate without joining in herself? Would anyone have noticed that the organizer of the evening's entertainment was too busy organizing to play along? Was it fear that had forced her hand? Or something else?

I studied her as she interacted with the band members at her table.

Wendell seemed particularly fond of her, referring to her with much more affection than a boss normally shows an employee. Was it possible they were a couple?

But if they're a couple, said the voice inside my head, *how come they don't hang out together?*

Could their deliberate avoidance of each other be a well-orchestrated maneuver? Was this how they kept their relationship a secret? By evading each other in public?

I slanted a look from Maisie to Wendell and back to Maisie.

Uff-da. Was the relationship Wendell refused to acknowledge — the one he swore he wasn't involved in — a love affair he was having with Maisie? Was it Maisie's room Bernice had seen him sneaking out of our first night at the hotel?

But what if the two of them *were* having an affair? They were consenting adults. Wendell wasn't married. Maisie wasn't marr—

The gold band on her ring finger caught my eye as she reached across the table for the water pitcher.

Geez Louise. Maisie *was* married.

This wasn't good. Wendell wasn't just having an affair. He was having an affair with a married woman who happened to be a subordinate in his company — an underling. Weren't there laws prohibiting behaviors like that in the workplace? Harassment laws or something? No wonder he denied the relationship.

"Be right back, folks," I said as I excused myself from the table. I scurried back to the restroom, locked myself in a stall, and dug out my phone.

Was I right about this or was I grasping at straws? Were Wendell and Maisie a couple? Could I find proof that they were?

I could access neither of their Facebook accounts, but Newton Lock and Key had both a Facebook page and a website, with photos of the company's various departments and the employees who manned them. Wendell appeared on the first page, sitting behind a massive desk with a smile on his face and a key as long as a shoebox in his hands. Below his photo was the caption *We've Found the Key to Success Here at Newton.* Subsequent pages included group pictures of the Newton employees in their various divisions. I spotted Otis, Gilbert, and Maisie in the production department, Hetty in accounts, Astrid Peterson in reception, Stretch and Arlin in shipping and receiving, and several of the other musicians in photos of the company's

Halloween party, Thanksgiving luncheon, and Christmas party. But I found nothing that would link Maisie and Wendell romantically.

I googled Wendell to discover citations he'd received for both his community service and his philanthropic efforts to build a municipal pool, a Little League field, a hockey rink, and an animal shelter. I found links from his name to an event schedule that listed where the Guten Tags would be entertaining in and around the state, along with the Little Bitte Band, the Brassed Offs, and Das Bier Band. Looked to me as if they traveled together a whole lot, which would have been perfect for Maisie and Wendell, especially if Maisie's husband didn't travel with them. If their appearances included overnight stays, well . . . how convenient was that?

I allowed myself a self-satisfied smile. I was so right about this.

I entered Maisie Barnes in my search field and, except for her name being mentioned as part of the Little Bitte Band, I got bupkis. But when I accessed the Iowa White Pages directory, I found her address, age, and the additional detail that she was related to Dale Barnes, who, I discovered after a search on that name, resided at the same address. So Maisie's gold band wasn't simply a piece of random jewelry. She was indeed married . . . . to some poor shmuck who was being cuckolded up the wazoo.

The confirmation caused thoughts to crowd my head like gumballs in a vending machine.

Had I attributed the wrong motivation to Zola's assailant? Had the purpose been to kill her not for what she *might* reveal but for what she'd *already* revealed? She'd dissected Wendell under a microscope, and he hadn't liked it. Did Wendell and Maisie want Zola out of the picture before she had an opportunity to broadcast the results of his disastrous reading to the other band members? Was that why Maisie and Zola had been best friends for all of ten seconds?

I stared at a phone number scratched into the stall's partition, mentally dazed.

But if Maisie and Wendell were a couple, why was Wendell hitting on Bernice?

Unless . . .

My mind kicked into overdrive.

Could Maisie have acted on her own and not told Wendell about her murder plot until *after* the fact? Wendell had admitted that Maisie always followed through and never disappointed — that she was his go-to person. But this time, could he have been so appalled by her deed that instead of offering his expected congratulations, he'd condemned her? Was that the reason he was fawning over Bernice? To make an obvious show of depriving Maisie of his affection? To punish her in the most public and hurtful way possible?

Which led me to my next question.

Were they even a couple anymore?

In the distance, I heard the first strains of oompah music ring out from the dining room, causing a muscle to clench involuntarily in my stomach.

If Wendell had dumped Maisie, she might be putting on a good act right now, but she was probably seething inside, a ticking time-bomb ready to explode. And if he was pouring salt into her wound by flirting with Bernice, then . . . then . . .

I stuffed my phone back into my shoulder bag and unlatched the stall door.

Then Bernice could be in grave danger. What was the old saying — in for a penny, in for a pound? If Maisie had killed once, she was already looking at capital murder charges, so she'd have nothing to lose by killing twice. Was there any better way to get even with a former lover than by offing his latest flirtation? Which meant . . .

Omigod. Bernice could be next.

I dashed into the hallway, startled by the sounds that greeted me. Foot-stomping so raucous, the floor vibrated. Whistling so shrill, my ears crackled. Clapping so loud, it drowned out the music. Was that the audience's intent? To muffle the band's presentation with an outburst of moblike behavior? Or were they simply aiming to muffle the sour notes of the one band member who lacked any talent at all?

Oh, geez. Poor Dad.

Fraught with anxiety, I raced into the dining room . . . to find the boisterous mob on its feet, arms intertwined, hips swinging, feet clacking, dancing in the aisles and between tables, gyrating to a polka that the Guten Tags' accordion player was pounding out like Myron Floren on steroids. His fingers flew over the keyboard and button board with wild abandon, creating a sound so exciting, so heart-pumping, his fellow band members simply stepped aside to give him room. The audience cheered. The audience laughed. Even the waitstaff deserted their posts to kick up their heels with the guests. He played with the ease of a lifelong musician and the confidence of a virtuoso — like Yo-Yo Ma on his cello, Ringo on his snare drum, Schroeder on his toy piano. His performance was flawless. Breathtaking.

Spectacular. But the only thing I could do was gawk.

Dad?

SIXTEEN

The lunch crowd adored him.

He received so many standing ovations, he was basically forced to play right through everyone else's slot. By the time we dragged him off the stage to board the bus, he'd depleted his playlist while the other musicians had gotten off not a single note, which kinda explained their grumpiness as they stomped out of the dining room. I volunteered to help Dad pack up while Wally and Etienne herded guests across the parking lot to the coach. I greeted him with a bewildered smile and the question of the hour.

"What was that?"

He looked burdened with guilt as he opened Astrid's instrument case and maneuvered the accordion into its foam insets. "I hogged all the time. You suppose the real musicians were okay with that?"

"Real musicians? Dad, you just entertained us with an hour's worth of flawlessly played polka music. You *are* a real musician." Although I couldn't have made that statement last night. "What did you do? How did you do it?"

He shrugged as he closed the lid and secured the locks. "I didn't look at the sheet music."

"Okay. And then what?"

"Nothin'."

"C'mon, Dad. Last night you couldn't buy a chord. Today you're inventing new ones. What changed?"

A one-shouldered shrug. "I did what I used to do before my teacher found out I couldn't read music. I just let my fingers play the songs I hear in my head."

I narrowed my eyes. "You mean, you play by ear?"

"Guess so."

"So . . . you can play anything?"

"Gotta hear it first."

"Holy crap, Dad. You're a musical genius! They should have treated you like . . . like a child prodigy when you were growing up."

He shook his head. "Before you can be a prodigy, you gotta know how to read sheet music, and I couldn't." He let out a rueful laugh. "They didn't think your ole dad was too bright back then, hon."

"Well, they were wrong, and now you've been discovered. You're going to be the next great sensation, Dad. I can see it all now. The seventies had the Rubik's Cube. The nineties had Tickle Me Elmo. The new millennium will have" — I opened my palm and panned across the headlines of an imaginary newspaper — "Bob Andrew, accordionist extraordinaire. You'll probably get your own action figure!"

Dad sighed. "Hope not. It'll be just one more thing the grandsons can sneak into the bathroom to clog the toilet."

I was all smiles as I escorted him through the dining room beneath the admiring eyes and congratulatory handshakes of the restaurant staff and guests. In the space of an hour he'd become king for the day. The toast of the town. The gold standard against which all other accordion players would heretofore be judged. "Spread the word," I advised the hostess on our way out the front entrance. "Bob Andrew. Windsor City, Iowa. He's available for weddings, anniversaries, football games, and bar mitzvahs."

Not that she understood a word I said, but the grin on Dad's face told me it made him feel pretty special.

Etienne met us at the rear door of the coach, and it was obvious that something was up. "The authorities in Munich have lowered the boom. They'll be meeting our bus the minute it arrives back at the hotel."

For the third time in as many days we trooped into the Prince Ludwig room, but we weren't expecting another commendation from the mayor. We were expecting to be grilled — a process that started less than a minute after we'd seated ourselves and been introduced to the officer in charge, Kriminaloberkommissar Axel Horn.

He spoke perfect English with no trace of an accent, which gave me hope that he might allow us to call him something other than Kriminaloberkommissar, which I suspected none of us could twist our tongues around. Standing in the front of the room with his arms folded and feet braced apart, he studied our faces as if his mere gaze could detect guilt like an X-ray could detect broken bones. "Before we begin, would anyone like to confess to the murder of Zola Czarnecki?"

Gasps of shock. Murmurs of disbelief.

Wow. Talk about cutting to the chase. Just one more example of German efficiency.

"Someone killed her?" cried Maisie. "But . . . what about her heart condition? Wally told us —"

"How'd it happen?" Bernice called out. "When they loaded her onto the gurney she looked okay, except for the fact that she wasn't breathing."

"Are you accusing one of *us* of killing her?" demanded Gilbert Graves.

"Yes," admitted Horn. "I am." He loosened the tie at his throat and unbuttoned the placket of his sport coat. He carried no notebook, iPad, or clipboard. This guy was apparently so well versed with the case that he kept all the details tucked away in his head. "Who are the smokers in the group? Please identify yourselves."

Heads turned left and right, but no one raised their hand.

"No smokers among you? Not even one?"

"Maisie Barnes smokes," Hetty offered helpfully.

"I do not," Maisie fired back. "I'm quitting. Everyone knows that."

"Frau Barnes?" Horn drilled her with a no-nonsense look. "Please show me what you claim not to be smoking."

"It's an e-cigarette." She reached into her shoulder bag and fished out the device, holding it above her head for his perusal. "No smoke involved. Just vaporized liquid."

"Do you refill the cartridge yourself?"

"Sure do. It's a lot cheaper than the

disposable prefilled kind. But what does my e-cigarette have to do with Zola's death?"

"Frau Czarnecki was poisoned with liquid nicotine, which is conveniently contained in a refill bottle for an e-cigarette."

More gasps.

Maisie, however, remained oddly impassive. "So?"

"So . . . were you carrying a refill bottle in your bag last night, Frau Barnes?"

"I always carry a refill with me."

"I'd like to see it, please."

She shook her head. "Can't help you."

Horn tipped his head slightly, as if to indicate checkmate. "So you disposed of the bottle after you poisoned Frau Czarnecki at the Hippodrom last night?"

Maisie stared at him, aghast. "Are you crazy? I *liked* Zola. Why would I want to kill her?"

"I intend to find out, Frau Barnes. But since you are the only member of your tour group who is known to be in possession of liquid nicotine, the mantle of guilt seems to fall squarely on your shoulders."

Maisie looked him squarely in the eye. "I don't think so."

"Really? And why is that?"

She sat up straighter in her chair. "Because at some point between the time I left my hotel room and the time our band left the stage last night, my refill was stolen out of my shoulder bag. I couldn't have poisoned Zola even if I'd wanted to. I had nothing to poison her *with.*"

"How very convenient. And I should believe you why?"

Her voice turned hard. "Because . . . it's the truth?"

"Excuse me." Mom waved her hand in the air. "Did someone we know die?"

"Besides," Maisie continued, "you can't pin this on me and make it stick. Nicotine refills are sold in every corner store. I'm not the only guest on this tour with exclusive access to them. I'm just the guest who got pickpocketed. And furthermore . . ." She heaved herself to her feet. "If someone in this room is the thief, I have a warning for you. If liquid nicotine comes in contact with your skin, it can kill you, so I hope you took some precautions when you used it because if you didn't, you'll be joining Zola in the morgue." She dropped back into her chair.

A nervous undercurrent swept through the room. Osmond rose politely to his feet. "If that stuff is so toxic, why do you carry it around with you?"

"Hey, no one uses it except me, and I'm always extra careful, so what's the big deal?"

"The big deal is, you just said it can kill us," huffed Lucille.

Maisie's voice grew tight. "Not if you avoid direct contact."

"What I want to know is, if that liquid is so toxic, why do you *smoke* it?" Tilly inquired.

"I don't smoke it. I vape it."

"What's that mean?" asked Nana.

"It means she smokes it," said Dick Teig.

"I do not! I don't even inhale."

"Just like Bill Clinton!" enthused Mom.

"You might as well be carrying unexploded ordnance around with you," Dick Stolee accused. He gestured toward Horn. "Don't you people have laws against carrying weapons-grade material around in purses?"

"Our tobacco laws apply to minors and vending machines, not to purses." Horn nodded toward Maisie. "Frau Barnes, perhaps you would show the other guests what the bottle in question looks like as a point of reference."

"I — uh, I don't have one with me."

He lifted his brows. "Was it not you who claimed to carry a refill with you at all times?"

"I stuck a fresh bottle in my shoulder bag this morning, but when we left the castle, my bag broke and just about everything fell out." She held her detached strap up as evidence. "I haven't seen it since. It's probably still rolling down the hill."

I exchanged a furtive look with Etienne, who'd stashed it in his pocket, then felt my heart nearly burst from my chest as I was struck by a sudden paralyzing fear. *What if the bottle leaks?*

"Well, that's just great," railed Dick Stolee. "What if some kid finds it lying on the side of the road and decides to play with it? *You* might know not to touch the stuff, but the kid doesn't. Victim number two, coming right up."

"There was *no* victim number one," yelled Maisie. "I *did not* kill Zola."

Kriminaloberkommissar Horn cleared phlegm from his throat like a faulty muffler expels exhaust — with ear-popping explosiveness. "Thank you," he said after every eye in the room riveted on him. "Since we appear to have reached a temporary impasse, I believe this would be a good time to re-create the scene of the crime. If you would be so kind as to ignore my lack of artistic ability."

He strode to the whiteboard that spanned the front wall and picked up a black marker from the tray. At the top of the board he wrote the word *Hippodrom.* Beneath that he drew three rectangles, each one over a yard long. "The rectangles represent the three tables you occupied in the festival tent last night. I've made them overly large to provide you plenty of space to indicate where you sat in relation to Frau Czarnecki. If you would be so good as to write your name in the location where you sat, it would be most helpful."

He recapped the marker and stared at the group.

The group sat quietly and stared back.

"I mean for you to do it *now,*" he barked. "Everyone up. Form a queue."

We merged into some semblance of a line, with Bernice pushing her way to the front and grabbing a marker. "Are your little boxes lined up from right to left or left to right?"

Horn blinked. "What?"

Bernice rolled her eyes. "I sat at the table closest to the partition. So, depending on your perspective, I could either be sitting at *this* table" — she flicked her hand toward the rectangle on the far right — "or *this* table" — the rectangle on the far left.

"If I could intercede briefly," said Etienne as he uncapped a marker. "My wife and I presided over tables one and two." He wrote our names in the center of the appropriate rectangle. "Our tour director, Mr. Peppers, was responsible for table three. I suspect this might help guests remember where they sat."

It helped the musicians. As for the rest of the gang? Not so much.

"I'm telling you, Helen, I sat right here." Dick Teig rapped his knuckle beneath the name he'd just written. "Table one. With Emily."

"You did not. You sat with Etienne and Dick."

"Stolee and I *both* sat with Emily. Tell her, Dick."

Dick Stolee sidled up to him and whispered out the side of his mouth, "Let it go, bud. That was today."

Nana picked up a marker. "Are we s'posed to mark where we was sittin' before or after we changed places?"

Horn strolled over to her. "When did you change places?"

"It was on account of them folks what thought we was celebrities. We had to pose for pictures, but when the food started comin' we had to sit down real quick, so we ended up in other spots on the bench."

"Write your name in the place you sat to eat your meal," instructed Horn.

"Should we write our name if we didn't eat anything?" asked Margi.

Horn regarded her oddly before focusing on Nana once again. "There were photos?"

"You bet. You wanna see? I got lots." She whipped her phone out of her jacket pocket. Horn turned around to face the room.

"How many of you took photos on your camera phones last night?"

Just about every hand in the room went up.

"I would like to see them. Please, form a queue behind the podium."

While the room erupted in another mass movement, I wrote my name on the whiteboard, then handed the marker to Mom. "You were sitting next to me last night, Mom, so you can write your name right here." I tapped my finger on the board.

"Why am I doing this?" she asked as she dutifully penned her name.

"To help the police with their investigation."

"What are they investigating?"

It took only a few minutes for Horn to examine a gazillion digital photos, a circumstance that related more to subject matter than German efficiency. "Did any of you take a photo of anything other than your own face?" he asked with frustration.

"Like what, for instance?" asked Margi.

"Like group photos. Table shots. Who was conversing with whom."

"I have a dynamite selection that I took at the site where that bomb exploded," offered Bernice. "Real Pulitzer Prize–winning stuff. You wanna see those?"

"For what reason?" asked Horn.

She shrugged. "You need a reason?"

He grabbed the edges of the podium, his knuckles turning white. "Has everyone posted their name on the board?"

Nods. Yups. You bets.

"I will ask once more. Would any of you like to confess to the murder of Zola Czarnecki?"

Head shaking. Shrugs. Blank looks.

A hand shot into the air. "I'd like to make a confession."

Gasps. The loudest of which was my own when I saw who'd said it.

"You are . . . ?" asked Horn.

"Wendell Newton." He nodded toward the whiteboard. "Table two. Trumpet player for the Guten Tags. I had a run-in with Zola yesterday in Oberammergau, so I wanted to 'fess up. She told my fortune, and —"

"Explain, please?"

"She was a self-proclaimed psychic. A fortuneteller."

"She preferred the term *clairvoyant,*" corrected Dick Stolee.

"Anyway," Wendell continued, "she told my fortune, and I didn't like what she had to say, so I reacted like a hothead and said some pretty unkind things. I shouldn't have lost my temper, but I did. I acted like a real jerk. Doesn't make me feel very proud. I'm usually pretty level-headed, but what she said just hit me the wrong way, and I overreacted. Emily witnessed the whole event, so she can verify what a dope I was. So I'd like to apologize to Emily for my bad attitude, and if Zola were here I'd apologize to her too. And I'm sorry for the bad example I set for all my employees who've come to expect better from me."

Horn lifted his brows in a questioning look. "Emily is . . . ?"

I inched my hand into the air. "Emily Miceli. Co-owner of the tour company."

"And the reason I'm telling you this," Wendell continued, "is because I might have been fuming with Zola yesterday, but I sure as hell didn't kill her."

Horn nodded. "Thank you, Mr. Newton. Anyone else at table two who didn't kill Frau Czarnecki?"

Otis, Gilbert, and Hetty shot their hands into the air, followed by Osmond, George,

Dad, and Dick Stolee. Helen Teig fired an impatient look at her husband before she whacked his arm. "Raise your hand, Dick."

"But I didn't sit at table two."

"Yes, you did."

"No, I didn't."

She hoisted his arm in the air for him. "My husband didn't kill her either. Dick Teig. Table two. Idiot."

"Does Mr. Teig play a musical instrument?" asked Horn.

"No," Wally spoke up. "Table two was a mixed bag — the Guten Tag band and several non-musicians. The other three bands sat at table three."

Horn studied the whiteboard. "How many guests on the tour in all?"

"Thirty-two," said Wally. "Including me."

Horn paused. "Then why are there only thirty names on the board?"

All eyes flew to the whiteboard. Gazes narrowed. Lips moved silently as everyone started counting.

"That's probably because them two women what aren't here can't write their names down on account of they're dead," said Nana.

An awkward silence flooded the room. Well, *duh*?

"Sorry," Wally apologized. "I gave you the

284

wrong head count. We're presently down to thirty guests."

"Yes," said Horn, "but last night at the Hippodrom Frau Czarnecki was still alive, bringing the count to thirty-one names. So would someone kindly show me where she was sitting?"

"I can do that," said Wally. "She was at my table."

As he grabbed a marker off the tray, Nana raised her hand. "S'cuse me, young man, will you be wantin' to know where we ended up sittin' after we come back from goin' potty?"

Horn stared at her, nonplussed.

"Personally, I think colored markers would make our seating-arrangement plan look much more attractive," said Margi.

"Hey, I've got some." Dick Teig removed two permanent marker pens from his jacket pocket. "But they're for emergency use only — in case Helen's eyebrows get washed off in a torrential downpour and she needs a touchup."

Mom squinted at the board. "Are those names in alphabetical order?"

"Would you mind giving us some idea about how much longer you're going to keep us here?" Otis called out to Horn. He tapped his watch with an impatient finger.

"We have an engagement this evening."

"Playing in one of the premier beer halls," boasted Stretch.

"Does anyone know what time?" asked a member of Das Bier Band.

"Six twenty," said Dick Stolee, reading the digital readout on his phone.

"But it's six twenty now," Lucille pointed out.

"Why wasn't anyone watching the time?" cried Helen. "We're late!"

"I'll be damned if I'm gonna get shut out of two performances in one day," swore Gilbert.

"It's every man for himself," bellowed Dick Teig as he led the stampede toward the exit.

Amid the chaos of instrument case grabbing, overturned chairs, and random shoving, I glanced at the large block letters Wally had printed on the rectangle representing table three.

ZOLA CZARNECKI.

He'd inserted her name at the far end of the bench.

Right next to Maisie Barnes.

SEVENTEEN

"Sitzen Sie Hin!" demanded Kriminaloberkommissar Horn.

They continued to charge into the hall like escapees from a burning building.

"SIT DOWN," barked Horn as the last of them squeezed through the door.

I wasn't going to waste my breath trying to explain to a law-and-order German that a dyed-in-the-wool Iowan would rather flout the law than be late. I doubt he'd understand. "They probably won't get any farther than the lobby before they reach an impasse," I said as I joined the men at the front of the room. "The bus isn't here to take them anyplace."

Eyes wild, veins bulging in his forehead, Horn let fly a string of German that exploded like firecrackers.

"They're usually quite law-abiding, Herr Inspektor," Etienne explained in a placating tone. "But since I've come to live among them, I've discovered that the guiding force in their lives is the clock. When a guest mentioned the time, it was all over but for the stampede."

Horn rebuttoned his jacket and tightened the knot on his necktie. "A group interrogation. What was I thinking? I'll need to speak to them individually then. At the police station. Tomorrow. And I apologize for asking, but the elderly woman with the — the facial boils —" He fluttered his fingers around his cheeks to indicate her disturbing countenance.

"She's not contagious," I snapped.

Wally cringed. "Can you work with us on timing? We'll have to juggle our schedule. We need a good two and a half hours to reach Kehlstein tomorrow, so the earlier you could conduct the interviews, the better it would work out for us."

Horn removed a card from his wallet and handed it to Wally. "That's the address. Give it to your coach driver. Interviews will begin promptly at seven o'clock in the morning."

Uff-da. I could hear the whining now. "What are the odds that you'll be able to coax more out of them privately than you did in today's group setting?"

"Slim. But that won't prevent me from trying. Your guests have dug in their heels.

288

They know nothing. They killed no one. But one of them will make a mistake. They always do."

I nodded toward the whiteboard. "How important is it that Maisie Barnes was sitting next to Zola Czarnecki last night?"

Horn turned to face the whiteboard, eyeing the name that Wally had written. "It's of no importance if I fail to place the nicotine in Frau Barnes's hand and prove that she used it to poison the victim. She claims her own refill was stolen from her purse. How do I prove otherwise? If Frau Barnes is not telling the truth, she's a very skilled liar."

"But is she your prime suspect?"

"I've not singled out a prime suspect, Mrs. Miceli. Every one of your guests will be under suspicion until they've been successfully cleared." He removed a small plastic bag. "Thank you for turning this over to me, Mr. Miceli. The lab analysis may be able to tell us if this is the same brand that killed Frau Czarnecki."

"And if it is?" I asked.

"Then we will have one piece of concrete evidence with which to work."

Etienne reverted to his police inspector's voice. "Ms. Czarnecki was scheduled to tell everyone's fortune after the Oktoberfest event last night, Herr Inspektor, so perhaps our perpetrator is someone who feared the woman might uncover a secret that could be irreparably damaging to them? It certainly speaks to motive."

"A plausible theory," commended Horn, "leaving me with the simple task of uncovering the deepest, darkest secrets of thirty American tourists."

"Twenty-nine," quipped Wally. "I don't have any secrets."

"Nonetheless. Forgive me for hoping your theory is wrong, Mr. Miceli" — Horn bowed his head politely — "because if you're correct, we may never discover who killed Frau Czarnecki. I'm a detective, not a mind reader."

"I was presented with a case in Switzerland some years ago that dealt with a similar issue," Etienne recalled, capturing Horn's undivided attention. "Perhaps you're familiar with the details." So while the two inspectors exchanged fish stories, I cornered Wally.

"Do you happen to be carrying in your bag of tricks a list of all the room changes we've had in this hotel since we arrived?" I nodded at the soft-sided messenger bag he'd propped against the wall.

"Yeah. I'm a notorious hoarder of useless

documentation. What do you want to know?"

"The night we arrived, what other guests were located on the same floor as Bernice?"

Hauling his bag off the floor, he set it on the podium and pulled out a file. He scanned a page at the back of a sheaf of papers. "Let's see: Bernice Zwerg . . . Bernice Zwerg . . . there she is." He continued scanning. "Okay. Easy enough. There was only one other guest on her floor that first night."

"Maisie Barnes?"

He shook his head. "Astrid Peterson."

"Astrid Peterson? But . . . are you sure?"

Margi Swanson hurried into the room in a breathless panic. "Officer! You've gotta come quick. Somebody stole our bus."

Was Wendell having affairs with both Maisie and Astrid?

We'd hoofed it to the beer hall in the old city, avoiding major thoroughfares and pausing a couple of times to watch street performers who, at the toss of an onlooker's coin, morphed from statue stillness to robotic animation like life-size music box dancers. The beer hall was more intimate than the Hippodrom had been, with lower ceilings, longer tables, and chairs rather than benches. But, like the Hippodrom, it was filling up fast with dozens of guests from other tour groups. The musicians stowed their instrument cases in a storage area, then joined the rest of us in the dining room, visibly champing at the bit to hit the stage. Excitement was too passive a term to describe their exuberance.

They were stoked.

"I think we should start out with everyone's favorite: 'Beer Barrel Polka,' " suggested Maisie, "then explode into the 'Maine Stein Song.' " She sat opposite me, next to Stretch, while I sat beside Arlin, the four of us holding down the far end of the table.

"But we haven't cleared our playlist with the other bands yet," objected Stretch.

"Yeah," Arlin agreed. "Wendell won't like it if we steal his thunder by playing all the good songs first."

"Wendell's a big boy," countered Maisie. "He should know how to handle a little disappointment by this period in his life."

"I'm just saying," repeated Arlin. "He won't like it."

Maisie grinned. "C'est la vie. I just slipped the maitre d' a cash incentive to let us play first, so the fix is already in. Just protecting our interests, fellas. First is always best. You know that. Am I right, Emily?"

I flashed a smile, trying to imagine what Maisie's reaction would be if she learned Wendell might have been two-timing her. "First is good . . . but last has its place. Like, say . . . with romantic relationships. Would you rather be someone's first love or last love?"

"Hmm," said Maisie. "Good question." Elbows on the table, she fisted her hands in the air as if they were the scales of justice. She opened her right palm. "On the one hand, being someone's first love leaves you with a life's worth of magical memories." She opened the left. "But on the other hand, being someone's last love means you're the one who inherits all the perks. So I'd have to say . . . I'd rather be someone's last love."

Interesting how she could make a statement like that while cheating on her husband. Boy, her conscience was really missing in action.

"My first love *was* my last love," Stretch announced proudly. "I married Verna straight out of high school, and we've been together ever since. Forty-five years now."

"They celebrated the big forty-fifth at the country club last summer," said Arlin. "What a bash. The champagne was flying."

"And the food!" Maisie dug out her

phone. "What a feast! A fountain of chocolate for dipping strawberries . . . smoked salmon . . . shrimp cocktail . . . caviar . . ."

"I scarfed down half a bowl of caviar before I realized it wasn't boysenberry jam." Arlin grimaced. "There's times when I swear I can still taste it. Who eats that stuff?"

Maisie began flipping through screens. "But the pièce de résistance was the ice carving — a supersized reproduction of an Iowa hog."

"It was big as a small mastodon," said Arlin. "Musta weighed half a ton."

"My folks raised swine," acknowledged Stretch, "so Verna and I had the carving done to honor their one contribution to our marriage." He smiled shyly. "Me."

"Here you go." Maisie handed her phone across the table to me. "Just keep flipping through. Arlin can tell you who's who."

"That's Verna and Stretch in front of the dessert table," said Arlin. "I suppose you could've guessed that."

I flipped to a new screen. "That's Bessie and Bob — Stretch's mom and dad — standing in front of the hog. Can you see the tears in their eyes? Emotion pretty much got the better of them when they saw that pig."

New screen. "All the kids and grandkids.

Don't ask me their names because I don't know — there's too dang many of them. That family of yours breeds like rabbits, Stretch."

New screen. Arlin chuckled. "A selfie of Maisie and Dale. How many years you two been married now, Maisie?"

"Ever since 2009."

My eyes widened involuntarily. Holy crap. Maisie's husband, Dale, wasn't a "he."

Dale Barnes was a "she."

A waitress in full Bavarian costume paused beside Maisie, leaned over to whisper something in her ear, and discretely handed her something beneath the table.

"But . . . he can't do that!" Maisie complained. "We had a deal."

"Es tut mir leid," the waitress said in an apologetic voice before scurrying away.

Jaw squared, lips pursed, eyes narrowed, Maisie held up the twenty-euro note she'd just been handed and regarded it sourly. "Chiseler."

"Does this mean we won't be going first after all?" asked Arlin.

The maitre d' strode toward the stage area and stood behind a microphone, his tuxedo and hot pink cummerbund making him look as if he belonged on the top tier of a wedding cake. "Ladies and gentlemen, I welcome you to the most famous beer hall in the Old City of Munich."

Applause. Hoots. Whistles.

"We've altered our scheduled musical entertainment for the evening due to a rather extraordinary circumstance. I received a telephone call late this afternoon from another restaurant alerting me to the fact that a musician blessed with truly epic talent will be joining us in this very beer hall tonight."

"Are we getting shafted by a local?" whispered Maisie.

"We can listen to the music of our beloved oompah bands at any time," he continued, "on our old vinyl records, on our iPods, on YouTube. But an opportunity to hear a true master only comes along once in a lifetime. So this evening, instead of asking the brave Americans who performed like heroes at the site of the explosion near the Marienplatz to entertain us, we would like to impose upon the goodwill of a single musician to delight us all with an evening of melodious magic."

"Is he saying we don't get to play at all?" griped Stretch.

Spines stiffened around the table as tensions rose and tempers frayed.

"Ladies and gentlemen, please put your

hands together to welcome the Mozart of the piano accordion, the maestro of the button keyboard, Bob Andrew!"

Uh-oh. This wasn't good. This wasn't good at all.

Submerged up to my chin in a snowscape of bath bubbles, I was happily reliving Dad's show-stopping performance in my head while coming to grips with the evening's most unexpected revelation.

I'd been so wrong.

Now that my blinders were off, I realized that Maisie and Wendell had *not* been engaged in a torrid affair. Maisie was blissfully married and batting for the other team, so she had no interest in Wendell's equipment. Of course, that didn't disqualify her as a suspect in Zola's murder, but it sure blew a huge hole in the motive I'd assigned her.

I was feasting on crow like Arlin had feasted on caviar.

Way to jump to conclusions, I scolded myself. But at least there was an upside to my miscalculation.

I didn't have to worry about Maisie knocking off Bernice in a fit of jealous rage.

I scooped up a handful of bubbles and blew them into the air.

So if Maisie had no reason to kill Zola, who *did* kill her? It had to have been one of the musicians, didn't it? It couldn't have been a complete stranger, could it?

I was so confused.

I poked my foot up through the bath water to tease the bubbles with my toe.

Despite Wendell's impassioned speech to Officer Horn, I wasn't quite willing to let him off the hook yet. He might not have been involved with Maisie, but he'd obviously been up to his ears in an intimate relationship with Astrid. I understood now why we'd found so much sexy lingerie hanging in her closet. Her nighties might have been old, but they were being put to good use on what I suspected was a regular basis. Heck, she'd packed enough of them to star in her own erotic film flick.

My toe stilled in the air as a wild thought danced in my head.

Omigod. You don't suppose . . .

I recalled an image of Wendell's super-duper camera — the one that had the ability to produce movie-quality video. He'd confessed to being a frustrated film director — an Otto Preminger wannabe. Was he dabbling with movie making? But not family movies — underground movies . . . Internet movies . . . racy flicks of Astrid in her retro-chic lingerie?

Eww. Had he turned Astrid Peterson into a starlet in the world of senior erotica? Was there even such a thing as senior erotica? And if there was, had Wendell been Astrid's producer, director, and videographer rather than her lover? In it for the art rather than the recreational activity?

An affair with a subordinate at his company was one thing, but if he had a secret life that revolved around filming and posting girly videos online, that was a whole other kettle of fish. If something like that ever leaked to the community —

Wendell would be washed up. Finished. A man with that much to lose would indeed have a great deal to fear from a psychic.

But if he had that much to lose, why did he risk having Zola tell his fortune in the first place? asked the voice inside my head.

Hubris? Had he been so convinced she was a fraud that he hadn't thought her capable of sniffing out his secret? But her prediction had apparently cut so close to the bone that her very presence on the tour became a threat.

So he'd killed her.

He'd pinched Maisie's nicotine from her handbag, and, at some point during the Hippodrom performance, he'd used it to poison Zola's food.

But how to prove it?

I stared at the dissolving bubbles, smiling when I hit upon a simple solution.

Why, I'd prove it the old-fashioned way.

I'd have my loyal band of computer whizzes and Internet hackers do the footwork for me!

I shot out of the tub, toweled dry, shrugged into my bathrobe, and rushed into the bedroom.

"Out so soon?" questioned Etienne. "I was going to join you."

I grabbed my phone. "Hold that thought." At this late hour, I couldn't call a group meeting, so I'd send out a bulk text: *NEED YOUR HELP TO CRACK ZOLA'S MURDER. PLEASE CHECK INTERNET SITES (LEGITIMATE OR NOT) TO LOCATE EROTIC VIDEOS OF ASTRID PETERSON. SEXY SENIOR FILMS. RACY RETRO FILMS. SHE PROBABLY USED FAKE NAME. KEEP RECORD OF CHARGES. I'LL REIMBURSE. THANKS. E.*

"Voilà." I set down my phone and dusted off my hands. "I have a new theory."

"Do you now." He yanked his shirttails out of his trousers and walked over to me. With a languid gesture, he loosened the belt at my waist. "I never fail to be fascinated by your theories." He coaxed my robe away from my neck and pressed his lips to the

300

hollow beneath my collarbone. "Shall we continue this conversation in the bathtub?"

Ting! Ting! Ting!

I grabbed my phone.

From Dick Stolee: *I LIKE THE WAY YOU THINK.*

From Helen Teig: *I WOULD RATHER PIERCE MY EYES WITH HOT POKERS THAN ACCESS ANY OF THOSE FILTHY INTERNET SITES. SO, WHEN DO YOU NEED THE INFORMATION?*

From Nana: *DO YOU KNOW GEORGE'S ROOM NUMBER?*

Etienne eased the phone from my hand before I could read any more. "But —"

I bit back the rest of my sentence as my bathrobe glided down my body to puddle at my feet.

EIGHTEEN

"I don't get your father." Nana sat beside me the next morning as we headed for the southeasternmost tip of Germany, where the Bavarian Alps rub shoulders with the Austrian Alps. Even though Dr. Fischer had said her skin condition would improve within forty-eight hours, I couldn't see much change. Her face was still a lumpy mass of boils and blisters. "When Bob was onstage in that festival tent, he couldn't play nuthin' but sour notes. Last night in the beer hall, you'da thought he was channelin' that fella what plays on *Lawrence Welk*. How'd he do that? Emergency visit to one a them Suzuki music schools?"

"The difference was he chucked the sheet music, which he's never been able to read, and went with his gut, or rather his ear, which he excels at. But why were you surprised? You heard him play for a whole hour at the Neuschwanstein restaurant yesterday."

"I couldn't hear nuthin' with them earplugs of mine. Shoot. I thought all the hullabaloo was folks tryin' to boot him off the stage." She reached into her jacket pocket and plucked out her earplugs, cupping them in her palm. "Guess you get what you pay for. I splurged on the real good ones what was labeled industrial strength. Cost me a quarter more."

I rolled my eyes.

"Don't go pooh-poohin' me. It adds up."

We'd arrived at the police station this morning at precisely seven o'clock and were back on the bus by eight without a single person being cuffed, jailed, or detained for further questioning. I guess it was pretty difficult to squeeze incriminating statements out of a couple dozen guests who hadn't spoken to Zola outside the meet and greet, so we zipped through the formalities at lightning speed. In deference to Mom's condition, Officer Horn allowed me to accompany her during her interview, which began at 7:16 and ended at 7:17 when she excused herself for a "quickie," which in Mom's lexicon meant to organize the clutter on the room's bulletin board. I took this as a hopeful sign that she really *was* getting back to normal.

When it was my turn, I tested out my "Wendell as X-rated videographer" theory on Officer Horn and was rewarded with a polite but incredulous nod. "Seriously?" That's when his grin appeared. "You Americans are such Puritans, one wonders how you ever reproduce."

Well, I still believed in my theory, even if he didn't, so my goal today was to see if any of the Internet research I'd initiated had hit pay dirt. The whole gang was pretty animated this morning, bright-eyed and chatty, so I was getting a positive vibe that maybe one of them had found evidence that would back up my theory. All I needed to do was steal a few minutes with each of them, starting with Nana.

I leaned close to her. Keeping my voice low, I asked, "Did you have any success last night?"

"Define success."

"With your Internet search."

She bowed her head, causing all three of her chins to pancake onto her chest. "I done what you asked, dear, but I got a question. Is there a difference between them sites what advertises erotica and the ones what say they're triple-X rated?"

"Uhh . . . I think erotica implies a higher

level of good taste. Like romantic fantasy blended with enticing costumes and soft music. The triple X sites are probably a lot more hardcore — like everyone's body parts are front and center, overinflated, and ready to go."

"No kiddin'?" She gave a little suck on her uppers that ended in a woebegone expression. "Dang. I think me and George was lookin' at the wrong stuff."

"You didn't see any familiar faces?"

Her voice dropped an octave. "Faces?"

I didn't allow this to disappoint me. I had ten more gang members to check out. The odds were in my favor.

Halfway to our destination, we stopped for a comfort station break at a rest area whose supply of newspapers included the Munich edition that carried the article featuring the unlikely senior-citizen heroes from Iowa. Front page. Above the fold. Complete with group photo in vivid color. Problem was, it was written in German, so none of us could read it other than Etienne and Wally, although I wouldn't put it past Dad to attempt a translation if he suddenly remembered that he'd learned German in another lifetime.

Etienne purchased every copy on the shelf and handed them out to us on the bus so we could follow along as he translated the article. We applauded when he finished, basking in the afterglow of phrases like "unparalleled courage," "selfless spirit," "indefatigable grit," and "unprecedented mettle."

"They're applaudin' our metal?" Nana asked me. "Lucille musta told 'em about her hip replacement."

The real show-stopper, however, was the photograph, which caused more than a little head-scratching.

"Who's this woman with the bristly hair in the front row?" I overheard Stretch asking.

"I don't remember her at all," said Arlin. "She probably photo-bombed our shot."

"Publicity whore," sniped Hetty.

The fact that Bernice no longer looked like the woman in the newspaper wasn't lost on me. If she continued to use Tilly's cream, she'd probably be crowned America's Next Top Model.

As the landscape on the horizon mutated from riverbed flatness to saw-toothed ruggedness, Wally fired up the mike. "We're heading toward the town of Berchtesgaden, which originated as a Benedictine monastery in the eleventh century but later became famous for its salt mines, spas, ski resorts, wellness centers, and the Third Reich. It was here where Adolf Hitler decided to build his private residence and, after rising to power, his entire government headquarters. Allied forces destroyed all the buildings in a bombing raid in 1945, but one structure did survive, and that's what we'll be seeing today.

"The locals call it Kehlsteinhaus, but after the war the American military dubbed it the Eagle's Nest, and that name stuck. It sits on the peak of a six-thousand-foot mountain, the Kehlstein, and was built as a personal retreat and official guesthouse for the führer to mark his fiftieth birthday. Hitler is reputed to have visited the place all of two times, so it seems it was a gift that was little appreciated. But Hitler's loss is our gain because you'll never find a more spectacular view anywhere on earth."

"How many bedrooms?" asked Dick Teig.

"No bedrooms."

Collective gasps.

"What kind of guesthouse doesn't have bedrooms?" asked Lucille.

"The kind where guests aren't actually welcome," said Tilly.

"How's the temperature six thousand feet up?" Stretch tossed out.

"Glad you mentioned that," said Wally. "It

snowed in the higher elevations overnight, so if you have an extra jacket with you, bring it along. We'll be touring the inside of the house mostly, but if you venture outside to walk along the hiking trails, you might find things a bit nippy, if not downright frigid. However, you'll be happy to know there are refreshments available should you need to purchase a hot drink to thaw yourselves out."

"What about our performance schedule?" asked Wendell.

"I talked to the man in charge this morning, and everything's a go. Ten-minute slots for each band, so whatever you do, remember to pick up your instruments from the storage bay before we transfer from our coach to the Kehlstein bus."

Head-bobbing. Scattered applause. Murmurs of discontent.

Nana leaned toward me. "Them other musicians wasn't real happy with your father last night, dear."

"Ya think?"

"If I played in one of them bands, I wouldn't be happy neither if I got canned in favor of some upstart what can't read sheet music."

By the end of Dad's solo performance, you could have cut the tension in the air with a knife. The other band members sat stone-faced, not only refusing to applaud but refusing to even acknowledge his presence the rest of the evening, as if he'd donned a cloak of invisibility condemning him to non-person status. Of course, Dad was kept so busy signing autographs for the beer hall clientele that he was oblivious to all the emotional undercurrents — not that he would have been any more aware if he hadn't been preoccupied. Dad's social awareness radar always seemed to be happily stuck in the off position.

"We've arranged for everyone to eat lunch in the Kehlsteinhaus restaurant," Wally continued. "I'll hand out tickets that entitle you to a discount on your meal, so hang onto them. They equal money in your pocket. Any other questions?"

"Yeah," Dick Stolee spoke up. "Are we there yet?"

Though we were headed in the direction of Berchtesgaden, we bypassed the town in favor of the Kehlstein bus terminus, which was our transfer point. The building was a pretty ordinary one-story structure that reminded me of the tourist information facilities that popped up along our interstate highway systems. But this building boasted a huge advantage over state-funded American tourist bureaus.

This building had shopping. *Oh, boy!*

Wally made a final announcement as our driver cut the engine. "I'd like the musicians to pick up their instruments now so we won't run into any delays when we board the Kehlstein bus. We have about twenty minutes to kill, so ladies, get ready to power shop. They sell all German-made products here — everything from candy and beer steins to boiled wool jackets and sweaters — so it's a good time to add onto that Christmas list you've started."

The doors whooshed open.

"Musicians to the outside storage bay. Everyone else, happy shopping."

We streamed out the exits in surprisingly orderly fashion, with no one clambering over anyone else to be first into the store. I was a little taken aback by their uncharacteristically laid-back behavior, but when I spied the Dicks interacting with their wives, I stopped to give myself a hard pinch because I couldn't believe what I was seeing.

The Dicks and their wives were holding hands — and not only that, they were doing weird kissy things with their mouths and making moon eyes at each other. *Omigod.* They were acting like newlyweds. Like . . . like they couldn't get enough of each other.

310

Like . . . like they actually *liked* each other.

"Emily." Margi Swanson caught my arm and pulled me aside. "About that research project you assigned us last night. I came up empty. I didn't see anyone who looked like Astrid Peterson, although I really couldn't tell what any of those women looked like beneath all the makeup and hair and veils and feathers and sludge."

Sludge?

A look of desperation crept into her eyes as she glanced from her hands to the store. "I need to run into that place really quick. I hope they sell hand sanitizer. I accidentally used all mine up last night when I was watching the mud wrestling."

Okay, negative results so far from Margi, Nana, and George, but the odds were still in my favor.

Satisfied that Mom was in good hands as she waited by the storage bay with Dad, I hurried into the shop and caught up with Tilly in the over-the-counter travel medication section. "Do you have anything for me?"

"A website address." She slipped me a piece of paper. "I recall Ms. Peterson's costume more than I do her face, so I can't be entirely sure, but this could well be a match. I suggest you watch it yourself."

311

"Omigod, Tilly. You're amazing." I gave her a quick hug.

"I've written lengthy monographs on the importance of romance and erotica in other cultures, but I've never had the misfortune of actually witnessing physical reenactments over the Internet at such close range." She pushed her glasses up her nose and blinked myopically at the array of medications on the shelf. "Tell me, dear, do you see any eye drops?"

Dick Stolee and Grace cornered me near the alpine hats. "Say, Emily, do you happen to have a picture of that Peterson woman? Grace and I wasted about three hours checking out those websites of yours before we realized we didn't have a clue what she looked like." He cocked his head like a puppy and lapsed into baby talk as he patted Grace's cheek. "Isn't that wight, honey-bunny?"

She let out a girlish giggle and rubbed against him. "Yes, that's wight, sweetie-weetie."

Was this *my* doing? *Wow.* Talk about unintended consequences. "I'm sorry, you guys, but I don't have a photo."

Dick shrugged. "Well, we're not about to leave you in the lurch. We'll just keep looking, won't we, princess? Who knows? Maybe we'll get lucky."

Grace giggled again and stared at her husband with doe eyes, indicating that perhaps she'd already *gotten* lucky.

Knocked off-kilter by the Stolee's metamorphosis, I was happy to see Alice in the book and tape section, looking neither desperate, myopic, nor lovelorn. "Anything to report?"

She hung her head. "Abject failure. I'm so sorry, Emily."

"That's no problem. I can't expect miracles when I make last-minute requests like this."

"I couldn't remember if Astrid was the lady with the red hair or the platinum white, so I googled oompah bands in Iowa thinking I might find a picture of her band, and that sent me to YouTube, where I ran across a video of a singing dog, and that sent me to a skiing squirrel, and from there I accessed a whole section on bloopers, and after I watched those for a couple of hours, I forgot what I was looking for in the first place, so I went to bed."

I nodded my understanding. "It happens to the best of us, Alice." But my favorable odds were rapidly disappearing.

I tracked down Helen and Dick huddled in a corner with the stuffed mountain rescue dogs, lost in each other's eyes. "Who has the most beautiful eyes in the world?" Dick asked in a lovey-dovey voice.

"You do," cooed Helen.

"No, you do," insisted Dick.

"No, you do," chirped Helen.

I wasn't even going to bother asking them what they'd discovered. It was obvious the only thing Dick and Helen had found last night was each other.

"Get a room," Bernice crabbed at them as she joined me. She shook her head. "See what you started? The Teigs pawing each other in public. The Stolees asking the cashier if she's got any cheerleading outfits and pompoms in stock. The old married couples can't keep their hands off each other. It's disgusting. Yuck."

"I think it's rather nice."

"You would. Say, you need to place an order for me with Tilly. I want a whole case of that compound I'm using."

"Uhh — that's going to depend on how many batches she's cooked up back home."

"Why does she have to make it from scratch? Can't she just order it ready-made?"

"I don't know if her New Guinea supplier offers it ready-made."

"We live in a global economy. If they want

to compete with the big boys, they'll have ready-made. So I'd like my order express-mailed so it'll be waiting for me when I get home." She smoothed her hand over her cheek. "I don't want any interruptions in the treatment."

I looked across the store to find Tilly chatting with Nana at the front entrance. "She's standing right over there. Why don't you ask her yourself?"

"Because that's why we pay you the big bucks — to troubleshoot for us. Get with the program, honey."

I smiled stiffly. "So how'd your research assignment pan out last night?"

"Are you kidding me? With all the spying the government does on our Internet activity, you're telling me to watch naughty videos? Are you crazy?"

"I wasn't asking you to watch the really naughty stuff. I only wanted you to access the material that's considered titillating without being gross."

"Devout Lutherans don't do titillating. We're above that." She paused. "No. Let me rephrase that. We don't mind doing it *ourselves,* we're just not big into watching other people do it. So are you going to speak to Tilly for me?"

"You got it." At least I could be counted

on to frame the request a little more politely than Bernice would.

"Good. Now, point me in the direction of the restroom. My next beauty treatment is due in two minutes."

I scrubbed Bernice's name from my mental list. Ten down, two to go. Tilly's information could turn out to be a wash, so my whole theory basically rested on the findings of Lucille and Osmond, who were nowhere in sight. *Please have good news for me,* I thought as I scoured the store for them. *Please have good news for me,* I thought as I noticed the commotion in the parking lot near our tour bus.

Uh-oh. What was up with that?

After delivering Bernice's request to Tilly on my way out the door, I arrived on the scene to find both Wally and Etienne trying to pacify the musicians, who were making noises as if they were about to stage an open revolt, rattling their instrument cases in a manner reminiscent of peasants wielding pitchforks and torches.

"You *promised* us," said Wendell in a growly voice.

"What kind of raw deal is this anyway?" griped Otis. "A promise is a promise."

Wally threw his palms up in a helpless gesture. "I'm sorry! I'm not the manager of

Kehlsteinhaus. I have no control over the event schedule."

"What's happening?" I asked Arlin.

"Oh, the head honcho at the Eagle's Nest place called Wally to cancel our appearance because he's getting an unexpected visit from the Bavarian yodeling team that won some big state championship last week. So they're on and we're off. I guess yodeling trumps American heroism."

"That's terrible!" Not to mention gut-wrenchingly disappointing.

"I say you phone that fella back and give him a piece of our mind," barked Gilbert.

Head-nodding. A rowdy chorus of *hear, hear.*

"Yeah," cried Maisie. "He can't disrespect us like this."

Etienne removed his cell phone and held it aloft. "I'll make the call for you."

A cheer rose up as he separated himself from the group to conduct the call. After watching him listen, gesticulate wildly, and listen again, we held our collective breaths as he returned with a response.

"He apologizes for this embarrassing yet unavoidable turn of events, but he's willing to make a concession as a gesture of good faith. His Twitter feed has been lighting up with accolades for a visiting American musi-

317

cian, so he's willing to shave some time off the yodelers' performance to accommodate a fifteen-minute slot for our famed accordionist Bob Andrew."

"No kidding?" enthused Dad.

You could say that was the proverbial straw that broke the camel's back.

Jaws dropped. Nostrils flared. Fists doubled.

However, instead of becoming an angry mob, the musicians withdrew into the kind of bristling silence that signals both outrage and retaliation, and, like an army of drones, they returned their instruments to the storage bay and stormed away.

Standing beside Mom in the parking lot, Dad watched them leave, his hand secured around the handle of Astrid's accordion case. He stared after them, mystified. "Was it something I said?"

"The Kehlstein bus is here!" Wally announced as the big red vehicle pulled into the car park. "Let's go, people. Everybody climb aboard."

NINETEEN

The twenty-minute bus ride to the top of the six-thousand-foot mountain was a nail-biting rollercoaster adventure around hairpin turns that dropped off into nothingness and through cavernous tunnels that had been excavated by an army of Italian stonemasons. Our driver navigated the narrow road quite admirably, hugging the mountainside like bark on a tree, so the trip would have been uneventful if not for the trumpeter for the Brassed Offs. Overcome by a fit of acrophobia, he screamed "we're all going to die" on every death-defying switchback, which was about every thirty seconds. Not that anyone blamed him for his outbursts. He'd never set foot off Iowa soil until this trip, so he didn't realize he had a fear of heights.

We exited the bus on a broad plateau beneath the mountain peak to find the temperature cool enough to chill our hands and turn our noses red. Snow clung to the craggy bluff that towered above us, capping the jagged rocks like sea spume and giving no indication that it would melt anytime soon. At the very lip of the bluff sat Adolph Hitler's mountain retreat, a modestly sized structure whose exterior looked too unexceptional to qualify it for a spot in a Parade of Homes tour. In fact, from what little I could glimpse, it looked pretty ordinary in a commercial sort of way, but you couldn't beat the location. There probably were not too many houses built at the top of the world.

"There's a footpath from the parking area that allows you to hike the final four hundred feet to the top," Wally called out as he herded us toward what looked like a railway tunnel left over from the Gilded Age. "But we're going to take the elevator instead. Follow me."

We scurried behind him, hugging our collars to our throats as we entered the tunnel through an edifice of grandly chiseled stone. Beyond the entrance, the tunnel seemed to bore toward infinity, slashing deep into the heart of the mountain. Chandelier lighting illuminated the space from overhead, casting shadows on the unpolished marble walls that arched around us. I was surprised how

320

quickly everyone was moving. I guess we were all excited about piling into the elevator to see the compartment where infamous Nazis once crowded together. Either that or we were anticipating piling *out* of the elevator and being first in line to find the baseboard heating units.

The endless passageway shunted us into a domed hall that had the look and feel of a ginormous igloo lit by old-fashioned wall sconces. The elevator attendant beckoned us forward, allowing half our group to file into the compartment before cutting us off. "I'll be bahk," he assured the remaining guests, his Arnold Schwarzenegger accent making me realize that we were so close to Austria, the locals might talk like that for real.

"Well, would you lookit that," said Nana as she seated herself on the elevator's luxurious wraparound leather bench. Above the cushioned backrest the walls were paneled with brass mirrors that glowed like liquid gold, as resplendent as the most ornate of Mad King Ludwig's chambers. Hitler's cronies had obviously spared no expense to outfit his twice-used retreat.

The cables began to whir. "Wheeee," giggled Mom, clinging onto Dad as we began our ascent. I guess she was feeling the same tingling sensation in the pit of her stomach that I was. After jerking to a stop, we clambered out into a small entrance hall and followed the sign that directed us to an opposite doorway. *Speisesaal* read the sign, with a translation below: original dining room. But it was a dining room no longer, having been converted into a European-style café, though I suspected the wood-paneled walls and checkerboard ceiling with its recessed wooden squares were all part of the original interior.

Every seat in the room was occupied. People drinking beer. People drinking coffee. Flatware clinking against plates. Voices raised in laughter. Waitresses scurrying back and forth. And nearly all the diners were wearing T-shirts stamped with the words Bavarian Yodeling Champions.

Aha. The famous yodelers.

While the rest of the gang made a beeline through the congestion to reach the opposite doorway, I grabbed Mom and Dad and shuffled them toward the counter where an aproned attendant, who looked as if he might be the chief cook and bottle washer, greeted us with a jolly guten tag.

"Would it be possible for my father to store his accordion case behind your counter for a short time? He'll be performing for your guests after the yodelers, but he'd prefer not to have to drag the case around while he's touring the house."

"*Ja, ja.* I play also, though not so well. You leave it right here." He rolled the case behind the counter. "Play loud so I hear you in kitchen. You want to see menu?"

"We have vouchers for the main dining room, so . . . this isn't the main dining room, right?"

He gestured toward the door at the opposite end of the room. "Main dining room that way."

"How clever of you to think of freeing up your father's hands like that," Mom commented as I led them through the café. "Wasn't that clever of her, Bob?"

Dad nodded. "Yup."

I gave my lips a self-satisfied smack. "That's why they pay me the big bucks."

We descended a wide staircase that deposited us into an octagonal banquet room that was even more crowded than the café had been and a hundred times more noisy. Windows the size of double beds filled six recessed bays on the exterior stone wall, and sound bounced off the natural stone like gunfire in an echo chamber. Clattering dishes. Shrill voices. Floor-scraping chairs. The only architectural elements that could absorb the racket were the wooden beams that lined the ceiling, but unfortunately they weren't getting the job done. I noticed an open fireplace with a raised hearth to our right, but since no one had bothered to light a fire, it failed to add any warmth to a space that was in desperate need of it, both physically and atmospherically. "This is the room where we'll be eating lunch," I instructed Mom and Dad before marching them down another staircase to a smaller chamber. "So, Dad, make a mental note, okay?"

"You bet."

"I'll make a mental note too," tittered Mom, sounding suspiciously like her old self.

There were so many tourists jammed into the smaller chamber that the only interior features I could distinguish were two massive windows that looked out over a panorama of blue sky and snow-capped mountains. A pleasant male voice was sharing what were probably pertinent historical facts over the room's speaker system, but I'd have to wait for the English version before I'd be able to understand him.

"Did you read the sign what's hangin' by the elevator?" Nana asked as she threaded her way toward us. "We can't take no photographs. Dang."

Mom tilted her head, her gaze drifting upward to the beams on the ceiling. "Where did you say we are?" Squinting suddenly, she lasered a look at Nana. "And don't tell me Space Mountain. We've already been there."

"Ladies and gentlemen, we welcome you to Kehlsteinhaus," the canned voice recited, "often referred to as the Eagle's Nest. The road that brought you here was constructed between the years 1937 and 1939 under the supervision of Adolph Hitler's deputy, Martin Bormann. It climbs two thousand feet in four miles and . . ."

I hit the mental pause button when I spied Lucille Rasmussen by one of the windows. "Gotta leave you, folks. Duty calls. Stick together so you don't lose each other." I pointed a threatening finger at Mom. "And no squirting Nana with hand sanitizer."

"The octagonal room serving as our present-day restaurant was originally purposed as a reception hall and conference room," the voice went on. "The marble fireplace was a fiftieth birthday gift to the führer from Italian dictator Benito Mussolini. After the war . . ."

"Lucille." I squeezed in beside her at the window. "Do you have anything to share with me from last night?"

325

"I certainly do." She retrieved an official-looking paper from the outside pocket of her purse and handed it to me. "I'll accept a personal check, but I'd prefer cash."

I scanned the note. "This is an invoice." My eyes riveted on the number in the Amount Due column. *"Eight hundred and thirty-six dollars?"*

"And twenty-four cents."

I would have said something else if my jaw hadn't crashed to the floor.

"I've included all the necessary details: name of video, amount of time spent watching it, charges and fees."

"Eight hundred and thirty-six dollars?" I wheezed.

"Who knew the X-rated stuff was so pricey, huh? And most of them were so short, I never felt like I was getting my money's worth. Highway robbery if you ask me. Glad I'm not the one footing the bill. Is the altitude bothering you, Emily? You don't look so good."

I opened my mouth but nothing came out except pathetic choking sounds. Lucille splayed her hand over her chest.

"I'm afraid I'm feeling a little nostalgic this morning," she sniffed. "Watching all those videos by myself got me to thinking about Dick. He's missed out on so much by dying the way he did. Two new grandchildren. The interview Katie Couric did with Sarah Palin. Facebook. Smartphones. Flash mobs. Can you imagine how gaga he'd be over today's technology? I can see him now." She smiled as a faraway look crept into her eyes. "Stretched out on his recliner. Cigar in his mouth. Electronic tablet in his lap. Charge card in hand. Enjoying an evening's worth of smut in the privacy of his very own man cave, confident that no one but North Korean hackers would ever find out about it. That would have meant the world to him." She gave her head a reverential bow. "I really miss the big guy."

"Lucille." Her name shot out of my mouth in a gasp. "For eight hundred and thirty-six dollars, please tell me you discovered a cache of Astrid Peterson videos."

She crooked her mouth in thought. "No Astrid Peterson, but I watched a ton of Ophelia Peterman. Would that work just as well?"

"An Allied air raid on April 25, 1945, destroyed the Obersalzberg headquarters," the taped voice narrated, "but the Eagle's Nest was spared. It was confiscated by the American occupation troops and on June 20, 1952, was given back to Bavaria. The terrace at the back of the building . . ."

"I really appreciate your input," I told Lucille, numbed at the prospect of making good on all the charges she and the rest of the gang had racked up. *Oh, God.* How was I going to explain this to Etienne? I heaved a sigh as my optimism took a nosedive. "Have you seen Osmond?" He was my one last hope.

"As a matter of fact" — she pointed straight out the window — "he's right over there."

Before I could hyperventilate over the possibility that Osmond might be outside, clinging to the face of a six-thousand-foot mountain, she spun me halfway around so I could see for myself.

There he was, in a room that branched off at a right angle to ours, standing behind an enormous panel of plate glass, taking pictures of . . . us.

I waved.

He smiled and waved back.

I stabbed my finger at him and with over-exaggerated lip movements instructed, "Stay right there."

He smiled and waved back.

"I've gotta catch him before he disappears. Thanks, Lucille." I skirted around the perimeter of the room and, as I opened the door leading to the terrace, got hit with a blast of frigid air that felt as if it was being piped in from the North Pole. The terrace was as long as an indoor shooting range, with a towering bank of windows that overlooked the sheer drop-off below and absolutely no evidence of baseboard heating units. They could build a road halfway to the stratosphere but couldn't remember to install indoor heating? *Geesh.* With geniuses like that in charge of military strategy, no wonder they'd lost the war.

With my breath steaming through my nostrils, I hurried toward the room's farthest window, where Osmond was snapping pictures of the mountainscape. "Talk to me before my toes get frostbitten, Osmond. Did you find anything last night?"

"Lots."

"Really?"

"Yup. How much time you got?" He accessed another screen on his phone. I hugged my arms to my body and stomped my feet to warm them up.

"Did you get hit with a lot of credit card charges?" I asked, dreading his answer.

"For what?"

"For watching the videos I asked you to watch."

He shook his head. "Didn't have to pay a cent."

Bless his little heart. He'd probably hacked into the sites. I wondered how he'd feel about offering Lucille an advanced tutorial.

"This here's the list I made for you. I'll send it to you as an email, but this is what I got." He handed me his phone. "Your message disappeared last night before I finished reading to the end. My fingers got twitchy and deleted it by mistake, but I got the gist, so we're good."

My hands shook as I cradled his phone in my palms. I skimmed the text. Paradise on a Budget in Tahiti. Private Island Luxury in the Heart of the Bahamas. White Sand Meets Turquoise Sea in Shoal Bay.

I looked up. "Uhh . . . Osmond? What is this exactly?"

"It's the exotic videos you asked for."

Exotic, not erotic. I hung my head. Oh, what a difference a consonant can make.

"And get this, Emily. Some of the resorts cater to seniors."

"I don't suppose you ran across Astrid Peterson in any of your videos."

"Nope. Was I supposed to?"

I handed his phone back. "Thanks for your time and trouble, Osmond. Good job."

"Are you looking to visit some of these

places, Emily? Because if you are, you can count me in . . . if I'm still alive."

Considering the dough I'd be forking over to cover this fiasco, I feared Destinations Travel might *never* be scheduling another trip.

"Yodelaaay-e-whooooo."

"The yodelers," Osmond enthused. "S'cuse me, Emily. I don't want to miss this."

The terrace cleared out within a half minute as visitors piled back through the interior door. I remained by the window, shivering as I took in the view. Evergreens drooping beneath their heavy mantle of snow. Clouds hovering like smoke rings above distant mountain peaks. Villages set in miniature in the valleys below. Wooded slopes. Avalanched rock. Fractured ledges. Sunlight gleaming on snow. Shadows darkening crevasses. Alpine lakes that sparkled like Norwegian fjords. I snapped a quick picture through the window and, with my teeth beginning to chatter, glanced toward the arched doorway that exited onto the outside terrace.

Dining tables sat snow-covered and unoccupied on the raised patio. A wooden guardrail flanked the cliff's edge, preventing guests from accidentally taking the six-thousand-foot express route to the bottom. A rough hiking path zigzagged to a nearby rise, where a simple cross stood proud and erect against a backdrop of unscalable bedrock. On a warm day the patio would have been an ideal setting in which to relax, but with today's wind, cold, and slush, I wasn't even tempted to go out, not that I could have even if I'd wanted to. The double doors were chained shut and padlocked. I guess the management was serious about wanting to avoid risk, accidents, and litigation when the weather was less than optimal.

I snapped a picture of the cross to include in Nana's Legion of Mary newsletter, then turned back toward the sound of yodeling, pausing to wonder if this would be a good time to —

Despite my plummeting internal temperature, I whipped the paper Tilly had given me out of my pocket and entered the website address into my browser. I rolled my eyes at the name of the video but, taking advantage of my moment of unexpected privacy, I girded my loins, charged the fee to my PayPal account, and hit play.

The first two minutes were so poorly acted, the film was almost comedic until the clothes came off and — *eww*. The next two minutes stunned me into silence, and the next five were so mind-numbing that I watched through one squinted eye while turning my phone upside down and right-side up, trying to figure out if the position they'd assumed was even anatomically possible. I mean, seriously, guys. *Eww.*

Two additional women joined the twosome, both wearing long braided wigs and dressed in Bavarian costumes not unlike the one Astrid had been wearing on the day she died. This must be what had caught Tilly's attention because one of them did bear a slight resemblance to Astrid, but she was at least a couple of decades younger and much less well endowed. Tilly's eyes really must have been bleary to miss that.

I fast-forwarded through a blur of entangled limbs to the end of the video and exited the site, disappointed at what a waste of time and money my hunch had turned out to be. Looked like I wouldn't be pinning Zola's murder on Wendell anytime soon. All I could hope was that Kriminaloberkommissar Horn was having better luck.

As I headed back toward the anemic warmth of the house proper, the entrance door to the terrace flew open and Mom rushed out, fanning her face with both hands. *Uh-oh.* "You okay?" I called out as I hurried toward her.

Making a beeline for the partition that divided the massive windows, she hugged it with both arms and pressed her forehead against the chilly stone. "Ahhhhhh."

I pressed my hand to her back. "Is the altitude making you lightheaded? Are you sick?"

"Emily, have I ever had a hot flash?"

"Uhh . . . you never mentioned that you had."

"Well, I'm having one now."

I regarded her flushed cheeks and sweaty brow with envy, wishing it were me. "Is there anything I can do for you?"

Without removing her forehead from the wall, she stripped off her jacket and opened the collar of her blouse. "Not a thing. I'm just going to stay like this until I cool off." She puffed up her cheeks and blew outward. "How long does a hot flash last?"

"I have no idea. You want me to google it?"

"No, no. Just leave me here and when the yodelers are done, come get me so I can watch your father play. If I'm still perspiring through all my clothing when you come back, you have my permission to shoot me."

"Aww. I'm sorry you're so miserable, Mom." I gave her back a little rub.

"Hot! Hot!" she complained, wriggling

her shoulder blades to oust my hand, which I snatched away immediately. Wow, I had so much to look forward to down the road.

"Can I bring you some water?"

"This is better than water," she said as she flattened the side of her face against the stone.

"Okay, then, you'll be standing on this very spot when I come back for you, right?"

"I'm not moving. If I do, I'm afraid I might internally combust."

I crept into the restaurant as unobtrusively as possible and found a viewing spot by Mussolini's fireplace. The yodelers were performing in a small area along the opposite wall and were so lively, they had the entire audience in a festive mood, even putting a smile on the mouths of some of our very own stone-faced musicians. Their songs were in German, with copious *yoooo-de-yos* and *yodel-lay-hee-hoos,* but the real fun began with the sing-alongs that included hand gestures reminiscent of the Chicken Dance. People stood. People sat. Hands fluttered like wings. Arms waved in the air. Knees got slapped. Fingers snapped. Hands swooshed down, faster and faster, until the audience burst out with laughter and collapsed in breathless exhaustion.

I could see why these yodelers were state

champs. They were masters of audience participation.

I was able to locate most of our tour group at tables scattered throughout the room. Looks like they'd used their vouchers to purchase the luncheon buffet and Oktoberfest-sized steins of beer, although the jumbo mugs might not have been the best choice since folks were having to leave the entertainment with some frequency to attend to what I could only imagine were internal plumbing issues. Etienne was keeping Dad company while Wally was sitting with Wendell and Otis in what might have been an attempt to either keep their displeasure from exploding or to prevent them from heckling the yodelers. On a personal note, the room was so crowded and getting so stuffy, I was actually starting to warm up!

When the choral leader announced a final song, I saw Dad get up and circle the room, heading for the café. Almost time to fetch Mom . . . and get something to eat myself. My stomach was starting to growl.

The final selection being a polka, we began clapping our hands and stomping our feet, which prompted the group to pick up the pace even more until the song became a frenzied race toward the very last *yodel-lay-hee-h—*

"My accordion!" Dad's voice knifed through the room. "It's gone!"

TWENTY

"I did not move case." The aproned counter attendant, who introduced himself as Felix, looked perplexed. "I set it here" — he slapped his palm against the wall — "behind counter. The Fraulein and parents watch me. And now, *poof!* Gone."

"Did you leave it unattended at any time?" pressed Etienne.

"*Ja,* while I was in kitchen, heating vegetables for chafing dishes."

"So anyone could have walked off with it when you weren't looking?"

"*Ja,* but the café, it was empty. All the peoples were in main dining room, listening to state champion yodelers." He scratched his head. "Why would visiting tourist take accordion? Big honking case is big problem to hide."

"Perhaps the intent wasn't to steal it." I exchanged glances with Etienne and Wally as I recalled the vengeful expressions on the faces of the musicians as they'd returned their instruments to the luggage bay this morning. "Perhaps the intent was to destroy it."

"Why would peoples want to destroy accordion?"

"To prevent someone from playing it." My eyes lengthened in a hard squint. "That someone being Dad."

Wally frowned. "You think one of the musicians deliberately — ?"

"Maybe you missed the look in their eyes when you made your announcement at the bus terminal, but I didn't. They were livid. So I wouldn't be surprised if this is their attempt at retaliation. If the professionals aren't allowed to perform at the Eagle's Nest, they're going to make sure that the lone amateur can't either — not here and not anywhere else for the rest of the trip."

"Do you think one of the musicians secretly took off with it?" probed Wally. "Or were they all in cahoots?"

"Shall we conduct a thorough search before we cast aspersions on half the guests in our tour group?" suggested Etienne. "I'll search the back staircase and first floor. Emily, check the ladies' room and non-public areas on this floor. Perhaps Felix would help you. Wally, talk to the elevator operator and check out the men's room. We'll meet back here in ten minutes."

We were done in eight.

There was no instrument case. Not in the anteroom behind the café, the adjoining kitchen, the private corridor that connected the two rooms, nor the public toilets. The elevator operator remembered seeing the silver case on the way up but hadn't seen it since. Etienne reported that no one had left it in a dark corner on the back staircase, and with the door to the ground-floor rooms locked, there was only one route the thief could follow. "Out the back door to the terrace. And from there" — he rainbowed his arm to indicate an object whistling through the air — "over the guardrail. I couldn't isolate any footprints, but it was evident that someone had kicked up a lot of slush on their way to the edge of the mountain and covered their tracks quite successfully. So I fear Emily may be correct. In all likelihood, Astrid Peterson's instrument case tobogganed to the bottom of the Kehlstein without benefit of a toboggan."

I shook my head. "That's pretty sad. The accordion that survives a bomb blast falls victim to ill tempers. Beware of musicians wielding wind instruments."

"We have no physical evidence that any of

our musicians are responsible, bella."

"So now what?" asked Wally.

"Have you found it yet?" Dad hurried toward us, all aflutter. "If I'm not ready to go on in five minutes, I'll lose my spot and the yodelers will get to perform another set."

Hoping to ease the blow, I looped my arm through his. "Dad, Etienne thinks someone with an axe to grind might have snatched your accordion and . . . and disposed of it."

His jaw came unhinged. "Why would anyone do that?"

"*Ja,*" boomed Felix. "I ask same question."

"Just a guess," I continued, "but I think your sudden notoriety might have twisted a few noses out of joint."

"Not to mention hurt some feelings and bruised a few egos," explained Wally.

"In other words, Daddy, the other band members might prefer that if a musician is to be singled out for celebrity, it not be you."

He nodded like a bobble-head doll. "I understand," he lamented, before adding, "but we need to find it in five minutes, so where should we look?"

"Sums of beeches," growled Felix. "You peoples wait here." He disappeared through the door behind the counter, returning a minute later with a full-size piano accordion in tow. "You take this." He thrust it at Dad.

341

"We show them sums of beeches. Ha!"

Dad's performance having been successfully resurrected, I'd seated myself at a table with Etienne and was enjoying his first musical number when I remembered where I should be right now. *Omigod. Mom.*

"I'm so sorry," I apologized as I peeled her away from the wall and helped her into her jacket. "Major emergency with Dad's accordion."

"What kind of emergency?"

"It disappeared."

She cocked an ear toward the restaurant. "Isn't that him playing now?"

"Yup. But it's a borrowed instrument."

"Why would your father's accordion disappear?"

"Nothing official, but we're guessing that in a fit of jealous rage, one of the musicians chucked it over the terrace guardrail."

"Really?" She rebuttoned the collar of her blouse. "I wonder if that's what the person I saw was doing."

"You saw someone outside on the terrace?"

She nodded. "While the yodelers were performing. The glass on that outer door is so clean, I got an excellent look at the person's face."

I grabbed her shoulders. "Who was it?"

She opened her mouth as if to tell me, then snapped it shut as the spark of awareness that had flared in her eyes suddenly died out. She heaved a sigh. "Can you give me a minute? Maybe it'll come back to me."

TWENTY-ONE

I sat next to Mom on the ride back to Munich in anticipation that she'd remember because she was suddenly recalling all sorts of things. What country she was in. What she'd ordered for lunch. Why the musicians were giving Dad the cold shoulder. Who the woman with the boils on her face was. Whose bright idea it had been to leave the accordion case in Felix's care in the first place. But she couldn't create a visual image of the person she'd seen through the terrace door.

"If I could reconstruct the scene with the same lighting and shadows and distance, I know I'd remember," she assured me. "Or maybe I should try smooshing my face against a wall someplace. That might jog something loose."

The musicians were officially peeved and grumpy when we reached Munich, a condition that deteriorated even further when we entered the hotel to find Kriminaloberkommissar Horn awaiting our arrival at the front desk.

"Do not return to your rooms," he instructed. "I have more questions before I allow you to depart Munich in the morning."

Groans. Eye-rolling. Grumbling.

"You should know the routine by now." He swept his arm toward the inner corridor. "The Prince Ludwig room, if you please."

"Have you had a break in the case?" Etienne asked him as the group trooped toward the meeting room.

"A break? No. A clue? No. An inkling? No."

Not even an inkling? Nuts. An inkling would have been good.

"I have exhausted my resources, Mr. Miceli, and have nothing to show for it. The background checks on your guests raised no flags, no suspicions. They *are* who they say they are. They *do* what they say they do. If they're harboring secrets, I doubt they're lurid enough to raise even one eyebrow. They are truly one of the most average, run-of-the-mill groups of individuals I have ever been tasked with investigating."

I wasn't sure if that was meant as a compliment or an insult. I narrowed my eyes. "So if you've got nothing, what further questions do you have to ask?"

He lifted his brows. "I am the youngest police officer ever to earn the rank of kriminaloberkommissar, Mrs. Miceli. When I finish with your group, you'll know why. Please." He tipped his head and motioned me forward. "After you."

"Are we all here?" he asked when we'd seated ourselves.

"We're missin' a few," offered Nana. "They're in the little girls' room goin' potty."

"Very well. We can wait." He eyed his watch. Tapped his fingers on the podium. Fussed with the knot of his necktie. "I believe you were scheduled to visit Kehlsteinhaus today. Did you have a pleasant experience?"

"It was great," said Wendell, his voice dripping sarcasm. "Last night our band got the shaft at sea level. Today we got the shaft at six thousand feet up."

"I thought we were supposed to be the toast of the town for our heroism," complained Otis. "What a crock. We're getting disrespected all over the place."

"I don't think it was *your* heroism that the town was toasting," Margi spoke up. "If I'm not mistaken, after the explosion you musicians all raced farther down the street to protect your instruments. It was the rest of us who risked our lives to perform triage in an unstable bomb zone."

"What of it?" balked Otis. "According to that fella who works for the mayor, it didn't matter what role we played. We're all supposed to be recognized as heroes — until some two-bit yodelers show up."

"Yodelers?" questioned Horn. "Are you referring to the Bavarian yodeling team? Did you know they won the state championship and will go on to compete in —"

"Hey, Mr. Inspector, are you ready to take a look at the crackerjack photos I took of the aftermath of the blast site yet?" Bernice held up her phone. "Documentary film—ready. Maybe you can suggest where I can auction them off."

After casting an impatient glance at the doorway, he hastened toward Bernice's chair. "Show me."

His expression grew puzzled as she flipped through several screens. "Who is this woman?"

"Me." She primped her hair. "Prior to the introduction of my beauty treatment."

"Where are the photos of the bomb site?"

"You're looking at 'em. This is me hovering over the guy who'd been operating the heavy machinery. See how sympathetic I look? This is me hunkering down beside one of the guys in the yellow vests. I had to watch where I was stepping because the place was like a swamp and I didn't want to ruin my shoes. This is me listening for the sound of sirens. This is me —"

Horn muttered something under his breath and stormed back to the podium.

"I hope you realize you're turning your back on some very important historical documents here," chided Bernice. "You've just blown your chance to immortalize the face of a former magazine model in the German press."

Maisie Barnes hustled through the door.

"Are you the last one?" Horn called out as she found a chair at the back of the room.

"One more behind me."

He checked his watch again. "We'll start without the straggler." Gripping the sides of the podium, he ranged a flinty look over the room. "Secrets. You all have them, and you believe you'll take them to the grave with you. But that's where you're wrong. Do you know how much information we're able to compile on you from public records that are available to us over the Internet? Through social media? Through Interpol, state intelligence agencies, and cooperative programs with the FBI and NSA?" He paused for effect. "We can listen to your phones. Read your text messages. Discover your deepest and best-kept secrets with little effort at all."

He was beginning to sound like Vincent Price in a sixties horror flick. The only thing missing was the maniacal laugh.

"My staff has been very busy today collecting data on all of you — one of you in particular. If you thought you could hide your secret from us, you were mistaken. We know." He made a slow visual sweep of the room. "We know all about you. So I give you a onetime opportunity now to confess your crime. I can almost guarantee that our judicial system will deal with you more reasonably if you take responsibility, here and now, for what you have done."

I could hear chairs throughout the room creak and rattle as people squirmed in their seats.

Dad raised his hand rather tentatively in the air. "Would this be a good time to report a theft?"

"That's being taken care of," Etienne called out. "I left our contact information with the management at Kehlsteinhaus should the instrument ever reappear."

"Someone stole your instrument?" Horn

349

asked Dad.

Dad nodded. "It wasn't mine. It belonged to the Peterson woman who passed away. I was just borrowing it. But one minute it was there, and the next, it was gone."

"What type of instrument?"

"An accordion. A real nice one too. Kinda like the one Myron —"

"It was her!" Mom sprang to her feet and pointed a damning finger at the doorway. "*She's* the one who stole it. *She's* the one I saw on the terrace."

Hetty Munk froze on the threshold, stuck halfway between in and out. She stared at Mom, mouth gaping and eyes aghast. "What are you talking about?"

"I saw you. At the Eagle's Nest. Outside the terrace door. It's all coming back now."

Hetty inched nervously into the room and shifted her gaze from Mom to Officer Horn. "I'm a little uncomfortable mentioning this, but Mrs. Andrew has been mentally incapacitated for the last two days. She doesn't even know where she is."

"Germany," Mom fired back. "My brain's been a little off, but there's nothing wrong with my eyes. It was you outside that door."

Hetty shook her head in denial. "The terrace was buried under snow, Mrs. Andrew. The temperature was freezing. *Why* would I go outside in those conditions?"

"To throw Bob's instrument case over the mountainside, that's why."

The musicians let out a collective gasp.

Hetty rolled her eyes. "That's absurd."

"You destroyed Astrid's accordion?" Wendell asked in disbelief.

"I didn't touch Astrid's accordion."

"You and Astrid were best friends forever." Otis's wistful tone couldn't disguise an undercurrent of condemnation. "How could you do something like that to the instrument she loved?"

Hetty fisted her hand on her hip. "I don't believe this! You're taking the word of a crazy woman over mine?"

"Amnesia is not classified as a mental illness," corrected Tilly, "so I take umbrage with your use of the pejorative term *crazy.*"

"What'd she say?" asked Arlin.

"That accordion was the only thing we had left of Astrid," snuffled Gilbert. "We could have put it on display at our gigs. We could have honored her memory by having her name engraved on a special plaque that we could attach to her silver case. We could have —"

"Give me a *break,*" whined Hetty. "Astrid, Astrid, Astrid. She's dead, all right? And fawning over her sainted accordion isn't go-

351

ing to bring her back. Deal with it."

Wendell shot to his feet, anger darkening his features. "You're glad she's dead, aren't you? You didn't like Astrid. All these years, you . . . you were jealous of her. Jealous of her talent. Jealous of her personality."

"And her looks," said Otis.

"And her lingerie," added Gilbert.

I sat up straighter in my chair. Gilbert knew about Astrid's lingerie? But how —

"If I was jealous, it was all your fault," she shouted at the three Guten Tags, stabbing her finger at each of them. "How do you think you made me feel when you'd bounce off happily with Astrid but trudge beside me like . . . like you were slogging through mud?"

"It wouldn't have hurt if you'd bought a few enticing outfits," suggested Otis.

"On my wages?" cried Hetty. "Are you kidding?"

"And Astrid always served treats," Gilbert reminisced. "Italian wine served at room temperature. Chilled specialty beer. Truffles she made herself."

"Café au lait mousse," reflected Wendell, sighing. "Raspberry parfait. Orange dreamsicle."

"Cheese spread and crackers," Gilbert continued. "Cheese logs at Christmas."

"*I* served you treats," defended Hetty.

"Yeah." Otis pulled a face. "Peanuts."

"I'll have you know that peanuts are a wonderful source of protein, dietary fiber, and omega-3 fatty acids," she countered. "They're much more heart healthy than artery-clogging café au lait mousse truffles."

Otis curled his lip with distaste. "What I meant to say was *unsalted* peanuts."

"Astrid was my Stepford wife," mused Wendell. "When I was with her, I felt tall and . . . and clever and interesting."

"She made me feel like a superhero," lamented Otis.

Gilbert smiled. "She told me I performed like a V12 diesel engine — smooth camshaft, unflagging throttle response, super flexible torque, and horsepower off the chart."

"*I* might have told you the same thing if you'd ever turned your key in the ignition," wailed Hetty. "I'm fed up with the three of you! Astrid got Superman and diesel engines. What did I get? Underdog and flat tires!"

Uff-da. Were they talking about what I *thought* they were talking about?

"Hold it." Maisie Barnes unfolded herself from her chair and stood up, an incredulous grin on her face. "Are you telling us that you're, what — swingers?"

The Guten Tags looked from one to the other as if realizing, only now, that they'd aired their dirty laundry in front of the entire room. Wendell puffed out his chest and hitched up the waistband of his pants. "Yeah, we're swingers. So what?"

The room exploded in a cacophony of gasps, snorts, and snickers.

"They swing dance?" enthused Osmond. "I used to swing dance."

"They're not dancers," hooted Dick Teig. "When they swing, they're not doing it on the floor of any grange hall."

"And they're not vertical," said Dick Stolee as he choked back his laughter. "They're horizontal."

"Like yoga class poses?" asked Alice.

"They're not doing yoga," Stretch translated. "They're pulling the old switcharoo. They're swapping partners for the purpose of — how should I word this? — engaging in intimate after-hours activities on a regular basis."

Nana raised her hand. "Is this a private club or can anyone join?"

Laughter. More gasping. Schoolchild giggles.

"Oh, grow up," railed Wendell, jaw hardened, voice increasing in volume. "I don't know what your problem is. Are we breaking any laws? No. Are we committing any crime? No. We're divorced. We're widowed. We're not cheating on our spouses, so it's none of your business how we spend our time after hours. News flash: single adults deserve as much TLC as you married folks, so how about you cut us some slack? You're not the morality police. Deal with it."

"Oh, my stars." Mom cupped her hand around her mouth and whispered in my direction. "He's not talking about TLC at all, is he? He's talking about S-E-X."

"The incidence of STDs in your age group has reached epidemic proportions," Margi offered in a quick public-service announcement. "So you fellas better be taking precautions and using prophylactics."

"Why do they need protection?" raged Hetty. "They come to my room, they eat my peanuts, they fall asleep. What do they need protection from?"

"Anaphylactic shock?" asked Alice.

"I never fell asleep on Astrid," Otis admitted in a proud voice. "Astrid knew how to entertain a fella."

"I never knew what she was going to do next," Gilbert pined. "She was so full of surprises."

Wendell nodded agreement. "When she wore that little nylon number with the lace

355

bodice . . ." He gave his lips a lusty smack.

"The pink or the white?" asked Otis.

"I cannot *believe* the time I've wasted on you three bozos!" shrieked Hetty. "It makes me want to spit. Did you get a thrill out of making me feel so . . . so unwanted? Did it make you feel manly to pander to Astrid's every whim? Do you know how much that hurt me?"

Otis looked unsympathetic. "It's your own fault for not —"

"Don't you dare place blame on me, Otis Erickson, you . . . you underhanded *sneak.* What were you doing with Emily and Etienne when they were packing up Astrid's belongings? You want to fess up to what you were looking for or should I take a wild guess and assume you were going out of your mind trying to find her journal?"

Hey, I'd had that theory, too, hadn't I? At some point in time.

"*You* were looking for her journal?" barked Gilbert, bristling at Otis. "What gave you the right? Weasel! I knew you weren't looking for any damn library book."

Otis's cheeks reddened like Christmas tree lights. "I wanted a keepsake. Something to remember her by."

"Bull!" shouted Wendell. "You wanted to see what she'd written about you. You wanted proof in her own handwriting that she liked you best."

"She *did* like me best," crowed Otis. "I was always her favorite. I didn't need to read her journal to know that."

"Then why'd you go looking for it?" taunted Wendell.

"I *told* you. I wanted a memento. Something she'd touched. Something she cherished. Something that might make me smile for the rest of my life."

"But you didn't find it, did you?" needled Gilbert with no small amount of snark.

Otis shook his head, bereft. "It wasn't there."

"That's because it was destroyed in the bomb blast," snapped Hetty. "Isn't that right, Emily? She was carrying it in her shoulder bag, so I guess you'll never know which one of you she preferred, will you? I don't know how you'll ever survive the disappointment. Gee, my heart bleeds."

Emotion drained from the trio like air from inflatable yard ornaments. They stared at Hetty. They stared at each other. "It's really gone?" asked Gilbert, looking as if he might burst into tears. He grew quiet, sullen. "I guess that explains it, then."

"Explains what?" Wendell asked him.

"Why I couldn't find it either."

"You went looking for it, too?" sputtered Otis. "Aww, hell, you're the one who trashed her room, weren't you? Geez, dude, you ever heard of restraint? You should have had more respect for her stuff. There was no need to tear up her room like that. Astrid would have been appalled."

"I was in a hurry."

Omigod. I'd been right. The room *had* been ransacked. I fired a look at Gilbert. "You should be ashamed of yourself."

"I'm sorry! I would've been more tidy, but I only had a small window of opportunity during the newspaper interviews, so I had, like . . . no time."

"How did you get into her room in the first place?" I demanded.

A collective snigger rippled through the contingent of musicians.

"We work in a lock and key factory," said Stretch.

"The operative word being *key,*" added Arlin.

"All my employees acquire a certain expertise after a time," Wendell spoke up. "Kind of goes with the territory."

"He means we're good at picking locks," said Maisie. "If we didn't work for Wendell, we could all become independent locksmiths."

"Or professional lock picks," offered Gilbert.

I regarded the faces of the musicians, my gaze settling on Wendell. "Did you pick my door lock too? Did you riffle through Astrid's suitcase looking for her journal?"

Wendell tucked in his lips, guilt stamped all over his face. "If I'd known what Gilbert and Otis had been up to, I wouldn't have bothered. Guess I was a little late to the party. I apologize for breaking and entering, but I swear I didn't take anything. I just . . . I just wanted to savor whatever Astrid had written about me, because despite what my two friends claim, I know for a fact that *I* was her favorite."

"You were not," grumbled Otis.

"That's bogus," spat Gilbert.

"You turkeys," blasted Hetty. "I'm *glad* Astrid's gone. And I'm glad her accordion's gone, too. You boneheads might have robbed me of physical contact, but that accordion of hers isn't going to gyp me out of another minute of performance time."

"You *did* throw it over the side of the mountain," bellowed Wendell.

"*Someone* had to! I did it for all of us — or did you want to spend the rest of the tour listening to solo performances from Emily's father?"

"Told you so!" cried Mom.

Officer Horn put a bead on Hetty. "Did you just confess to destroying Frau Peterson's accordion?"

She bobbed her head. "You bet I did."

"In that case, I'm placing you under arrest on two counts of criminal activity. Theft and vandalism." He produced his handcuffs as he crossed the floor and slapped them around Hetty's wrists.

"You can't arrest me. I watch *Law and Order.* You need the owner of the accordion to press charges against me, and she can't because she's dead."

"A minor point," noted Horn. "We'll address it at the station."

Margi waved her hand over her head. "Excuse me, Officer. Can you charge her with Zola's murder, too, so we can get out of here? Dinner's in an hour."

"I didn't kill Zola!" swore Hetty.

"Do not move from your seats," warned Horn, his body language threatening.

But the fuse had already been lit.

Alarm began to creep through the room.

Nana stuck her hand in the air. "Can them fellas tell us how they decided what girl got to swing with 'em on what night?"

"Oh, sure," said Gilbert. He removed his wallet from his pants pocket. "Our company

360

keys." He waved a key like the one Wendell had shown me in the air. "All employees at Newton get a key with their name engraved on the back. So after our band finished a gig that called for an overnight stay, us guys would toss our keys into a hat and the girls would pull out the two lucky winners."

"Astrid picked winners," sniped Hetty. "My winners always turned out to be losers."

"You s'pose that system would work just as well if the names was on sticky notes?" asked Nana.

I bowed my head and covered my eyes. *Oh, God.*

"Say, fellas." Bernice's voice assumed a breathiness that made it sound less scratchy and more seductive. "Now that you're short two playmates, will you be accepting applications for replacement models?"

"Fifty-seven minutes until dinner," alerted Dick Stolee.

Horn narrowed his gaze as he probed the anxious faces before him. "I am warning you to remain seated."

"Is this like a time-out?" asked Lucille. "I always made my kids do time-outs on chairs in the kitchen."

"Do we have to sit here until every one of us tells you a secret?" questioned George.

"There is only one secret I'm interested in hearing," said Horn, "and that is which one of you killed Frau Czarnecki. When that secret is revealed, you'll be dismissed."

"So it *is* a time-out," groaned Lucille.

"Does anyone remember that old quiz show *I've Got a Secret*?" asked Tilly.

"I loved that show," said Nana. "But I don't recall none of them contestants ever admittin' they whacked someone."

"How big a secret does it have to be?" asked Alice. "Can it be a small secret like a woman's dermatologist talks her into having a Botox treatment at her last appointment? Or does it have to be something bigger like, say, the same hypothetical woman throws her old DVD player out in the regular trash rather than pay the fee to have it recycled?"

"I *told* you she had cosmetic work done," Grace Stolee squealed to Helen. "Crow's feet don't disappear on their own like that."

"Fifty-four minutes until dinner," announced Dick Stolee.

"I have an idea," suggested Dick Teig. "How about we all write down a secret on a slip of paper and toss it into a hat. Then Officer Horn can read them off one at a time and let us try to guess whose secret it is. If we guess right, we get to go to dinner!"

"When he reads the one about the dermatologist and the Botox treatment, I hosey first dibs on guessing," said Margi.

"Does our secret have to be sordid or would mildly disgusting be acceptable?" questioned Lucille.

"Can we guess our own secret," asked George, "or would that be considered cheating?"

"Good idea," applauded Margi. "That would really get us out of here fast."

"Excuse me, Officer," said Osmond, "but can I be excused to visit the facilities?"

"Ditto for me," said Helen.

"I've gotta go, too," said George.

A fine sheen of sweat appeared on Officer Horn's upper lip. His eyelid began to twitch. His Adam's apple bobbed erratically above the knot in his tie.

As if closing in for the kill, the group shot their hands into the air with desperate pleas of "me too, me too" echoing through the room.

"Fifty-two minutes," shouted Dick Stolee.

"*GO,*" bellowed Horn, apparently deciding that the spontaneous failure of two dozen aging bladders could be more catastrophic than a delay in his interrogation.

They raced to the door as if they were running from the bulls on the streets of Pamplona. "They have no intention of coming back, do they?" Horn asked the handful of us who remained in the room.

Etienne shook his head. "I believe you've lost them until after dinner."

"I have to go too," insisted Hetty.

"*You* may use the facilities at the police station," Horn told her.

"If you've no objection, I'd like to accompany Ms. Munk to the station," said Etienne. "She may find herself in need of an advocate."

"Fine. But I'm not through here, Inspector Miceli. You can expect me back in this room at eight o'clock sharp, and I will expect your guests to be here with full bellies and empty bladders. One of them is a cold-blooded murderer, and before this evening is out, I promise you, I will find out which one."

I hoped he changed his methodology. If he didn't, the only thing he could promise was a never-ending time-out.

TWENTY-TWO

After making a brief pit stop in my own suite, I stopped off at Mom and Dad's to console Dad a little more about the loss of Astrid's accordion and to reassure myself that the return of Mom's memory hadn't been a fluke.

"Is this the honeymoon suite?" asked Mom as she looked out over the city of Munich through the slender floor-to-ceiling windows.

Uh-oh. She wasn't starting to slip away again, was she? "Why do you ask, Mom?"

"Because there aren't any magazines on the coffee table. Newlyweds are so busy with other activities, they don't need reading material." She gave the bare table a forlorn look. "A half dozen or so would have been nice. I can just imagine how out of order they would have been."

I smiled with relief. Yup. She was back.

She checked her watch. "I'm through in

the powder room, so we should be heading down to dinner, Bob."

Dad sat on the sofa, head bent, moping. "Yup."

I sat down beside him, cradling his hand in mine. "How about when we get back home, you and I go shopping and buy you a brand-new accordion? I bet you could even start your own oompah band. Just think of the places you could play — the senior center, the church, the bowling alley, that supper club out on the highway, the —"

His head popped up with jack-in-the-box quickness. His down-in-the-mouth expression faded. His lips softened into a smile. "I could, couldn't I?"

"You're darned right. No more hiding your talent, Dad. You need to share it with the world."

He mulled that over for a half second. "You suppose I could just start with Windsor City?"

I gave him a peck on his cheek. "You bet."

"Well, would you look at this?" Mom stood at the kitchen counter, bursting with excitement as she fingered a tall stack of Dad's mini videocassettes. "They're not labeled." Ecstasy lit her every feature as she gathered them against her chest. "We can't have that, can we? Do either of you have a pen?"

Aww. This was so reassuring. Her OCD was back, too. "Dinner's in thirty minutes, Mom."

"*Psssh.* This will only take me a minute."

Dad threw his hands up in the air and shot me a woeful look. "There goes dinner."

"You know what'll happen if you don't leave now, Mom. All the good seats will be taken."

"Will you text your grandmother and ask her to save a couple of seats for us?" She removed Dad's camcorder from its case. "No, wait. Don't bother. With her complexion the way it is, people are probably still afraid to get too close to her, so we'll just sit in the empty chairs that'll be at her table."

"Dad can't wait that long. He's famished. Right, Dad?"

He nodded. "Yup."

Mom began removing the cassettes from their stack and lining them up in a semicircle on the counter. "Five minutes. That's all I need." She clasped her hands, smiling at the arrangement. "They're speaking to me."

I strode across the floor, locked my hands around both her arms, and gently marched her away from the counter. "You need to relax, Mom. You're recovering from a major neurological upset. The last thing your doctor would want is for you to overdo."

"But classifying material is relaxing."

"I'll tell you what. I'm holding off on dinner until Etienne gets back, so why don't I hang out here, go through Dad's tapes, and label them for you? It'll give me something to do."

Her lower lip looked as if it might be gearing up to quiver. "But *I* wanted to do it."

"By tomorrow Dad'll have another big stack that needs to be labeled, so you can have at it then. Right, Dad?"

"Yup."

Twisting her head at an impossible angle to cast a lingering look at the counter, she relented grudgingly. "Do you know what to do? The main title should be *Germany* with the month and year, and beneath that should be subheadings listing the city, attraction, and minute markers for each separate —"

"I know the drill," I said as I coaxed them toward the door. "I'll catch up with you a bit later, and unfortunately, at eight o'clock, I'll see you in the Prince Ludwig room again."

"Whatever for?" asked Mom.

"Officer Horn is coming back to finish his

368

interrogation. Wally's going to make the announcement at dinner. I'm just giving you a heads-up."

"That Munk woman is in jail all because of me," lamented Dad. "It's embarrassing. Makes me feel like a stool pigeon."

"Maybe another bomb will explode," Mom said, waxing philosophical. "Trust me. It'll help you forget."

Tilly was ambling down the hall as I scooted Mom and Dad out the door. She raised her walking stick in greeting. "Are we all headed in the same direction?"

"I'm not, but Mom and Dad are."

"Good. We can walk down to dinner together. Marion will catch up in a minute. And by the way, Emily, about that request from Bernice. The cream is available ready-made but you'd better tell her to preserve what little compound she has left because we're being cut off."

"You can't order any more?"

She shook her head. "I just received a text from my supplier. He's in a snit about the outrageous hike in overseas shipping costs, so he's decided to boycott his local carrier. Forever."

"He can't just stick Bernice with the charges?"

"You're missing the point. It's not about

money. It's about principle."

Oh, joy. And I was the one who'd have to break the news.

"He did say he'd be quite willing to sell Bernice as much product as she'd like, but she'll have to fly to New Guinea to pick it up."

Like that was going to happen. "Okay. Thanks for trying, Tilly."

"I'm afraid I had the easy part. You're the one who has to deal with the aftermath."

My digestive system screamed out for a roll of antacids as I headed back into the room. Bernice's discontent would be epic. I could hear her now. The snarling. The ranting. The griping. The bellyaching.

You've got this, said the little voice inside my head. *Remember? This is why they pay you the big bucks.*

There is no amount of money worth the scene this news is going to cause, I told the voice. Although once I'd made that admission, I realized there actually *was* an easy way to avoid having to play a part in her meltdown.

I'd text her.

Later.

Yup. I was good.

I packed Dad's photographic stuff into his camcorder case and dumped it all out on the sofa. Settling in for the long haul, I removed the first tape from its plastic case, popped it into the camcorder, flipped open the display screen, and pressed the play icon.

The chimes of the Marienplatz carillon rang out, rising above the errant sounds of voices oohing and ahhing. The view on the screen focused on the glockenspiel with its trumpeters and jesters and mounted knights charging at each other. I fast-forwarded to the place where the red knight toppled backward over his horse's rump. Laughter. Hooting. A jumpy shot of the dispersing crowd. More fast-forwarding. A classic image of Mom smiling for the camera and Nana curling her lip into a sneer. Another crowd shot. Then pavement. Dad's pant leg. Mom's shoes. Other people's shoes. More pavement.

Dad was obviously still struggling to master the art of switching from recording mode to powering off.

Water. Water running down the pavement. A phosphorescent yellow vest. Okay, he was back on track again. A John Deere backhoe loader. Jackhammers lying by the curb. *KA-BOOOOOOOOM!* A jerky image of exploding earth, then the screen went black.

Heart racing, I set the camcorder down

and inhaled a deep breath, feeling unexpectedly rattled. I was surprised at how unsettling it was to relive that moment, but I
fought off the feeling by reminding myself
what had come after — how the gang had
banded together to react to the crisis. Dad
hadn't caught their efforts on tape, but it
was something they could be proud of for
the rest of their lives.

The tape ended there, so I took note of
the minute marker, then annotated the label
exactly as Mom has suggested. Germany.
Date. Munich. Marienplatz. Glockenspiel.
And the marker where the section ended.

I didn't label the explosion in the hopes
that once Dad learned how to download a
tape to the computer and burn a CD, he'd
edit it out. None of us needed to hear the
sound of that explosion ever again.

Over the next hour I became a one-
woman labeling machine. Hohenschwangau. Horse-drawn carriage. Hike up to
Neuschwanstein Castle. Courtyard of Ludwig's Castle. Berchtesgaden. Winding road.
Eagle's Nest from parking lot. All of this
footage interspersed with long minutes of
bus upholstery, brick walkways, blue sky,
and an endless array of footwear.

I popped a new tape into the machine.
The Oktoberfest grounds filled the screen.

Honkytonk music. Fairway rides. Flashing lights. Delighted screams. I fast-forwarded until I arrived at an interior view of the Hippodrom tent. Oompah music with a side of "ZICKE, ZACKE, ZICKE, ZACKE, OI, OI, OI!" Revelers standing on benches. Our group huddled around our three assigned tables. Carousel horses hanging from the ceiling. A five-minute interval of the banner draped across the bandstand. A close-up of a group of Germans shooting pictures of us with their phones. Platters of food arriving. More platters of food. Maisie, Stretch, and Arlin on stage, playing their first beer song. Their second song. Their third song.

I fast-forwarded until I saw the Brassed Off Band replacing them on stage, which must have been about the time Dad got tired of filming because while I could hear the Brassed Offs play, the only scene the camcorder was recording was a static view of the food platters and beer steins on table three. As I was about to hit fast-forward again, I caught a sudden movement on the tape — a hand passing over the beer stein at the end of the table. Surreptitiously. Subtly. As if shooing a fly away. *What the — ?*

I hit pause, angled the screen to minimize glare, and scrutinized the frozen image.

There was something in that person's hand that looked suspiciously like —

I hit play for two short seconds before pausing again.

Omigod. Omigod. Omigod.

It was a bottle. A mini bottle. It disappeared in the person's palm as quickly as it had appeared, but I didn't need to read the label to know what it was.

Maisie's e-cigarette nicotine refill.

Holy crap. This was it! The incriminating evidence. On tape. Without realizing it, Dad had caught Zola's killer red-handed, destroying the myth that there were no perks to be gained from human error.

Heart pounding, hands trembling, I grabbed my phone and called Etienne but was immediately shunted to his voicemail. "I know who our killer is," I said in a rush of words. "Dad has it all on his camcorder. Get back here as soon as you can with Officer Horn."

I picked up the camcorder again and stared at the paused profile of the person who had killed Zola, not understanding the motivation. Why? What would prompt an all-round nice person to commit murder? I'd seen photos of all the employees at Newton Lock and Key. Was there a clue I'd missed? Something so obvious that it was hiding in plain sight?

I googled the Newton website once more, accessing the photo galleries from each department. There was our killer, looking as amiable and innocent as —

My phone chimed with a text alert. Not Etienne, but Wally: *NEED YOU IN THE DINING ROOM. IT'S BERNICE. SHE'S GONE BALLISTIC OVER SOMETHING TILLY TOLD HER.*

Nuts. The very situation I'd been hoping to avoid. Bernice obviously confronted Tilly about the beauty compound thing hersel—

The beauty compound thing. I froze, my gaze riveted straight ahead as the fog suddenly cleared.

Uff-da. The missing piece of the jigsaw. It wasn't the picture gallery at Newton that held the clue. It was the *other* pictures.

Grabbing my shoulder bag, I raced into the hall, pelted down the back staircase, and skidded into the dining room, out of breath and frazzled. I spied Nana and Tilly first, at a table for two in the center of the room. Bernice occupied a table for six next to them, the only female amid five male band members who looked to be plying her with wine and hanging on her every word. Wally met me at the door.

"I may have gotten you down here for nothing. She's stopped shouting. And the guys seem to be teasing her out of her snit, but she scared the bejeebers out of the poor waitress and flung some pretty colorful words at Tilly. You have any idea what's yanked her chain?"

"Yup. She was having a grand time at the ball when Tilly ruined her evening by telling her that the clock was about to strike midnight."

He narrowed his eyes. "I don't get it."

"You would if you were hoping to be Cinderella for the rest of your life."

He pulled a face. "C'mon. Are you saying all this fuss is over a fairy tale?"

I shook my head. "It's about shipping costs, actually." I shielded my mouth with my hand. "You might want to wait here for Etienne and Officer Horn. I suspect they'll be arriving momentarily."

I marched over to Bernice's table disguised as the cheery tour escort in charge of spreading goodwill. "Hi, guys. Enjoying the buffet?"

Otis, Wendell, Gilbert, Stretch, and Arlin offered spontaneous nods and grunts. Bernice eyed me suspiciously. "Is this a social visit or did someone rat me out?"

"Let's just say I'm glad to see that tempers have cooled."

"Ratted out. Bet it was Tilly."

"I'm sorry you can't get your hands on any more cream, Bernice, but that's not Tilly's fault."

"Says you."

"Did she explain to you about her supplier?"

"Exorbitant shipping costs. What a crock. She wants to keep the stuff all to herself and freeze me out."

"She's telling you the truth. Have you mailed a package recently? Prices are through the roof. Even for teeny-tiny items."

"Pfffft."

I glanced across the table at Arlin and Stretch. "Tell her, guys."

"She's right," admitted Arlin. "In the last ten years, the base price to mail a package cross country has quadrupled, and international fees have skyrocketed."

Stretch nodded. "The company's had to funnel a lot more money into our department just to meet basic operating costs."

Wendell slanted his mouth at an irritated angle. "It's a real kick in the pants when your fastest-growing department is shipping. We're getting killed on both ends, paying premium prices for what we receive and losing revenue dollars for what we ship out, because that's one of the big perks with doing business with Newton. We've always offered free shipping. Although if prices continue to rise, we might have to rethink our business model."

I trained my gaze on Wendell. "The increase in your budget pays for more than just shipping."

He frowned. "What do you mean?"

"I'm pretty sure it pays for luxuries you had no idea you were funding." I lasered a look across the table. "Isn't that right, Stretch?"

He stared at me, dumbstruck. "What?"

"Wasn't some of that shipping budget spent on ice sculptures and caviar and shrimp cocktail and a chocolate fountain for dipping strawberries?"

His complexion turned ashen. Wendell arched his brows. "You wanna tell me what she's talking about, Stretch? Because I think she just announced that I was the one who paid for your anniversary bash." His gaze darkened. "Did I?"

"Hell, no," choked Stretch. "I'd sooner cut off my right hand than cheat the company. You know that, Wendell."

Otis canted his head toward the boss. "Seeing as how Stretch is a southpaw, a statement like that doesn't hold much water, does it?"

Wendell gestured toward Arlin. "You're

the one who works with him eight hours a day. You have anything to add to the conversation?"

"Sure do. I've been working with Stretch for most of my life, and I can say, without exception, that he's honest as the day is long."

"See there?" reasoned Stretch. "Arlin can vouch for me. We go back —"

Arlin raised his forefinger in the air. "Except . . . I've been wondering about this one curiosity for a few years now. Stretch and me have compared our paychecks. We make the same amount of money right down to the penny. So how come the wife and me are riding around in a Dodge Dart, and him and Verna are driving a Lexus?"

"For cripes sake, we didn't buy the thing," sputtered Stretch. "We're leasing it — for medical reasons. Verna's chiropractor said a luxury car would lessen her back problems, so we made the sacrifice."

"Some sacrifice," quipped Arlin. "What about the addition you built onto your house? Was that a medical necessity too? You had that done during the recession, when no one could afford to do anything."

"And that's exactly why the builder offered me such a great deal," said Stretch. "He needed the work. You can't believe the favor I did by hiring him."

"You're right," Arlin wisecracked. "I can't."

Wendell fiddled with his silverware. "Did you have to rent the venue for your anniversary bash or do you have an actual country club membership?"

"We signed up in the worst of the recession, when they were bleeding members, so they practically paid us to join. You wouldn't believe the money we've saved, especially on their all-you-can-eat weekend buffets where the grandkids eat for free."

"What's the head count on the grandkids now?" asked Gilbert.

"An even dozen, with number thirteen due in a couple of months."

"How come you're the only person who ever seems to run across these great deals?" asked Otis.

"It's not me, it's Verna. That woman can sniff out bargains like a bloodhound. She says you've gotta read the fine print to find the deals, so that's what she does."

"Considering the size of your paycheck, seems to me she's not bad at squeezing blood from a turnip either," mocked Arlin.

Wendell shifted his gaze to me. "Would you mind explaining how Stretch ended up in your crosshairs?"

In the distance I heard the wail of sirens and knew that help would be arriving any minute, which emboldened me to answer Wendell's question.

"Sure. It was after I saw the video."

"What video?"

"The one that Dad accidentally filmed at the Hippodrom when he thought his camcorder was turned off. The powering on and off thing is kind of a chronic problem with him, so we find a lot of surprises on his tapes — dirt, rocks, pavement, shoes — but this time the surprise footage showed Stretch emptying Maisie's liquid nicotine into Zola's beer stein in vivid color, with enhanced digital sound. Who knew, huh?"

"That's a lie," cried Stretch. "You're trying to frame me. Offering me up as the sacrificial lamb. You doctored the tape or photoshopped the images or —"

"Feel free to mention that to Kriminaloberkommissar Horn when he arrives." I checked my watch. "Which should be any minute now."

A hush fell over the table for a stunned moment before everyone started talking at once.

"You really killed that woman?" Otis croaked.

"You're so screwed up, man," said Wendell.

"I knew there was some funny business going on all these years," insisted Arlin. "I just knew it."

"You've really stepped in it now, Stretch," warned Gilbert. "Stuck in a German prison for the rest of your life? Good luck trying to pick *those* locks."

Stretch boosted himself to his feet with such force that he knocked over his chair, which crashed to the floor with a resounding thud. "Do you know who that redhead was? She told me on our walk over to the Hippodrom tent that she was an accountant. But not just any accountant — she was the accountant who was going to conduct our next company audit! Do you think my books would have passed muster with her? Did you hear her predictions? She never missed. She would have found me out — ruined me. It would've been all over. You couldn't have hired a normal CPA?" he yelled at Wendell. "You had to hire an accountant with a minor in psychic ability?"

"So you admit killing her?" accused Wendell.

Air steamed from Stretch's nostrils like fire from a dragon. His eyes grew skittish. His chest heaved. Gasping for breath, he leaped over his chair and grabbed the closest thing he could get his hands on: Nana.

Yanking her out of her chair, he pulled her against him, braced his forearm across her collarbone, and grabbed a steak knife from the table. Eyes wild, spittle gathering at the corner of his mouth, he poised the tip of the knife at her throat. "Don't anyone move."

My knees went gimpy. My mouth went dry. He wouldn't hurt Nana. He *couldn't* hurt Nana. Where were the police?

I threw my hands up as if surrendering. "Just take it easy, Stretch. No one's moving. Everyone's cool. My grandmother's done nothing to you, so I'm asking you to put the knife down and let her go."

He shook his head. "You people don't know what my life's been like." His voice was high-pitched, desperate. "Nothing was ever good enough for Verna. She couldn't settle for what everyone else had. *Nooo.* She had to have bigger. Better. Brighter. Faster. Nothing but the best made her happy, and if she wasn't happy, she made my life a living hell, so I had to keep her happy. I *had* to."

"By robbing my company blind?" yelled Wendell.

"You never missed what I took," Stretch

fired back. "And you never had the family I've had to support. The kids. The grand-kids. If those kids of mine had found good jobs, I might've been able to cut back, but what are they doing? Working at fast food joints. Working at big box stores. Minimum wages with no health insurance or benefits. So guess who pays for all their doctors' appointments? Grampa. Do you know how many ear infections kids get every year? And the eye doctor. And the dentist. I'm gonna have to put braces on every one of them because they don't share one straight tooth among them. They're the most snaggle-toothed brood God ever put on this green earth. And then there was the anniversary party. Do you know how much it costs to have live lobster flown in from Maine? And here's the kicker: Midwesterners don't even like lobster!"

"Excuse me, young man," Nana said politely through stiffened lips. "I'll write you a check for a thousand dollars if you'll poke your knife someplace other than my neck. I don't want no blood gettin' on my new sweatshirt if your hand slips."

He replied by tightening his grip on the knife. His eyes grew darker, more crazed.

"How about a million?" asked Nana. "My checkbook's right there in my handbag."

"Here's what I want," he said in a menacing voice. "I want a helicopter to get me out of here. Right now. And no tricks or my hand might just slip."

"Don't you need no money?" asked Nana. "You're gonna need cash once you get to wherever you wanna go."

Stretch hesitated as he considered her suggestion. "Yeah, good idea. I want, like, a hundred thousand dollars in euros." He nodded to me. "Go ahead. Make the call to Horn. Tell him my demands."

I tried Etienne again. Where was he? The sirens had stopped. Shouldn't he be here by now? Unless . . . the sirens had been heading to another emergency. Uh-oh.

"I'd ask for more money," Bernice snuffled. "A hundred thousand is small potatoes. It won't last you a month, especially going into the holiday season. Do you have any idea what a good ski resort in Bavaria will cost you during Christmas?"

"Ask for half a million," Dick Teig called across the floor. "That way you won't have to pinch your pennies so much."

"It'll take longer to collect half a million," said Osmond. "I bet he doesn't want to wait that long."

"Don't forget to ask for clean underwear," said Margi. "Being on the lam is no excuse to ignore basic hygiene."

"And a toothbrush and floss," shouted Helen. "Ignore your teeth and they'll go away."

"And pajamas," said Lucille. "You don't want to embarrass yourself if a fire breaks out at your hotel. Unless you hide out in a nudist colony, in which case no one will probably notice."

Etienne still didn't answer. I waved my phone at Stretch. "I — uh . . . I'm having a little trouble with my phone."

Nana waggled her eyebrows at me and darted her eyes all around her sockets.

Omigod. She was trying to send me a message.

She parted her lips slightly. Pressed her tongue to each corner of her mouth. Wriggled her nose. Crossed her eyes.

"What about food?" asked George. "Could be a long helicopter ride to where you're going. You might want to ask for a few snacks."

Stretch mulled this over. He trained his crazed eyes on me. "Ask for snacks — maybe some of those hundred-calorie bags of cookies and crackers or something."

Nana wriggled her nose again and rolled her eyes. What was she telling me? She was going to sneeze? Her eyes itched? *What?*

And then she cracked a mischievous smile, and I knew exactly what she was going to do.

She was going to take him out.

She hadn't earned a brown belt in tae kwon do for nothing.

"You want to request any snacks?" Stretch asked Nana.

"I'm fond of them marshmallow Peeps, but they're hard to find outta season. How come you're askin'?"

"Because you're coming with me. You're my insurance policy, Grandma. From now on, you and I are joined at the hip. So wherever I go, you go. If anyone attempts to hurt me, I hurt you first."

Boos. Hissing. Jeering.

"Dickhead," yelled Maisie Barnes. "Why don't you pick on someone your own size?"

It had probably escaped Maisie's notice that Nana was the only person in the room who *was* his size.

"If you wanna stay healthy, young man, you better let me go now," Nana said calmly.

This was it. She was going to stomp down on his instep, spin around, and deliver a roundhouse kick to his jaw. I held my breath and waited for her to strike.

"Is that a threat?" snickered Stretch.

"You bet."

He laughed. "If you think an old woman like you can actually hurt someone like me, you better readjust your thinking, Granny."

Uh-oh, she hated being called Granny. So maybe this was it. She'd stomp on his instep, spin around, and land a tornado kick to his gut.

"Are you gonna let me go?"

"No."

"You'll be sorry."

"I'm quaking in my boots."

"Don't say I didn't give you no warnin'."

This *had* to be it! She was going to stomp on his instep, spin around, hammer his chest with a reverse side kick, and knock him to the floor.

My heartbeat thundered in my eardrums as I waited for her to strike. I held my breath and waited . . . and waited . . .

So how come she wasn't doing anything? What was *wrong* with her? Why wasn't she taking him out?

She gave a loud suck on her uppers. "Truth is, young man, I got a secret of my own to share."

"You might as well spit it out," encouraged Stretch. "It's the last chance you'll ever have to share anything with your friends."

"Okay. I'm apologizin' to everyone in the group on account of I been hidin' the truth.

You know when I told you I wasn't contagious?" She heaved a guilty sigh. "I lied."

"Ehh." Stretch thrust her away from him as if she were a live electrical wire.

"Now, Til!" cried Nana.

Tilly raised her cane and walloped him across the back of his knees before reversing direction and thumping him across the bridge of his nose. Legs buckling beneath him, he collapsed onto the floor in an unconscious heap.

George popped out of a nearby chair and hog-tied Stretch with several napkins he quickly tied together. I pushed through the panicked guests who were stampeding from the room as I raced to Nana's side and smothered her in my arms. "Omigod! I'm so glad you're safe! But why didn't you just take him down with your roundhouse kick?"

She straightened the shoulders of her sweatshirt and dusted off the front. "I didn't wanna tear out no seams in my sweatshirt." She glanced at the mob rushing out the door. "How come everyone's leavin'?"

"They apparently don't want to catch what you claim to have."

But Mom and Dad weren't among the fleeing horde. In fact, as Etienne and Officer Horn rushed into the room, Mom hurried toward us, arms spread wide — but instead of joining us in a group hug, she stopped in front of Nana to squirt a stream of hand sanitizer down her sweatshirt.

Brows arched and eyes narrowed, she drilled me with a self-satisfied look. "I told you she was contagious."

TWENTY-THREE

"So when did Stretch steal Maisie's liquid nicotine?" Tilly asked Etienne.

It was close to midnight, but we were so wired that a bunch of us were still hanging out. Officer Horn had paraded Stretch off to jail and released Hetty with a slap on the wrist and a stern warning to keep her paws off other people's property, no matter if the people were dead or alive. The Guten Tags were so happy to have their clarinetist back that they approached both Hetty and Dad with white flags and, in a flurry of apologies, set about restoring their band to its full musical capacity. There were still performances to be given over the course of the tour, so they realized they had two choices: set their petty grievances aside and take the stage as a united group or remain miffed and not participate at all. I applauded them for being classy enough to mend fences and was touched when they decided that since

Dad no longer had an instrument, not even a borrowed one, they'd all pitch in to buy him a new one.

Funny thing about people. Just when you think you have them pegged, they do something to surprise you.

"I'd expected Mr. Doozey to be quiet and withdrawn on the ride to the police station," Etienne said in response to Tilly's question, "but quite the opposite occurred. He was absolutely chatty. Nerves, most likely. He was quite forthcoming about his exploits — how easy it was to slip his hand inside her shoulder bag on the walk to the Oktoberfest grounds and snatch her nicotine refill. The crowds were suffocating, if you recall, so all of us were getting bumped and tugged, which suited his purpose entirely. He was in panic mode about incapacitating Zola, so he was improvising on the fly."

"When'd he dump the stuff into Zola's drink?" asked Nana.

"I can answer that," I said. "After Maisie, Arlin, and Stretch finished their performance, Maisie and Zola took off for the ladies' room. Remember? They weren't gone that long because they decided to use the men's room, but it was still long enough for Stretch to poison Zola's beer. Which reminds me." I glanced at Dad. "When Officer Horn asked to see everyone's photos of the Hippodrom tent, why didn't you show him yours?"

Dad elongated his features as if he were Stan Laurel reacting to Oliver Hardy. "He asked for camera photos. All I had was video."

You had to love my dad. He was just so . . . literal.

"What I wanna know is, how'd that fella steal so much money from his company without no one noticin'?" asked Nana. "Don't they do no audits?"

"I'm no expert in the art of embezzlement," said Etienne, "but I suspect he juggled two sets of books and manipulated the shipping charges to his own advantage. He's been perpetrating the ruse for years, so he apparently became quite adept at it."

I startled as the desk phone in our suite rang out with an annoyingly shrill tone. "That's probably for me," said Etienne as he crossed the floor to answer it.

"It's almost midnight," Mom reflected in a disapproving tone. "Who's calling him at this late hour?"

"He's still conversing with Zola's and Astrid's families about transportation arrangements to fly their bodies home, so it could be either a call from the States or his

Munich liaison. Since this is our last night here, the officials in Munich might feel compelled to tie up any loose ends."

"Sad thing about those women." Mom boosted herself to her feet and pulled Dad off the sofa with her. "I'm so sorry for their families. I shudder when I realize it could have been members of our own family who were killed." She graced me with a teary look. "We're all very lucky, aren't we? A little bruised and battered but very, very lucky." She blinked away her tears and forced a smile. "And on that note, your father and I are leaving."

"Us too," said Nana as she and Tilly stood up. "Six o'clock for luggage outside our door?" she asked me.

"Wish it could be later, but we have a long drive ahead of us tomorrow."

"I think for our next trip we should visit a place where we don't have to drive such long distances," proposed Mom. "Someplace small like Lichtenstein. Or Rhode Island."

Nana shook her head. "You can suggest all you want, Margaret, but it won't do no good. Bernice is already lobbyin'. She's got her heart set on New Guinea."

"Too many bugs," Mom declared as I escorted everyone to the door. "Too many snakes. Too much humidity." She stuck a warning finger in Nana's face. "You are *not* traveling to New Guinea, Mother. How would I ever keep track of you in the jungle?"

Nana riffled through her handbag, fishing out the wrist strap Mom had bought at Pills Etcetera. "I s'pose you could use this." She handed it back.

"My toddler tether! I was wondering where that went. Oh, good. Now, tomorrow when we get off the bus, we'll give this another try. Aren't you thrilled that we'll be attached again? So you can go anywhere and look at anything, and if you need something, I'll be right there at your side to take care of it. Isn't that exciting?"

"You bet," Nana deadpanned. "I'm about to break out in handstands."

But I could see the little twinkle in Nana's eye. As much as she despised Mom smothering her, I think being a nonentity had bothered her even more. Guess it was like the proverb said: "They wooed her and she resisted; they neglected her and she fell in love."

I closed the door behind them, relieved that things were slowly getting back to normal.

Whatever normal was.

"Who was that?" I asked when Etienne hung up the phone.

"The front desk. They were inquiring if we were still awake because they're sending someone up with a delivery for us."

"What kind of delivery?"

"We'll know in a few minutes."

I stepped into the bathroom to brush my teeth, popping out five minutes later when I heard the bumpity-bump squeak of a familiar set of wheels. I stopped in my tracks, jaw slack, staring.

"You've gotta be kidding me."

"It apparently has more lives than a cat." He released the handle of Astrid's rolling instrument case, then took a step back to inspect it with a critical eye. "Doesn't look too much the worse for wear."

A small dent was punched into one corner and several irregularly shaped scratches were etched across the top, but it looked as if it had sustained less damage in its six-thousand-foot descent down the Kehlstein than average luggage sustained going through O'Hare.

"I can't believe it. Did the delivery person offer any explanations?"

"Only this." He held up an envelope. "Would you like to do the honors or shall I?"

"Please." I gestured for him to continue.

He gave the contents of the note a quick scan. "It's from the manager of the Eagle's Nest. 'Dear Mr. Miceli, I am happy to return your case to you before you leave the immediate area. A hiker discovered it lying on one of our mountain trails early this afternoon, surprisingly intact. Please accept our good wishes that the accordion inside has not been seriously damaged. With sincere regards.' And he signs his name."

I winced. "Do you think it's damaged?"

"Only one way to find out."

He set it on the sofa, released the locks, and threw open the top. We did a quick visual inspection, searching for dents, missing buttons, or damaged piano keys. "Wow," I marveled, "is it just me or does it look as if it's in perfect condition?"

"It's not you. It looks as good as new. At least, from this angle." Peeling away the Velcro straps that immobilized it within its molded foam interior, he lifted it out and turned it gently upside down. "No damage to the underside either. I don't know where Astrid bought her musical equipment, but this is one damned fine instrument case. Looks like your father won't be needing a new accordion after all."

"What's this thing?" I pointed to the tail

end of a pink ribbon that was wedged in the crack where the foam insert was tucked into the case. "Looks a little out of place, doesn't it?"

"Is it attached to anything?"

Squeezing the satin between my forefinger and thumb, I tugged slowly, surprised when the entire foam insert lifted up to reveal the object to which the ribbon was attached: a slender book that was emblazoned with a riot of garden flowers and stamped with the words My Journal.

"*Omigod.* I don't think Astrid's journal was destroyed in the bomb blast after all. I think we just found it!" I lifted it out of its hidden compartment and opened it up to the first page. "The beginning date is inscribed as July two years ago." I flipped through a few pages, taking note of her tiny handwriting and short entries. "Will the police need this for any reason or should we simply turn it over to her family with the rest of her belongings?"

"Astrid was never under investigation, so the authorities would have no use for it. But I do wonder if she made any observations that would help Wendell as he begins to clean up his embezzlement mess."

I handed it to him. "Sounds like police work to me."

While he settled into a chair with the journal, I picked up the foam insert and was about to tuck it back into the case when something broke loose from beneath it and thunked onto my foot.

A wad of bubble wrap as long as my forefinger and as fat as a sausage. I plucked it off the floor. "Uh-oh. There might be damage after all. Look what just fell out of the foam insert."

"What is it?"

"Something cocooned in bubble wrap." I unraveled several layers before I uncovered the surprise in the center. A small bottle of clear liquid with an eye-dropper cap. I flashed it in Etienne's direction. "I don't know what it is. Nose drops? Eye drops?"

"Does it have an odor?"

I unscrewed the cap and sniffed. "It doesn't smell good enough to be perfume, but it doesn't smell like medicine either." I screwed the cap back on. "What do you suppose it is?"

He held up a finger in a "hold that thought" gesture as he scanned a passage in the journal. Then another. And another. Muttering something under his breath the entire while.

I shot him a frustrated look. "What?"

"This entry is dated July twenty-second.

'We rocked tonight at the gig in Winterset. I put Wendell down with his favorite café au lait mousse truffles and Montepulciano wine and he slept like a baby until I woke him at six.' "

"She 'put him down'? Meaning she put him to sleep?"

"That's my interpretation."

My eyes widened with a sudden memory. "She was carrying truffles in a side pocket of her suitcase — a whole bag full — but they'd melted in the plastic, so I threw them away. Do you suppose they were laced with whatever she used to induce sleep?"

"Seems fairly likely, doesn't it?" He leafed through more pages. " 'July twenty-ninth. A huge crowd in Spencer and great accommodations at the hotel. Gilbert devoured my cheese spread and drank two glasses of wine, which was enough to knock him out until dawn. I pumped up his ego about his prowess for a solid ten minutes, so he was feeling pretty good about himself when he left.' "

"Holy crap. She *did* drug them."

" 'August fifth. Otis is going to be crushed if I don't select his key tonight. He so enjoys our chats about politics and religion — all the topics you're supposed to avoid. If he's the lucky winner tonight, I might reduce his dosage so we can talk a little longer before he falls asleep. He's packed on a few pounds lately, so when I cuddle against him in bed, I'm reminded of the days before my Jim got sick, when we'd cuddle like spoons. Funny, the little things you miss when you find yourself widowed.' "

I stared at him, gobsmacked. "So . . . there was never any actual hanky-panky going on? Even though the guys *thought* there was?"

Etienne smiled. "A clever woman, Astrid Peterson. She apparently stroked their egos by feeding them stories about their manly exploits when all they actually did was eat, drink, and fall asleep."

"You don't think they ever questioned why they couldn't recall the evening's activities with as much detail as Astrid?"

"She inflated their egos so convincingly, made them feel so physically gifted, why would they ever question her? They wanted to believe every word she told them, whether they could remember or not. It was genius really. She got what she wanted most — an evening of companionship and cuddling that harkened back to the days when her husband was still alive. And they were given a chance to sustain the kind of fantasy that I imagine every man over a certain age craves — affirmation that he can still perform like a tiger in the bedroom. It was the perfect symbiotic relationship."

"I assume she never told Hetty what she was doing?"

"That would have been too risky. But I'd be willing to bet that Hetty never told Astrid about what was happening on her end either. She was probably too embarrassed to admit that the only thing the guys were interested in doing when they were with her was nodding off."

"Seems like a lot of hoopla to hide the fact that the only activity the Guten Tags were engaging in was sleeping." I held Astrid's mystery bottle up to the light. "Her bottle is just about full. Do you suppose this is what she used to knock everyone out? Poured it into their wine? Slipped it into their beer? Mixed it into the truffles? A home-grown sleeping potion maybe? Wendell told me she grew some pretty unusual plants in her garden. He said she was so happy all the time, he wouldn't be surprised if she was growing marijuana."

Etienne skimmed more pages. "If she concocted the brew herself, then you'd think she might make mention of it in one of her entries. Perhaps a plant that flourishes in the summer and needs to be harvested in — aha. 'September second. My valerian has grown especially well this year. A bumper crop to insure continued sweet dreams for my boys. Time to get busy. Life is good.' "

"Valerian? You want me to google it?"

"I think we know what it does, bella, and how effective it is."

I gave him an anguished look. "So is it our responsibility to tell the guys that their nights of passion with Astrid were all a sham? Or do we tuck her journal into her suitcase and never mention it again?"

"It depends on whether we choose to preserve the gentlemen's fantasies . . . or shatter them."

I flashed a sly smile. "You know what I'm going to say, right?"

"As an honorary Midwesterner, I'm proud to say *you bet.*"

Crossing the floor to the kitchenette, I turned Astrid's bottle upside down and poured the contents down the sink. The guys would never learn which one of them she liked best — at least, not from Etienne or me. And that was okay.

There were a few things in life that were just plain no-brainers.

Happily, this was one of them.

ABOUT THE AUTHOR

After experiencing disastrous vacations on three continents, **Maddy Hunter** decided to combine her love of humor, travel, and storytelling to fictionalize her misadventures. Inspired by her feisty aunt and by memories of her Irish grandmother, she created the nationally bestselling, Agatha Award–nominated Passport to Peril mystery series, where quirky seniors from Iowa get to relive everything that went wrong on Maddy's holiday. *From Bad to Wurst* is the tenth book in the series. Maddy lives in Madison, Wisconsin, with her husband and a head full of imaginary characters who keep asking, "Are we there yet?"

Please visit her website at www.maddy hunter.com or become a follower on her Maddy Hunter Facebook Fan Page.

The employees of Thorndike Press hope you have enjoyed this Large Print book. All our Thorndike, Wheeler, and Kennebec Large Print titles are designed for easy reading, and all our books are made to last. Other Thorndike Press Large Print books are available at your library, through selected bookstores, or directly from us.

For information about titles, please call:
  (800) 223-1244

or visit our Web site at:
  http://gale.cengage.com/thorndike

To share your comments, please write:
Publisher
Thorndike Press
10 Water St., Suite 310
Waterville, ME 04901